*Some Measure of Happiness*

Lee Wicks

# Some Measure of Happiness

SINGING DOG PRESS

MONTAGUE

SINGING DOG PRESS
30 Center Street
Montague, Massachusetts 01351
www.singingdogpress.com



This is a work of fiction. Names, characters, places, and incidents (with the exception of the bombing of the Twin Towers in New York City on September 11, 2001) are either products of the author's imagination or used fictitiously. Any resemblance to actual persons, living or dead, events or locales is entirely coincidental.

In alphabetical order my heartfelt gratitude goes to my colleague and friend, Jessica Day who read draft two, offered much needed encouragement, and proofread the final draft; Danae DiNicola and Lizzie Doubleday who also served as readers; Elinor Lipman who read a small segment and found my lead sentence buried on page three; Janet MacFadyen; a keen-eyed proofreader who became an inspired editor; Mary Ellen Shaughan, a busy poet and writer who got me started and made sure I kept going: and James Whitbeck who allowed me to use his lovely painting on the cover. My husband Roy Rosenblatt, my daughter Ali Wicks-Lim, her wife Jeanette Wicks-Lim, and my grandson, Mason Wicks-Lim, are an enduring source of love and inspiration and I thank them for always listening to my stories.

I am grateful to Jamie O'Connell of Tiger Press for producing this book and discounting the price so that the Dakin Pioneer Valley Humane Society can benefit from the sale of this book.

Finally, special thanks go to Robert Moorhead, artist and chair of the art department at Deerfield Academy, who donated his precious time and expertise to design this book.

*To the Dakin Pioneer Valley Humane Society for their great work caring for animals in search of their forever homes.*

# *Prologue*

## *Cooper Hill, Vermont*

## *March 2001*

WHEN PEOPLE HEARD ABOUT WHAT HAPPENED, they said, "Not that wonderful family," as though somewhere a family existed that deserved such a fate. When Jack Walker remembers that Sunday, the colors come back to him first: a gray blue winter afternoon too warm to snow, too cold to rain, golden light pouring out onto the patchy snow from the windows of their home because they'd lit all the lamps, dark green pines marking the wood line that surrounded their clearing, a gravel driveway bordered by dirty snow, and a dingy kitchen floor.

All that morning he'd wasted time wondering if a new coat of wax would do any good or if he needed to strip it completely. The wood floors bore the scuff marks of boots and a dog needing her nails clipped. Wonderful dog. With his usual care, Jack had researched breeds and chosen a Newfoundland for its gentle nature. Conway Titty, he and his wife Cate had called her, because she was such a plump round puppy, still eager to nurse long after her litter mates had been weaned. Their twins, Molly and Zeke, had learned to walk by hanging onto Conway's fur. Conway had simply looked over her shoulder and then walked forward slowly while the babies toddled along. They should have called her Nanny, Jack said. Cate thought the dog had more patience than she would ever possess.

It had been a long Sunday, and after a while, even with all their board games and stories and puzzles, the kids became restless. Cooking a big dinner had been Jack's idea, inviting friends to share it had been Cate's. Jack started to cook, and Cate made the calls. Washing the vegetables and taking turns kneading the bread dough had distracted Zeke and Molly for a while, but then nobody had anything to do but wait.

"I wish we had a TV," Zeke said. Jack pretended not to hear him. "Everyone has one but us," Zeke said. "Mom wouldn't mind if we only watched videos." This was news to Jack.

Cate broke an uncomfortable silence and said, "Who wants to go sleigh riding?

Jack had cleared the run and the trail that led to it the first year he and Cate bought the land, even before they began building the house. He'd slashed a narrow lane through the forest and made a wide clearing about five-hundred yards from the house site. On late summer afternoons when the light filtered down through the leaves, it looked like the path led to an outdoor cathedral. He'd spent a lot of time tracing the angle of the sun before he chose that particular place on their forty acres. It overlooked a small pond, and he made a fire circle there so they could camp out on the spot and then cook breakfast and watch the fog lift from the water. They brought the twins there when they were just six months old, strapping on cross country skis and bundling the babies, one each, in snugglies against their chests. In early spring, the sound of peepers drew them all to the edge of the pond. Conway swam out and back, always watching the children, ready to nose them in towards shore if they ventured beyond safety. Molly and Zeke threw rocks and trekked around in the mud to see what they could find, while Jack and Cate held hands. Jack liked to say, "I'm the luckiest white boy in America—it's all blueberry pie and ice cream, this life we have."

While they pulled on boots and mittens that Sunday, the kids begged Jack to go with them, but he couldn't and didn't really want to. The bread was on its second rise and he had to keep an eye on the chicken.

"I get to go all the time," he said. "Let Mommy have some fun today."

Cate went to town each day to work at a clinic where pregnant women without health insurance came for prenatal care. She had guided countless lives into the blaring light of the world, coaxing women in labor to breathe, relax, and let nature take its course; but when her own turn came, Molly had decided to enter feet first. Cate tried yoga; she did somersaults in the pool and finally agreed to try a process in which doctors attempt to turn the baby from outside by pressing and pushing. Nothing worked. She labored for nine hours and delivered Zeke, and then Jack donned scrubs and held her face in his hands while a surgeon cut into her and pulled their howling daughter into the cold operating room. It had been surreal, with Cate smiling bravely at one end of the table and her body all open at the other end. He had not expected so much blood, and Jack had a moment when he thought he might faint, but then he heard Molly cry right along with Zeke. Both of his bright pink babies got the highest Apgar scores possible and took to the breast without a bit of coaxing, and when Cate went back to work, they gulped their bottles, too.

Fatherhood claimed him immediately, as nothing else ever had. Jack never felt a moment of fear caring for their sturdy little bodies that plumped up on breast milk day by day. He bathed them, swaddled their wild-waving arms and legs, and brought them to Cate like neatly wrapped packages; and during the long nights with Molly, who suffered from colic, he lost all interest in teaching. In the first week of August, he called the headmaster at Burnside Academy to say he wouldn't be back—an unheard of act since he'd already signed a contract, but tolerated due to Jack's long association with the school. Cate loved the idea. Leaving her job never entered her mind.

And it had been fine, more than fine, but a day can seem long to an adult with two small children, particularly a man who had the habit of reading long complicated books while listening to classical music. When he had the chance to spend an hour alone on a Sunday afternoon, Jack grabbed it.

"Daddy," Molly said, "It will be more fun if we all go."

"But no fun to come home to a burned dinner," Jack answered.

"Even Conway wants you to go," Zeke said. The dog was staring at Jack with a longing look.

"You couldn't just put the bread in a cool place to slow down the rising?" Cate asked. "You could turn the stew off for an hour; what difference would it make?"

"Yeah, Daddy, and we could have hot cocoa and you could go

down the hill fastest," Molly said.

"Next time," he promised. "Anyway, somebody needs to be here when our friends arrive."

"I wish Lizzie was coming," Molly said. "We won't have any fun without her. You and everybody will just talk and talk." Lizzie was Claire Westfield's teenage daughter from her first marriage, and the twin's favorite sitter.

Jack felt himself agreeing with Molly. Four more adults would suck the silence from the day. It would be hard to get the kids to settle down. Cate would drink too much and fall asleep the minute she hit the bed, and all day long he'd been thinking of making love to her.

"It will be fine," Cate said. "We'll have fun. But we have to get going now."

Jack watched them wind their way down the path. Cate pulled the sled with the twins riding. Conway followed. Jack put a little more wood in the stove and lifted the towel to check on the bread. It had developed a taut, slightly shiny surface, meaning he could put it on the oven anytime. He used his sharpest knife to make a slash down the middle of the loaf and brushed it with egg yolk and water, and sprinkled caraway seeds along the groove. He checked the stew and added a little stock. Then he meandered over to the stereo and took his time before choosing Brahms, just the right sound for a late winter Sunday. For months, he'd been pecking through Robert Caro's biography of Lyndon Johnson, and it was interesting to find himself liking the man who had been so demonized during the Vietnam War. With an intoxicating sense of luxury, he pulled an old quilt around himself and curled up on the sofa.

When he took the loaves out of the oven, almost all the light had faded. Cate and the kids had been gone more than an hour, which was unusual. Molly and Zeke loved the idea of sledding, but inevitably got snow in their boots and wanted to come home after a run or two. He waited another fifteen minutes before heading out, knowing Cate would be annoyed when they met on the trail. She always accused him of being over-protective. Still, she might need help with two cold and worn-out kids, and the temperature dropping fast.

He followed their trail to the top of the hill, and then life as he had known it vanished.

All the colors were gone, leaving a black dog, black water, grayish ice. Conway was diving, then surfacing, and then diving again. She had been bred for this and she would not stop until stopped. Paralyzed, he didn't know whether to run back to the house or to the pond. He heard the sound of a car bumping its way up their steep rutted driveway; he heard the car door slam, and then he began to run. In no time, Linda Brickman was there with Tom, her overweight husband, trudging behind. She shouted to him to go back and get help.

By the time Claire Westfield and Andy Spenser arrived, Jack had slid out onto the ice, trying to move carefully towards the hole, but Conway had bared her teeth and a growl never heard before kept Jack away. By the time the divers pulled the bodies out, Andy, who was a doctor, knew that it had been too long. Even though the ambulance screamed away with Jack inside, Jack knew, too. Claire and Andy drove straight to the hospital. Linda and Tom went back to the house and turned off the oven and tamped down the wood stove, and then went to the hospital.

The police examined the sled marks and concluded that they had all had gone down together. Their combined weight along with the slickness of the hill had made them go faster than usual. The sled did not stop at the snow bank at the bottom, but raced up and over it and onto the ice. Jack wondered exactly what part of the Brahms concerto he'd been listening to when they settled themselves on the sled, probably laughing. Jack wondered when Cate understood the danger. Jack wondered if Conway had barked; and would he have heard her if the music had not been playing? Jack wondered if he would ever eat dark bread again or be able to bear the smell of chicken stew. Jack hoped it had been fast. He could not bear thinking of his children or Cate, terrified and dying slowly.

Two weeks later, after the funeral, after his parents and Cate's parents were gone, after he'd worked his way through the casseroles that had been left at the house, and made one trip to town for coffee and a few other things, he brought Conway to an animal shelter in Russell, two towns over. She would not stay away from the pond, and he could not stand it. He'd call and call and finally have to go get her and there she'd be, looking out as though she was longing for every fine day they'd spent at that spot. Looking like she might still jump in and find them. One day, she sat there in an early spring storm and two inches of wet snow piled up on her head. Her lemon-sized dog brain could not fathom the picture that lived in her giant heart. She could still smell them. Jack would coax her back to the house and feed her, but as soon as he let her out, she'd be back there, like a dog in China he'd once read about who went to the train station to meet his master every day and then continued for fifteen years after the man died. He told himself it was for her own good. She needed another family to care for; she needed a family with kids. At the shelter they wanted to know his reason for giving her up, a purebred dog with papers and no health problems. Was she aggressive? Had she bitten someone? They had a form and couldn't leave any spaces blank.

"I'm moving," he said. "They won't let dogs live where I'm going," which turned out to be more or less true.

Conway, who knew nothing but trust, followed the attendant into the hallway lined with cages. She looked back once. Her deep brown eyes peered from her soft muzzle, and Jack bent down one last time to fondle the huge head. "Good girl," he said "You're a good dog. Go now." And Conway did as she'd been told.

In less than a day, he knew he'd made a huge mistake. He had hung her leash and collar on their usual hook, and every time he opened the door the wind rattled her tags. On his first night alone, he kept going to the door to call her in. He missed hauling her back from her vigil at the edge of the pond and telling her, "It's alright girl. You did the best you could," until she was finally willing to trot along with him and come in and have her treat. One of his dog books had said that you should never reward a dog without asking for some trick. It helped establish a hierarchy and made them secure. But Jack always thought Conway deserved a treat for merely being alive and kind when she had the power to snap his hand off at the wrist.

What was she thinking, sleeping on the concrete floor in the dark kennel filled with the plaintive barking of the other dogs? He imagined a jail with hardened convicts telling a new inmate there was no way out. He imagined her lying flat as she often did with her face between her paws. When he and Cate had tried, without success, to get her to stop begging at the table, she had assumed that posture and looked up at her people—the hungriest dog in the world. "Poor starving dog," Cate would say. Molly would giggle, because in fact Conway was fat, and the vet had warned them that the giant breeds did not live long and had even shorter lives if they were overweight.

He decided to give himself a day, but the second day was no better than the first and on the morning of the third day he drove over to the shelter where the same woman who had pushed paper across the counter with a disdainful look eyed him warily and then seemed pleased to tell him that Conway had already been adopted. They'd had a family on a waiting list for a long time that had been looking for a dog like Conway. "But certainly there's some kind of waiting period," he'd said. "Don't people get a chance to bring a dog back if it's not working out?"

"They do," she said. "We can call you if they decide they don't want her." Jack knew that was not likely. Who wouldn't want Conway? They would not have any second thoughts until she started shedding, and if they were really dog-lovers it wouldn't change anything.

"Can you give me their number?" he asked, thinking he could call and explain everything and surely they would understand. The woman said she could not do that. It was against their policy. She had hard eyes. She did not know his story. Had he chosen the shelter in Cooper Hill, someone might have given him some slack. Someone might have put a wait order on the adoption just in case he changed his mind. But he'd chosen this distant shelter to avoid having Conway adopted close to home where she might run off to the woods and the pond. Something in his face brought forth a little pity, and the woman told him that Conway had gone to a very good home. The shelter screened all families. The people who took her had three children, one a sweet toddler. Conway had seemed happy when she got into their car.

When he and Cate got a dog in the same month that the twins were born, people said they were crazy, but they were not crazy; they were celebrating. There had been fertility treatments and blood and sorrow all along the way. The irony that a woman who'd helped so many babies into the world could not have her own had tormented them. And then after six years and almost giving up, healthy full-term twins. Twins and a puppy that soon outweighed both babies. A puppy that let Molly chew on her ears. Now Conway had children again. Good for her.

As a nurse-midwife, Cate had assisted with prenatal care and births and also abortions. She had believed in choice with all her heart, but the procedure, as it was called, always seemed like a savage reversal of everything nature intended, and she often came home afterward and tried to describe the hollow eyes of the women in recovery. Jack had asked if they weren't relieved, and Cate had said, yes, they were. They had good reasons for what they'd done, but they were also empty. When Jack left the shelter for the second time, he thought he understood.

On the chance that he might drive by some house and see Conway playing in the yard, Jack took a ride around Russell, but then he asked himself what he might actually do if he saw her romping with some boy or girl who was deliriously happy to have a dog at last. Conway would run to him all fur and wet nose; he'd crouch down and wrap his arms around her and then glance over her wide back to see tears brimming in a child's eyes, a child who would already be crying *Mama, Mama, come here!* At the next set of lights, he turned around and headed back to the highway, which took him to a small road that became a lane that led to his long muddy driveway.

* * *

A tragedy like Jack Walker's denies privacy. The press crawls all over it. They find your friends and get pictures of your kids and plaster them on the front page of papers. They make a simple lifestyle look like a weird choice and imply neglect. Why hadn't Cate wanted to stay home with her kids? Had something secret and ugly pulled Jack from the classroom? Jack could not stand it. He posted No Trespassing signs on the land and came to town only when he had to. Well-meaning people said it would help if he resumed a normal routine, but he could not remember himself before fatherhood. If he'd had his way, he and Cate would have had eight or nine kids, so the first grandchild might appear before the youngest child left home. They had been talking about adopting some kids who were hard to place. All that land and the big garden and plenty of money—why not?

The dean of faculty at Burnside Academy called after a certain amount of time to tell him he would always be welcome. The Burnside family was waiting to welcome him back. Jack declined politely. Instead, Jack cut cordwood and calked the windows on the house. He cleared a small field, patched a leaky spot on the roof and then went to work inside. One day when the sun was warm, an awful smell drew him to Molly's room and then into her closet where, in the pocket of her rain slicker, he found a collection of clam shells from a trip to the shore they had made in the fall. It had been raining softly when they walked the long flat beach at low tide. Molly and Zeke had found the little blow holes clams make and dug into the gritty sand for them. He and Cate had held hands. Her hair, normally stick straight, had curled in the mist.

When the house sparkled inside and out and it would have been time to mulch the flower beds for winter, the need to leave overcame him. The real estate market was booming, and the place sold in less than a week for three times what he had paid for it; and the first thing the new owners did was raze the house so they could build a bigger one on that spot. He went to watch on the day the bulldozers came. The speed of the demolition astonished him. By the end of the day, the foundation hole had been filled in and the earth raked smooth, like a neatly covered grave.

Jack could have gone anywhere, and he considered many possibilities before choosing to move into the village of Cooper Hill, just six miles from the land he'd sold. Being in a place where everyone knew your story felt safer than going somewhere where eventually someone would pry it out of him. Also, even though he didn't feel much like being with people, he didn't mind being near them. He remembered how Conway would sometimes follow him from room to room and simply lean against his thigh. He liked the people in Cooper Hill whom he and Cate had known together. He might just lean against them a little.

Cooper Hill was surrounded by farm fields and bordered by two rivers. It had just one store, a library, a post office, and a pretty town common bordered by narrow streets named after dead presidents and nut trees. When you came into the town from the hills above, the tidy old houses gleamed white in the sun. Up close there was a lot of peeling paint. The scale felt right. Jack found an apartment over the store that faced the common. Linda and Tom Brickman, Claire Westfield and Andy Spencer, and a few other families lived within shouting distance of his porch. He liked to watch their comings and goings, and on the night of September 11, he sat with them all at the bar at the Cooper Hill Inn and watched that image of the planes flying into the towers play over and over again, against the voices of reporters who had nothing but bad news.

The anthrax scare came next, then war. It seemed like a time when people should pull together. Linda and Tom, and Claire and Andy invited Jack to their homes often and came by to see how he was doing, but Jack just looked at them, almost as if he didn't know what they were talking about. And after a while they left him alone.

On the first anniversary of the accident, Cate's family created a foundation in her honor to provide travel stipends for college students interested in women's health. Jack spent hours reading through applications from wonderful young people who wanted to go to Africa and educate women about the dangers of female circumcision, or work at health clinics in Appalachia or the Bronx. He wrote personal letters to every applicant and attended the awards ceremony that spring.

In this way, three years passed quietly in Cooper Hill for Jack, who learned that he was not one of those people who heals quickly. He filled each day tutoring neighborhood children or caring for people's pets when they had to be away. If he saw someone trying to lift a heavy piece of furniture into a truck, he helped. When mean Maud Crowe was kneeling in her garden pulling weeds, she often found Jack at her side. She thought that help from a younger person was her due and wasted no time on thank-yous, and this suited him fine. On the mornings after snow storms, he helped people dig out. He had no concerns about money. What he'd gotten for the land plus his trust fund was more than enough.

# *Part One:*
# *Cooper Hill, 2004*

## *August*

On a quiet Saturday in early August, 2004, Jack Walker ended up alone and uninvited in Linda and Tom Brickman's stunning house. Linda had called to say she had two painted kitchen chairs to donate to the Old Home Day's auction; she said she'd leave them on the porch and he could come by any time. When he arrived on that Saturday, the chairs were not there, but both cars were in the driveway. First he checked the garden. They had a deep and wonderful yard filled with perennial beds. The phlox were tall by August, and Linda could easily have been crouching among the beds, but she wasn't there and neither was Tom. He went back to the house, looked in the window, and saw the chairs in the hallway. All was quiet and he wondered if Linda and Tom were upstairs on the third floor where Linda had an office. He knocked but there was no answer. They didn't have a doorbell. He tried the door, found it unlocked, and stepped inside to call upstairs. Silence.

He had not been inside this house for years. It felt wonderfully cool, sheltered from the afternoon sun by the wide porch and a trellis of climbing morning glories. The kitchen counter was spotless, and a bowl of tomatoes and baby eggplants looked like a painting. Next to the door, a small basket overflowed with mail. Jack learned that Linda and Tom subscribed to the *New Yorker*, had an account with American Express and VISA, had their teeth cleaned twice a year, and paid their oil bill on a twelve-month cycle. Numerous charities had sent letters of appeal. A card from the vet indicated that their cat was due for a checkup. He put all the envelopes back in order and paused with the door ajar to take in the slight smell of curry, the vegetables, an apple-green bowl filled with blue hydrangeas on a table covered in pale yellow linen. He loved the apple-green bowl, which reminded him of Scarlet O'Hara's dress of apple-green watered silk.

In the first year of his marriage he had bought Cate a silk scarf in that same color, and it made her eyes an even darker green. Too practical to go out and buy bowls of flowers or silk scarves, she had still loved it when he brought these things into their world. Jack lingered for a moment over the memory and was startled when something brushed against his leg. Greylock, Linda and Tom's huge gray cat, raced past him and out through the open door. Damn! He had been asked to care for Greylock on more than one occasion and knew how this cat could move. He had no chance of catching it. It ran around the side of the house and into a mass of ferns. Feeling stupid and sorry, Jack spent about half an hour trying to coax the animal into range so he could grab it and put it back in the house, but he failed.

This was the moment when he might have left a note for Tom and Linda. He could have taken the chairs and let them know that Greylock was out, but he felt guilty for sifting through their mail. He didn't know what had come over him. It broke an unspoken rule. You never trespassed like that, not even with close friends. It was like peeking into someone's medicine cabinet. And so he left without the chairs and with an unsettled feeling.

On the town common people were hanging lights and building the booths needed for Old Home Days, a three-day harvest celebration always held on the third weekend in August. Linda and Tom, who'd gone for a long walk, stopped to talk to their neighbors and admire other gardens. They'd met Claire and Andy, and Linda had managed to persuade Claire to come for a cookout. Then, as soon as they turned into their driveway Linda remembered the chairs. She felt the familiar and annoying flush of heat to her face.

"How can that be? I said I'd put the chairs out and then it only took me a minute to forgot all about it"

"They're small. We can carry them up the street," Tom, her sweet husband, offered.

"I even brought them into the hallway, and then I walked right past them. How could that happen?" Linda couldn't seem to let it go.

"You have lots on your mind," Tom said kindly. His kind voice was starting to annoy her. Linda spotted Greylock sleeping in the ferns. "Didn't we leave him in?"

Tom shrugged. "I thought so."

"Me too. I put the chairs in the hallway, and then I saw that she had no water. That's why I forgot to take the chairs out to the porch. But I'm sure she was drinking when we left." These days Linda had what she called pudding brain. It was caused by lack of sleep from menopausal night sweats. It made perfect sense to her that a woman in London was acquitted for murder due to menopausal rages.

"Maybe he went down the cellar and out through the bulkhead," Tom said. Linda didn't answer. The bulkhead was a possibility; he also might have slipped past them when they left. It didn't matter now. She could not solve this today because she had to check the wine glasses to make sure they had no spots, and she had to iron some cloth napkins before Claire and Andy came over. Overall the house looked okay. She'd cleaned in the morning, watered the garden, and picked the tomatoes and the eggplants. If Tom went to the stand for some corn, they'd be fine. They had all the other vegetables they needed in their garden.

"What are we making?" Tom asked

"I thought I'd marinate some tofu and do a stir fry," This time Linda smiled, trying to sound perky, knowing Tom would not be happy.

"Again? I'd be happy to run to the store for some chicken or a few steaks."

"Tom, you *promised*," Linda said. Tom's cholesterol test had come back a little high, and the doctor wanted to put him on drugs. The side effects scared Linda, and ever since, she'd been cooking only vegetables and grains and oatmeal for breakfast, even in the summer. They ate pasta and Quinoa and flax, white beans and black beans, brown rice and polenta, and nuts by the handful. In the last six months, Linda had gained eleven pounds on all the starch and Tom had chronic diarrhea from the roughage, but Linda would not give up until his next cholesterol test. He kept telling her the extra pounds looked good on her, but she did not believe him. Tom just wanted her to be fat to keep him company. At forty-eight it was bad enough to look in the mirror and see that your upper lip was disappearing and that small hairs had begun to grow from your chin. Buying new pants in size twelve was a disaster, and she wanted a piece of lean meat as much as he did, but she would not give in.

"A little chicken now then wouldn't change anything," Tom said, sounding a little whiney.

"You don't know that. Anyway a little chicken today and a steak tomorrow and then what? You have to at least give this a chance." In addition to the rabbit diet, Linda had bought a treadmill and put it on the porch and timed Tom to be sure he put in at least forty minutes a day. She did, too. Sometimes she felt like a huge demented hamster.

"And what if it's the same when I have my next test in six months?"

"In six months we can talk about it. Stop sulking, I'll make the tofu taste like chicken," Linda said, and she began to make a marinade.

Tom gave up as she knew he would. "Where are my car keys?"

"On the hook by the cellar door," she said, "Yours have a blue tag, mine is yellow, and the spare key is green."

"When did we get color-coded?" He sounded amused.

"Oh, last week when I saw them at Staples."

"What's next?" Tom asked smiling.

"They have these little stickers that I thought would be good to use on jars we leave in the fridge, so we know how long stuff has been in there."

"Do you know you're a little crazy?' Tom asked, still smiling.

"Not as bad as my mother, though; she put our socks in the drawer in little plastic bags so we wouldn't get the pairs mixed up."

A week after Old Home Days had ended Jack sat on his porch and heard the jangle of a dog leash. He didn't need to look up and over his porch rail to know that Andy and Claire were walking Nina, or at least trying to, as they always did between six and seven in the morning. Their daughter Lizzie, who usually walked the dog, had run off back in July, leaving only a vague note. Claire looked gaunt. Right before Nina started pulling her down the street, she waved and stared into his face and it made him uncomfortable. The yearning look in Claire's eyes signaling that she thought they were now bound together in tragedy put him off. Jack went inside and refilled his coffee cup. In an hour or so, Amanda Sloane would come by in her power-walking outfit, a pair of Spandex pants and a bright yellow shirt tight as skin, and she'd be all plugged into her iPod. Shortly after that, the sound of mowers would begin. The mowers and trimmers could ruin the serenity of a Sunday morning, unless you knew how to take them. Jack just let the noise mute all loss and turned to another section of the paper.

He thought this year's Old Home Days had ended with a more than usual sense of well being for everyone but Claire and Andy, and nothing would be right for them until they had some news from Lizzie. Unlike some years, the weather had been perfect. A week of terrible heat had been broken on Friday night by one of those storms that show the silver undersides of the leaves and turn the sky black at four o'clock. The annual dance recital and band concert had been called off and that was a disappointment, but the next morning was clear and cool and talk of the bear was constant as everyone waited for the Saturday morning auction to begin.

The bear had first been seen in a yard over by the post office. From a distance it looked like a very large dog. Claire had been the first to see it as she restrained Nina, a skittish hound mix who would have pursued it to her death. Bears had been around all summer, but on the other side of the highway. A small thrill had passed though the auction-goers at the thought that it might come back at any time, and one woman remembered a story about a bear in a nearby town that had gone for a swim in a private pool. The homeowner had found it side-stroking back and forth in the turquoise water, calm as could be, and she'd kept quiet and watched until it climbed out and shook off like some paunchy old man. Others had tales to tell about raided bird feeders, rabid raccoons, and the ever-present deer who had a taste for the most expensive ornamental trees.

Inside this mild complaining lived gratitude. Nobody's house had burned down in the winter, no couples had divorced, one cancer had not come back, and a suspicious breast lump had been just a cyst. All the old people and some of the new ones missed Lenny and Stewart, but they had both lived into their nineties and died at home; and that too was a gift.

Jack had gone to the auction and bid on the same chairs he'd been seeking at Linda and Tom's place the week before, and he was sitting in one thinking about more coffee. It tasted and smelled so wonderful but too much jangled his nerves and made him grouchy. He restrained himself. He stood and stretched and looked down the street. The watering system that Linda and Tom had installed this summer went off on a timer, even though their lush lawn looked fine. Ever since they put it in, there had been the perfect amount of rain, mostly at night, every couple of days. Across from them, Mary Higgins was out weeding her vegetable patch, and Jessica Higgins, who had taken Mary's name when they married, busied herself deadheading flowers. But both had their eyes on their daughter, April, a four-year-old in a long tie-dyed tee shirt that served as a nightie. She had a tangle of pale brown curls, milk-white skin, and blue painted fingernails. Jessica had not approved of the polish, but Mary had argued that April had to have some choices in order to gain self-confidence, and they had finally compromised by finding non-toxic nail polish and a yoga class for children so that April could grow up having pride in her body, adorned or unadorned by commercial products.

April hunched over the sidewalk with a basket of chalk by her side, drawing stick figures. It troubled Mary that none of April's drawings included people of color, except for green, yellow and pink. For some time she'd been thinking that they ought to move to a more diverse community. Jess had absolutely no interest in moving. She'd bought the house long before she met Mary, plastered the walls and refinished the floors herself and, with diligent composting, enriched the soil so that their tiny garden yielded abundant produce from late June through September. She left parsnips in the ground to sweeten over the winter and dug them in the spring. She planted late kale and harvested it through the snow. The perennials that lined the front fence and the borders of the small lot would take years to reproduce somewhere else.

And, most of her dog-training clients lived nearby.

Mary and Jessica both noticed that April's nightie was bunching up in the back, exposing too much thigh and creeping towards her bottom. Mary spoke first, "April, wouldn't you like to go in and get dressed? We can have some breakfast and then you can draw some more."

April pretended not to hear.

"April, I know you heard Momma. Come in NOW," Jessica said. April had learned to call Mary "Momma" and Jess "Ma."

Mary frowned at Jess. She didn't believe in direct orders like you would issue to a dog. "The sidewalk is scratching you knees. You'll feel much better in a pair of jeans," Mary said.

Jess gave Mary a *this-could-go-on-forever* look, believing that children needed clear guidelines and that providing constant choice only led to insecurity and the feeling that no one was in charge. Though her perspective on child rearing was shared by much of the world, it did not help, in terms of her relationship to Mary, that she trained dogs for a living. Every time she tried to impose any discipline at all, Mary accused her of treating April like a pet. In conversation with anyone *but* Mary, Jess would say that a four-year-old and a puppy had more in common that one might think, but she knew she could never say this to Mary.

Even though Mary tried very hard to keep everything even, she was the birth mother and it showed most of all in matters of discipline. However, Jess spent the most time with April since she cared for her during the day and met with desperate pet-owners on weekends and weekdays after five when they got home from work. Without saying anything more, she simply put down her clippers and went to April. She picked up the basket of chalk, took April by the hand, and asked her to come help make pancakes.

April said, "What kind?"

Jess said, "Blueberry," and they went into the house.

Jack, who'd been watching all this time, smiled at the scene even though every child reminded him of his. Only another cup of coffee could stop that line of thought, and he got one and then returned to the porch and cast his gaze further down the street to Claire and Andy's house, where the garden had not been well-tended this year. Before they turned into the driveway and out of sight he saw Claire place Nina's poop bag in the trash bin. People noticed and appreciated the fact that she picked up Nina's waste, especially because of its size. Nina weighed close to ninety pounds and she produced amazing long, wide, well-formed turds that sometimes spiraled into glistening brown mounds that would have been awful to step on. Again, memories of his children assaulted him as he pictured himself scraping dog shit from the deep groves on the sole of Molly's sneakers. Memories such as this, trivial, sometimes ugly, sometimes so slight that he could barely catch them as they passed through his mind, had been relentless all summer, leaving a slight tremor in their wake.

Sunday, quiet for now, and early. Hours stretched before him. He hadn't vacuumed his place for two weeks, shirts filled the basket he set aside for ironing, his car could use a washing, he had to go grocery shopping, his parents would be expecting a Sunday call. He wanted to walk to the river for a swim before the cool late summer nights made the water too chilly. He wanted to ride his bike, make love to someone for hours and drink some cold white wine afterwards, read a big complicated book, stay right there on his porch and watch the day unfold, take a nap, download photos from his digital camera, check out new cars, and cook something for later in the week. Certain choices precluded others. Can't cook anything till you go shopping he told himself, can't think of trading in the car until you clean it up. Without choosing the nap, he let his head fall forward and he dozed off to the distinct smell of pancakes browning in butter.

## *September*

Every time he passed Linda and Tom's house, Jack wanted to be inside again, alone. He had not felt so compelled since a long ago summer at his grandparent's house when his grandfather told him that boys who played with themselves could go blind. Finally, on a Tuesday when both cars were gone and midday silence had settled over Cooper Hill, Jack could not stop himself. He looked up the empty street and down and then carefully let himself in, so that this time the cat could not escape. Greylock barely moved, but watched him closely through slit green eyes. Jack didn't particularly like cats, but this one impressed him. His size alone gave Greylock a presence. Plus, something thrilled him about having a witness. The cat continued to watch him although he was doing next to nothing. Now that he was inside, his reason for coming escaped him. He supposed he wanted that same feeling that came to him last time, a sense that beauty and order survived in small private spaces, perhaps a clue about how other people lived their lives. He didn't think he and Cate had ever seen their second floor. They'd always settled around the dining room table for hours.

He began to make his way up the stairs and stopped to look out the window on the first floor landing. He could see the whole length of the quiet street until it dipped down near the river. There had been a time not so long ago when everyone didn't have to work so much. This street would have been filled with children playing and young mothers talking or hanging up laundry, but now the very young went to day care, old people lingered in places where strangers cared for them, and the well-loved houses stood mostly empty all day. At three a small straggle of children would walk home from the elementary school, just a block off the common. Cooper Hill Elementary only went through third grade and existed in constant peril since the building needed expensive repairs and didn't meet disability access requirements. But every year, those Cooper Hill parents who believed in small local schools and did not want their children bussed to nearby Woodside argued ferociously to keep it open. Other Cooper Hill parents sold their houses when their children got to school-age, and moved to a town with a better school system. Or they sent their kids to private school, or bet on success in the school-choice lottery. As a result, Cooper Hill had just a few children and an unusual percentage of couples with no children at all. As he stood there with golden September sun pouring in the window, through the leathery leaves of the oak tree by the side of the house, he envisioned Molly and Zeke at eight, riding two-wheelers; he would have brought them into the village of Cooper Hill to learn, the dirt road on the land outside of town being unsuitable for riding.

Before he could continue to the second landing, Jack heard a scraping sound on the first floor and turned to see Greylock squatting in the litter box. The problem was that his hind end hung over the edge of the box. The cat looked blankly at the wall and strained while its waste went straight to the floor. Afterwards the creature spent about five minutes scraping at the kitty litter trying to cover what was not there and then walked away with a job-well-done attitude. What an awful mess to come home to, thought Jack, and then he pulled a length of paper towels off the role and cleaned the mess before letting himself out. With this thoughtful act, Jack prevented the conversation Linda dreaded, the one that began with Tom saying, "It might be time to let him go, honey. Twenty-two is very old for any cat."

Linda Brickman would always think of the eighties as the decade of lonely women. To the members of the Cooper Hill Book Club who had gathered at her house on a fragrant fall night, she said, "It was crazy. Marriages suddenly fell in on themselves like an overcooked soufflé, mine included." Linda loved telling stories about her first husband, who had never once laid a hand on her but when his temper flared, and almost anything could set it off, she cringed and had therefore spent too many years smoothing all the wrinkles in their life to keep Jeff from screaming *Motherfuckingcocksuckingson-of-a-bitchwhoreflamingasshole.* He had once screamed this on Christmas Eve as they were setting up the tree, because his efforts to make it perfect had failed. He had sawed branches from the lower portion and drilled holes in the bare spots and inserted the limbs after he'd put glue on the cut ends, but the glue did not hold and the weight of the ornaments pulled the branches out.

They broke up after he fell in love with someone else, and the night Linda told that story she had the book club laughing so hard that Claire said she'd wet her pants if she didn't stop. The story had a perfect ending. He'd made a fool of himself over a much younger woman, and after four years of living together she came home one day and told him she was gay. Not only that: he was so stricken he went out in his car (they actually had matching cars) to visit all the places that had once been special to them, and on that trip he got into an accident and sent the little Civic into a guardrail. And that would have been enough, more than enough, except that three months later his house burned down. Yes, the very same house he and Linda had shared and he had later shared with the baby slut, as Linda called her. It was delicious. Linda always ended the story with, "Yes, there is a God."

Linda and Tom had met because of Greylock. Six years after her divorce she had moved to Brooklyn where she sold real estate, and she'd met Tom at the animal shelter on the day she adopted what was then a small grey kitten. At the time Linda didn't like cats, but figured she'd love a kitten and then also love it when it became a cat. She thought that loving a cat might pave the way towards loving a man again, if she could find one in New York who was not married, gay, or recently divorced and going through one of those transitional periods where he could not limit his affections to just one person.

On his adoption certificate, she named her kitten Greylock after a beautiful mountain in western Massachusetts. She'd been there once to visit a friend, and they had climbed it on a foggy day and felt like they were in England.

"Great name," said Tom who would become her husband in less than a year. "I used to have a business in Western Mass."

"What kind?"

"I was a contractor. I built the shops in malls—you know how all the Gap stores and Victoria's Secrets look alike? I made sure they did."

"That doesn't sound very exciting," Linda said.

"It wasn't. That's why I'm not doing it anymore."

"So what do you do now?" For some reason Linda found it easy to ask personal questions of this stranger.

"I make warehouse lofts into condos."

"And that's better?"

"Some days. I'm getting tired of polished granite counters and stainless steel stove tops." Linda laughed. She lived in an old Brownstone in Park Slope with all the charm in the world, but the pipes groaned, and the radiators hissed, and the old windows let the wind right in. Her so-called three rooms were tiny. She'd spent hours thinking of those lofts fitted with huge new windows and infused with light. She then did something a woman living alone in the city should never do and invited a stranger to help her bring the kitten home. She needed to buy food and a dish and a water bowl and kitty litter, and she did not have a car. Nether did he. He came with her by subway all the way to Brooklyn without mentioning that he lived on the Upper West Side.

Linda still enjoyed recounting all the details of what came next, how she easily eclipsed the other girl friends; how he chopped and she minced while they made dinner. If they decided to go for a walk on a rainy night, he found the keys while she located the umbrella. Best of all, when she confessed that she imagined a future with white canvas sofas and uninterrupted sleep, meaning she didn't want children, Tom had said he felt the same way.

In six months they were living together in his large apartment; a year later they left the city and moved to Cooper Hill. Now Greylock had arthritis and could no longer groom himself. His once luxurious coat had spiraled into dreadlocks that pulled against his skin. He had to have his coat clipped on occasion, and then he got cold. Tom and Linda no longer let him in their bed because he liked to pee there. Sleeping on top of the heat register, he demanded excessive heat throughout the fall and winter. At night when they set the thermostat lower, Greylock howled like an outraged tenant. Linda, suffering from menopausal night sweats, slept on the coldest winter nights with the quilt thrown back and the windows open while the furnace churned away and Greylock enjoyed sauna-like heat in the guest room.

It had surprised her that Tuesday afternoon to find the smelly paper towel wrapped around an unmistakable mess of Greylock's in the trash. Was it possible that she had cleaned this in the morning and forgotten? She'd been forgetting so many things lately she could barely keep track: first those chairs, then her glasses, which she lost three or four times a day, then the car keys—she took care of that by hanging the color-coded hooks on the wall. Still, she didn't forget things that concerned Greylock. Tom must have done it, she concluded, but she didn't thank him because she did not want to be the one to start that conversation.

Jack barely got past hello and goodbye when it came to his neighbors, but put him in front of a classroom or next to a small struggling boy and he had no trouble at all finding the words he needed. On a fall afternoon with the brightest light and sweetest air anyone could imagine, Jack took a deep breath and tried to distract the child across the table from him from lunging for the right answer. He said, "So what you need to do while you're reading is ask yourself what are the main ideas. There are a lot of facts to get straight, but they won't make any sense if you don't understand the ideas behind them."

Eric Darling, a twelve-year-old whose asthma had kept him out of school a lot, had already told Jack that he had the worst name in the history of the world, and everyone at school hated him because he couldn't do sports, and he'd rather be outside than inside his house with a tutor. Eric glared at Jack and took an apple from the fruit bowl. They had been going over one chapter for half an hour, and still Eric couldn't answer the questions on the homework sheet. Jack saw how he was clenching his hands and taking short, shallow breaths. Knowledge, like his breath, got stuck inside this boy and tensing himself only made it worse. Jack pushed the textbook to the other side of the table.

"Forget about history for a minute, and take a look at this apple. Say you wanted to grow a tree full of these. You'd have to know a lot about apples and orchards, fertilizer and pests, soil and water conditions; but first you'd have to have the idea of the apple, right?"

Eric looked dubious.

"Hold that bite in your mouth for a minute before chomping down and tell me what you taste."

"Apple," said Eric

"Sweet or tart?"

"Tart"

"Mealy or crisp?"

"A little mealy."

"Can you imagine why that might happen?"

"I'm not an apple farmer," Eric said, sounding tired and a little sulky. His mother, who was listening from the kitchen, wondered where all this was going.

"You don't need to be an apple farmer or any one thing to use your mind and imagination," said Jack, "Now tell me something more about mealy apples."

"They seem dry," said Eric.

"And?"

"Maybe a little soft, like old lady's arms," offered Eric.

"So, if you were an apple farmer, what would you do to keep your apples from getting mealy?"

"Maybe I'd make sure they had plenty of water, and then I'd try to pick them and sell them when they were just ripe." Jack smiled. "Am I right?" Eric asked.

"Don't know," said Jack, "I'm not an apple farmer either, but those were very good ideas."

"But what difference does it make, if you don't know if I'm right or wrong? That's just stupid."

"Why? Farmers didn't start out with books about farming. They got ideas and tried things and when something worked, they knew it was a good idea. They had to be thinkers as well as farmers." Jack then turned back to the history textbook they'd been studying earlier.

"Okay," he said, "now forget about apples and pretend that you're the President of the United States, and thousands of people have no work, and people are starving. What would you do?"

"I'd make some jobs," said Eric.

"And if you didn't want proud people to think this was just charity, how would you explain all these jobs?"

Eric beamed, "I'd call it the New Deal, and everyone would think they were part of this new big thing."

"Exactly," said Jack, "What kind of jobs would these be?"

With that question Eric named all the TVA and CCC projects that he had read about but could not retrieve from memory at the beginning of the session. His mother, listening in, thought: the man's a genius.

With that, Jack considered this a good day. For whatever people could afford, he taught almost anything: U.S. history to Eric, Italian to a sixty-year-old woman who wanted to travel to Italy but not without knowing the language, piano to Amanda Sloane who had wanted music lessons all her life, good old-fashioned arithmetic to kids struggling with the new math. What he would not do for any price was SAT or AP prep, or any tutoring that involved giving some kid an edge over another, particularly in pursuit of admission to certain colleges. He'd had more than enough of that.

Jack had a PhD in philosophy, a Masters in U.S. History, and an MFA in English literature. He could write and read in French, German, and Italian. What he didn't already know he could learn and then teach. It seemed he'd been doing it his entire life— first with his younger brothers, later in high school where kids in the honor society helped the ones who were struggling, even later as a part-time job in graduate school, and then at Burnside Academy with some of the most talented kids in the country. Massive movements in history revealed themselves to him as outcomes of social, political, or economic causation—or more often a combination. Learn the geography of some part of the world, he once told his students, and you can predict its future. A deep harbor will bring trade and money. Water will make a desert bloom. His students never needed to cram for exams. His lectures and the discussions that followed filled their minds with vivid images of the landscape, personalities, and power struggles that shaped history. All they had to do was relax and write it down.

His afternoon with Eric made him think about his prep school.

Burnside would be good for Eric; the boy needed some space away from his hovering mother, a little breathing room, so to speak.

When Jack finally earned his doctorate and Cate had run out of patience, he gave serious thought to his future and found himself drawn back to Burnside Academy: a beautiful place with Georgian brick buildings and swaths of green lawn, where bells marked the time, young voices came together in song, and tradition held everyone in thrall. Two days after he'd been born, Jack's father had written a letter to the director of admission and the director of development, letting them know that Jack Walker III was on his way as his father and grandfather before him. Jack's dad brought him to the ancient lovely campus often and Jack grew up knowing that his mother would pack his bags during his thirteenth summer and off he'd go. Much later, when the twins were born and Jack resolved to never send them away, he wondered about his mother and the other mothers who had married sons of Burnside; did they know from the beginning that they'd have to give up their children at such a tender age?

Yet his adolescent soul had been well-tended there. Not a single moment of homesickness had ever bothered him, and because he had all the right clothes and could show his new friends pictures of his father and his grandfather in old yearbooks, but most of all, because he could play three sports (having been groomed at a private day school that had a history of getting kids into Burnside), he made friends easily. By his senior year he developed the required cynicism, but as the years went by he'd become nostalgic, especially when thinking of his teachers. Not a single college professor had come close to the high school teachers he'd loved. College professors seemed like lazy slobs compared to faculty who also coached and lived with students and never turned a troubled kid away, even if you knocked in the middle of the night, as he had done just once when his mom was in the hospital and he couldn't sleep.

Burnside loved to have alumni come back. The school had unsuccessfully hired public school teachers and even college professors attracted to free housing, hand-picked students, and lush surroundings and lost them just a few years later as astonishment set in and they realized what was required. Teaching, coaching, and living in a dorm—a job description called the triple threat—ensured the intimate faculty student contact that made the school work, and few people could handle it. Less than a week after he'd sent in his resume, Jack got a call from the dean of faculty. He went to talk to him, and then he and Cate came for a second visit in which they were given a campus tour and a chance to meet all the senior administrators and the student leaders. He visited a class and met with the athletic director who was pleased that he could coach soccer, swimming and lacrosse. They signed the first of what would be seven one-year contracts, and in late August of that year they moved into a small apartment in a boys' dorm. By year three they had a much larger apartment, and had they stayed and done dorm duty for ten years, they would have secured one of the old homes and lived without teenagers overhead.

They should have stayed there, is what Jack thinks now. It was so safe. Children played on the Quad, faculty families ate with the students in the dining hall. "Just teach and care for these kids, and we'll take care of everything else" was the message the school delivered to the faculty. No leaves to rake or snow to shovel, no roofs to fix nor homes to paint. No grocery shopping necessary. No gardens to destroy the green vistas. It had been fine for a while, then Cate said she hated Burnside because they had no privacy, and Jack served on too many committees, and the students barged in any time they needed something, only they really had no need of anything. Having no experience with prep schools, she found the entire culture odd, the self-satisfaction, the dowdy clothes the faculty wives wore, and the elitism. Nothing Jack could say could convince her that high school should cost more than thirty-thousand dollars a year. He continued to argue for what he called a life of service, but she had planted doubts.

"Look at your class list," she said one night, "It's like a list of Fortune 500 companies."

The next day he surveyed the kids in his second-period U.S. history class and saw the heir to a huge pharmaceutical company, a girl whose last name was the same as a nationally-known brand of shoe, a boy with the same name as an oil company. Well, he thought, these are tomorrow's leaders. I can have an impact here.

Cate quickly disabused that idea. She always had her shit detectors tuned to high. She said, "Oh yes, they'll do a little community service while here, and they'll serve on some non-profit boards when they get out, but they'll also use their money to elect presidents who roll back estate taxes and cut funding for public education, and they'll do it while they write checks to the Metropolitan Museum of Art, and in their spare time they'll raise funds so Burnside can have a field house."

He had not crumbled all at once, "Growing up in Greenwich doesn't make you a model of egalitarianism, you know."

"At least I went to public school," Cate said.

"Some public school. Every kid there lived in Greenwich. Did they bus any kids in from some other town? When exactly did they start offering French, third or fourth grade? I forget. Burnside has kids from the inner city, kids who never walked through the door of your high school."

"Yes, and all the financial aid is a good thing, but it does not address the structural problems."

"And what does?" Jack asked, "What revolution hasn't ended in bloodshed with the formerly oppressed becoming the oppressor? Where are the labor unions people fought so hard for? Even Ben and Jerry's abandoned their pay formula and hired a pricey CEO. In Sweden, conservatives are winning elections." He could have gone on and on.

"None of that changes the fact that I hate it here," Cate said in a ferocious whisper. As long as school was in session, they never raised their voices in the dorm. "I will not let you turn this into an academic discourse on revolutions. You always do that; you intellectualize everything, and you are not hearing me. I can't breathe here. I have no friends here. I want to plant flowers and know I'll be living in the same place a year from now. I want to go grocery shopping and cook. This WASP kibbutz is not my idea of a community."

"When did you start wanting to cook?"

"I have always loved to cook," Cate answered, truly surprised.

Jack raised an eyebrow, a gesture she sometimes found sexy. "I couldn't even turn around in our old apartment; that's why I never cooked there, but I'm a good cook. Jack, please let's stop arguing and think about it just a little bit. Do you really want to grow old with a whistle around your neck every afternoon and a row of kids jogging behind you like imprinted ducks? You have a PhD. Are you going to use it to lecture me on labor history? What about research, what about writing, what about real conversation? All anyone cares about around here is if Burnside beat Deerfield or Andover last week and by how much."

Jack would always remember that argument, word for word, because, after two miscarriages, he and Cate had just that morning decided to try again for a baby, and their sex had been profound and brand-new, and he'd thought they were heading for a wonderful day.

Then the fight, out of nowhere it seemed. No, not from nowhere. Cate got mad because she'd put a note on their door asking the girls (they had changed dorms again) not to knock unless there was an emergency, and then one knocked because she needed change for the clothes dryer. It didn't bother Jack because they had finished making love, but Cate couldn't let go of the fact that fifteen minutes earlier that interruption would have been terrible.

"We would have ignored it," Jack had said. Her hair was all tangled. Her green eyes were bright and her smell still lingered on his fingers. They had decided to forgo the Sunday brunch and make pancakes. He didn't want to see the day ruined.

"But it might have been a real emergency, a fire or an injury. That's the trouble with this place. We are always on call. If you wanted this, you could have been a doctor." Frustrated tears began to roll down her perfect cheekbones.

June, July and August remained good persuaders but Cate did not give up. For a year she led him on rides through the hills around Burnside, and gradually they found themselves looking into farmhouse windows at twilight, with Cate wondering out loud what it might be like to live in your own house and grow your own food and know that the sum of your days added up to a well-stacked woodpile, an abundant garden and aching muscles. She planted a longing for self-sufficiency;

and Jack started to feel that Burnside owned them and lulled them into complacency with all the benefits. Finally what got to Jack were the parents, competitive strident people who thought of themselves as advocates for their children and interfered with every aspect of their kid's lives. Johnny should have more time on the field. Brooks needs a larger room. Trip's math teacher doesn't understand him. Sloane could have a trip to Europe and a new Saab if she got into Harvard, but when she got into the University of Vermont instead, her parents bought her a ten-speed bike.

In the very last week of the summer of 1997, Jack and Cate saw the For Sale sign on the land in one of the hill towns. Forty acres with woods, fields, and a small pond, enough wood to heat forever, enough cleared land for a garden and some goats. They used "it" the money in Jack's trust fund—and paid cash. "It" had always been there but rarely discussed. At the age of fourteen, Jack had come home from Burnside for Thanksgiving vacation after his father had had his first heart attack. He sat him down to reassure him that whatever happened, he and his mother would be fine, and he showed him his portfolio.

The rows of numbers had meant little to Jack and finally he asked, "What does all this mean?"

And his father, who looked pale and sickly had said, "Son, what it means is this: you will never really need to work and your children won't either and probably their children will be set for life, depending on how this is managed."

It was too much for a fourteen-year-old. Why study then? Why care about where you went to college or what you might want to do with your life? He returned to school dazed and might have gotten himself into all kinds of trouble, but he'd confided in his house master, who turned out to be a kind, wise man with a trust fund of his own, and this man had persuaded him that the money gave him the freedom to lead an exemplary life. He would not need college loans. That money would be available for people in need. He could choose a career without worrying about his income. He could be an artist or marry one. He could be a social worker or a teacher or even an intellectual and never need to work for a company that made gadgets for the military or a financial firm that robbed pensions. This teacher had given Jack an idea of goodness.

The land gave form to that idea. They could lead a simple life there, and maybe he would find what he wanted to do. After the closing they bought a bottle of wine and camped there on the last night before they went back to school. A week after the opening of school madness at Burnside, Jack made an appointment with the headmaster and got permission to live off campus after another year in the dorm. Normally this would not have been permitted, but the school was having a hard time housing the entire faculty and Jack had a long family history with Burnside. The Walker Endowed Fund helped to pay for the teaching fellows program, for one thing. For another, the director of development had plans to ask for a significant gift to the endowment. That fall Cate got pregnant. They broke ground for the house in October before the ground froze and moved in early spring just weeks before Cate gave birth. It was a crazy time. A new house, infant twins, a puppy; they were way off the charts in terms of stress, and none of it penetrated their joy.

Joy, such a simple word. Jack thought that Molly should have been named Joy, and on his worst days his only comfort came in knowing that almost every second of her life was joyful. Zeke's too. The babies slept with Cate and Jack, despite his parent's warnings, and never cried themselves to sleep. His rosy babies walked a little later than some others and seemed content for the longest time to crawl backwards until they bumped into one another. They talked first to each other in their own language and then began naming the whole world and speaking in sentences before they were two.

For quite a while Jack and Cate congratulated themselves daily on their decision to leave Burnside. With a dozen teenagers living upstairs they would never have had the time they needed for their own family. And didn't some of the older faculty seem trapped? The ones who waited too long and then wouldn't leave because they had a sabbatical coming, and then couldn't leave because their kids would be attending Burnside in just a few years, and then lost all options because who would hire them at fifty? No, Jack and Cate had been bold and made the move early and everything they hoped for had come to pass.

Except now three of the four were dead, thought Jack. And could the sum of those perfect years equal the long life they should have had? Just a few months before the accident, Cate had begun complaining that they lived too far from town, and the dirt road that turned to mud each spring was impossible, and heating with wood was giving her a sore throat all winter. Beautiful, difficult Cate. On that Sunday of the accident, Jack and Cate had been hissing in whispers about the fact that he thought their life was perfect and she did not when she suddenly said, "I can't do this any more. I need some air. Who wants to go sleigh riding?"

Bicycling back to his place from the tutoring session at Eric's house, Jack thought about all this and might have had one of his very bad nights, except that along the way he met Claire and Andy in the company of Jess Higgins, the dog trainer, who was trying to teach them how to control Nina, who had pulled Claire down twice in the last week because the paperboy had ridden past them. Nina hated the paperboy so much that she could smell him from blocks away. She knew the car his mother drove on rainy mornings when he could not cover the route on his bike, and she growled and lunged at the car. If she was in the house when he came by, she'd follow him from window to window, barking and scratching the sills.

Nina didn't mind Jack's bike at all. He slowed down and she pulled on the leash to get closer. Jess told Andy and Claire not to let her do it. "You're in charge, not her. Make her wait, keep her in a sit-stay until you decide to walk over to Jack." But the directions came too late as Nina had already reached Jack.

Andy called," Nina come. Nina sit. Stay."

Jessica said, "That's no good. You just gave her three commands at once. She thinks you're confused and she's ignoring you. At this point, let her sniff Jack and make believe it was your idea all along."

Nina pressed herself against Jack's leg and gazed at him adoringly. He gave her a treat.

Claire said, "Look, you see, she's not the least bit aggressive and she isn't afraid of bikes; it's just the paperboy. Jess, I think you need to come by in the morning some day to see how bad she is."

"Have you tried taking her out with training treats?" Jess asked.

"We've tried everything," Andy answered, "Treats, cubes of chicken, cheese. If the paperboy rides by nothing distracts her."

Claire thought some history might help, and she told Jess about the black-hooded sweatshirt the paperboy wore in winter and how he swerved and tossed the papers overhand. Nina hated any arm-raising motions. She got upset and barked at the TV if they watched tennis or baseball. If she and Andy danced in the house, Nina jumped between them and tried to pull them apart. She had walked nicely with Lizzie, but not with anyone else. "She has a scar over her right eye," Claire said. "I think she was beaten before we got her."

"That may be so," said Jess, "But it doesn't excuse her behavior. You two have a right to demand good behavior. She just has to know you're serious."

At that moment, Nina, who had been placidly licking Jack's hand, lunged at Maud Crowe, the town's aging post mistress, who had stepped into the street to avoid the small group onto the sidewalk. Maud had a son in Iraq, a crucifix over her bed, and an America flag hanging from her porch. She had no use for all the new people in Cooper Hill, and she considered someone new until the family had been around for a generation or more. She hated the pagan May Day celebration and the way women would nurse their babies in the post office or anywhere else, if they felt like it. But what disturbed her most of all was the way people in line at the post office would go on and on about the war and everything that was wrong with America, as if everyone just automatically agreed with them. Then they'd come up to the counter and smile at her while she weighed their packages, and they had not a single word of apology regarding how rude they'd been, right there in the U.S. Post Office with red, white and blue everywhere.

Maud said, "I hope you have a bag with you in case that dog soils the sidewalk." She addressed her remark to Jack, and it pleased him that she treated him as badly as every one else. Jess had taken Nina's leash and pulled her into a sit-stay with one firm gesture and a liver treat. Andy and Claire looked amazed. Jack swung his leg over his bike and rode off.

Peddling towards home, he thought about how much Cate had liked Cooper Hill and their friends. She'd liked anything that took them away from Burnside for a night, and when they weren't on dorm duty, they had enjoyed many an evening with Claire and Andy and Linda and Tom doing nothing much. The village offered a store, a post office and paved roads, enough to know you lived in the country but without the isolation. The town had never been rich. With one or two exceptions, people had built Capes and two-story Colonials, unpretentious places. They could have settled here back when they chose the land. But THE LAND, as they had jokingly called it when the list of things to do seemed unbearably long and THE LAND seemed like a demanding monster, had become a myth. And they could not let it go.

Jack passed Maud's house and laughed to himself. Some salesman had made a killing in Cooper Hill in the 1950s. Anyone who could afford it had covered their clapboards with asbestos shingles and installed combination storm/screen windows. Walking down the street it was easy to pick out the old people from the newcomers. New people removed the layers that hid the simple beauty of the houses. They pulled linoleum off bedroom floors to reveal wide-pine boards. Maud thought it looked like a lot of work for no good reason and she didn't hesitate to say so if she passed by a house while people were working.

Maud continued on her evening walk around the block thinking about how much she disliked that Claire Westfield and her husband Andy what's-his-name. None of them had the same names anymore. Claire stood on the town common on Friday nights with about a dozen other women, silently protesting the war. How dare they talk about life and war, she thought, feeling her face turn warm. Each and every one of them would have an abortion in a minute and never look back, but they felt entitled to stand there in black clothing silently protesting the loss of life in Iraq, where her dear son had placed himself in harm's way. Maud sometimes prayed for these misguided women; she also prayed that the Lord would lift the hate in her heart. She prayed for company and comfort. She prayed from habit. And she prayed from fear, but all those hours on her knees at church and by her bedside in the dark did nothing for her anger. She'd been singled out to live a hard, unhappy life, and she would never know why.

After Jess waved goodbye, Claire and Andy continued on their own with Nina, who had decided to walk like a dog in a dog show just to prove that she could.

"What are we having for dinner?" Andy asked.

"Salmon. I feel like we ought to invite Jack over sometimes," Claire said.

"Because?"

"He's alone all the time; he must be ready to start getting out, and I feel like we have more in common with him than anyone else."

Right then Nina saw a squirrel and lunged. Because he was trying to pay attention to Claire, Andy let her pull him sideways.

Claire said, "Jess told us not to let her do that."

Andy tugged on the leash and pulled Nina close to his thigh. He said, "All we have in common with Jack at the moment is that we once spent a lot of time together. Honey, if anything happened to Lizzie, we would have heard. She's hiding out with one of her friends."

"I called all her friends."

"They lie for each other. You know that."

"Their parents wouldn't lie." Andy didn't have a good answer for this right away.

"She could have friends we never met. She knows people from all over the country. I'll bet she's in some great New York apartment with some family that lives in Switzerland half of the year," he said.

"But I still can't understand why we haven't heard from her. It's not like Lizzie at all."

Claire bent down and rubbed Nina between the ears. Her curly red hair tumbled into the dog's face. He could see her grey roots, which she usually covered every six weeks. Claire's shoulder blades stuck out like tiny wings. She once had the broad shoulders and slim waist of a swimmer, but she was beginning to look tattered. Andy wrapped his free hand around the back of her neck and rubbed gently. Claire's taut body felt like it would break if she couldn't find some way to relax, but Andy couldn't find any words to make things better. How could he explain his own irrational conviction that Lizzie was fine? He had no evidence, and he had no religion, yet he believed this completely.

The one thing he knew was that with enough people around and enough wine, Claire could stop worrying about Lizzie for an hour at a time, but after long hours with his patients and even longer hours at the clinic, he had no energy at all, and no matter how hard he tried, he found dinner party conversation unbearable. It was just a lot of well-read people agreeing with each other, referencing the week's issue of *The New Yorker* or *The Nation* or *The Times*, as if reading about a problem in any way addressed the problem, as if one more proclamation about the disgraceful Bush White House could magically travel across town and change Maud Crowe's mind. Jesus, he thought, had anyone ever had a name worse than Maud Crowe? But then, it suited her, she swooped around town like something cackling and nasty. Some people would think about her hard life and find compassion, but Andy did that enough in his own practice and at the clinic where lack of money, education, and good sense put women in harm's way, whether they were dealing with an unwanted pregnancy or a long-undiscovered breast lump.

Andy liked being with people when there was something to do. Back when they went to Jack and Cate's place, there had always been a project. Before the twins were born, Lizzie helped Cate in the kitchen or stacked wood with Jack. After the babies came Lizzie watched over them. Conway and Nina ran through the woods and splashed in the pond. Together the two couples had raised the walls for the barn, canned a winter's worth of tomatoes, stacked wood on crisp fall days, shelled beans, stripped corn, and eaten feasts at the end of a long and productive day. After the accident, Claire had hoped they could still spend time with Jack, but the balance had been lost and the memories made it awful. Then Jack got rid of Conway, and Claire thought it was about the worst thing a person could ever do. Lizzie had tried to persuade Andy that they should take her, and Andy had refused. It was hard to say why. An amazing thing then occurred to Andy: Conway could be dead by now or very, very old. How had the years gone by so fast?

Holding tightly on to Nina, watching the last light leak from the October sky and the bats flee from the church steeple, feeling the frailty of Claire beside him, Andy decided to try harder. She was suffering and so was he, but he'd found reserves of strength that had surprised him. Not so with Claire and Lizzie, who had pretty much bludgeoned each other last summer... It all went back to Cate, who still haunted their lives. Saint Cate, Claire sometimes called her. "If we could all die tragically at the age of forty-two then everyone would be remembered as perfect," she'd said to Lizzie back in July, right before Lizzie left.

Later, when he and Claire had gone to bed, Andy stretched out on his back and crossed his hands on his chest. He figured he'd put himself to sleep by telling himself the whole story again. He'd known Cate, who worked with him at the clinic, before he met Claire. In fact, Cate had introduced him to Claire when she decided their affair had to end. Andy had been sorry and relieved. He'd begun to feel trite: doctor has affair with nurse—handsome friendly husband suspects nothing. And anyway, Cate really loved Jack. She and Andy had slipped into their relationship in a careless moment. Once it started, Andy and Cate gave it more meaning than it deserved. First it made them feel great. Then it didn't, and Cate, always practical and pragmatic, broke it off first and delivered Claire and her sweet daughter, Lizzie.

In the beginning the friendship between the two couples had felt odd to Andy. Cate had slept with both men. Claire and Andy knew, and Jack did not. Andy would watch Jack stoke a fire, pour the wine, run his hand through Cate's heavy hair, and sometimes Jack seemed like an innocent fool, so full of enthusiasm for his tools, his wood lot, and the books he'd acquired on home schooling. It was as if three of the four were playing a game Jack didn't know, but the unease wore off over time and disappeared when Linda and Tom joined the group.

For years the three families spent most of their free time together. It had surprised Andy that Lizzie didn't protest, but she always welcomed a visit to Jack and Cate's. An only child, Lizzie made the Walkers into the big family she always wanted. Cate knew before Claire when Lizzie got her first period. Jack taught Lizzie to drive. When Lizzie got her first yeast infection and worried that she might have some sexually transmitted disease, she went to Cate. And after she and Claire had been shopping for a dress for a formal dance at school, Lizzie couldn't be certain about their choice until Cate had approved.

After the accident, Claire and Andy were so stunned by grief that they left Lizzie to handle hers on her own. Stoic Lizzie, who had not let herself cry at the funeral. Considerate Lizzie who had made three meatloaves for Jack to put in his freezer, but then couldn't deliver them and asked Andy to do it. Responsible Lizzie, who set her alarm for five so she could walk Nina before school. Guilty Lizzie, who believed with all her heart that the accident would never have happened if she'd gone over that day and taken the kids out on their sleds. Two days after the funeral, she went to school, earning honor grades, as usual. With Jack's encouragement she'd gone to Burnside as a day student and thrived there. It was spring and she went out for crew and worked herself to sinewy strength. When she wasn't rowing or ladling out food at the soup kitchen in Woodside, she studied. She had everyone fooled.

On the other side of the bed Claire turned and kneaded the pillow and threw off the covers. In a few minutes she pulled them back over her shoulders and turned again.

"Can't sleep?" Andy said.

"It will be Halloween soon."

"I know."

"Then Thanksgiving and Christmas."

"We'll be okay." Andy said, his voice thick.

"No, we won't," answered Claire. "It's hard to believe we'll ever be okay again. I can't stand to be at work. This time last year everything was fine. Lizzie was a senior. I saw her at school everyday and tried to let her have her space, but sometimes she'd sneak up on me in the library and bring me chocolate. Being at Burnside where everyone is afraid to mention her name is horrible." Claire stared at the ceiling for a few minutes and then tossed the covers back. "I'll never sleep. I'm going for a walk. Don't worry about me; I'll be back in a while."

Andy knew not to protest. He listened to the rustling of her getting dressed and heard the kitchen door close quietly then tried to put himself back to sleep with the rest of the story.

Secretly, discreetly, Lizzie began drinking in her freshman year at Burnside. For years nobody knew. In her senior year, she was accepted by Princeton early decision, and in the spring elected by her classmates to give the graduation speech. One month before graduation she got caught drinking in the day student lounge. She'd brought the vodka to campus mixed with fruit juice. Because of her good record, she was suspended for a week and allowed to graduate with her class, but they withdrew the honor of delivering the student commencement address. Claire and Andy had been upset, but surely Lizzie wasn't the first or the last kid to get in that kind of trouble, especially in the spring of senior year. They worried about the graduation parties, but Lizzie had told them she'd be fine; she'd learned her lesson. Then Claire and Andy got the terrifying call from one of Lizzie's best friends. They'd gone to a party at a house in Vermont. The parents had taken all the car keys and offered beer. Lots of kids had brought their own stuff, including Lizzie. Lizzie had passed out and nobody had thought much about it until they couldn't wake her up. She was in a hospital near Brattleboro.

Lying in bed, missing Claire and wondering how long she'd be gone, Andy tried to remember the exact details of that time. Again, Lizzie sobbed and begged for forgiveness. Again, they'd let it go with warnings. She'd been so lucky they'd said. Kids her age died of alcohol poisoning every year. They talked about AA. Lizzie straightened her spine and nearly spat. "I am not an alcoholic. Shit, Mom, kids drink. Like when did you come out of your cave?" Claire and Andy started watching her closely. Claire went to an ALANON meeting, but the children described there didn't sound like Lizzie. They weren't going to Princeton in the fall; they didn't row eights on swollen spring rivers. She let herself hope.

Lizzie had had a summer job as a lifeguard at a day camp. She went out with her friends in the evening, almost daring Claire and Andy to say anything. Then one night she was pulled over and issued a DUI. Her license was suspended, and Claire had to drive her to and from work every day. Claire had suffered so during those silent furious trips that Andy took over, but Lizzie didn't say much to him, either. In late June they tried family therapy. Lizzie had not wanted to go. Andy finally resorted to threats and told her she'd be grounded until August if she refused.

In therapy Lizzie had blamed everything on Claire. It seemed that inside their smart, achieving addicted daughter lived a lost girl who had felt abandoned by her father when he and her Mom divorced and then by her mother after Cate's death, right when she needed her most. About a week after their second session, Claire found a vodka bottle stashed in Lizzie's laundry basket, and they had fought.

A furious Lizzie said, "If Cate was my mother she wouldn't be searching my closets like some spy." And that was when Claire called her friend Saint Cate, and her daughter stopped talking. Instead, Lizzie spent all her time in her room or on the phone and prowled the kitchen for leftovers only when she knew Claire was not in the house.

On July 6, a day seared in both Claire and Andy's memory, Lizzie left in the middle of the night. A terse note let them know that she had called Princeton and asked to defer her admission for a year. She didn't say where she was going or when she'd be back, and Claire had not known where to begin. She could be anywhere; she had friends in New York and California and everywhere in between. She could be living on the streets or in the hospital again. Every time the phone rang, Claire and Andy lunged for it.

Andy heard Claire come in. The church bells rang three times. He waited for her to come up, but she settled on the sofa instead. When he first heard her sobs he thought he ought to let her be, but when they tore from her throat in howling pain, he went downstairs and wrapped himself around her trembling body. Andy rocked Claire back and forth. The sobs would subside for a moment and then surge again. He'd held Lizzie in just this way when she was thirteen, and he and Claire had decided to take her out of the local public school and enroll her at

Burnside. She didn't know anyone there. The boarders ignored the day students, she wailed; everyone knew that. She had cried and begged, overwhelmed with sorrow and he'd held her tight until she cried herself out, knowing she needed a better school, and he'd been right. He'd been right then, but all the consolation he wanted to give to Claire now could not be guaranteed. He could only say words, over and over, "It will be alright; we will be alright," without really knowing that at all.

In the morning Claire urged Andy to go ahead and play tennis with his buddy, Peter. Then, alone and exhausted from the night before she paced, smoked three cigarettes in a row, and thought about calling Linda. She felt like she'd called too often seeking comfort, and though Linda often had wise things to say, she had never had a child. Sometimes Claire wanted to spit her soothing words back to her, and then she felt awful, because Linda tried so hard. She would have called her other friend Melanie if she was home, but she'd gone off to Alaska to paddle around killer whales and hike close to grizzly bears. One of these days she'd go with her on one of these trips. Andy didn't believe her. He didn't think she was tough enough, but Claire felt herself getting tough. One way or another she would find out what happened to Lizzie, and if the news was very bad, she wouldn't care what happened to her; she'd be fearless in the face of bears and killer whales, and if Lizzie came home safe and sound, it might be her turn to take off.

Claire logged on to her computer. When Lizzie left, the police had not helped at all. Oh, they listened politely and took a recent photo with them, but Lizzie was eighteen; there was no evidence of foul play. She could not be counted as a missing person. So Claire had taken matters into her own hands and opened an account on My Space. She had posted a picture of Lizzie and asked, "Have you seen my daughter?" She'd told some, but not all of Lizzie's story. Since she'd begun this project, the world of the Internet had revealed itself as weird and cruel. A psychic had offered to locate Lizzie if Claire could send her a scrap of hair, even an old hairbrush would work. All kinds of people, who might have been real or writing under false names, said they'd seen her. In

California, the mountains of North Carolina, New York City.

At first Claire had been eager to follow every lead, until she checked the dates and realized Lizzie could not have been in all those places at the same time. That Saturday she got the worst message of all. A man wrote, "I have seen your daughter. She was taking it up the ass from a guy with the biggest cock you've ever seen while sucking the cunt of a woman who was bathing in a golden stream from another woman who was eating the shit of the man standing over her." Horrified, Claire logged off. Then she logged back into her account, took down the picture and closed it. She felt horrible. There was no way she could know how many sick disgusting people might have captured Lizzie's image and used it in ugly ways. You could do anything with computers these days. She knew that from her work at the library. She spent countless hours with students warning them about posting pictures of themselves and using these personal networking sites. Burnside had been looking for ways to block them. And despite all that, she'd fallen for it and opened herself to this kind of abuse and exposed Lizzie to the underside of the world, sick emails from strangers. Thank God she hadn't told Andy.

Jingly from too little sleep and too much coffee, Claire considered the day. She was supposed to be in Woodside at eleven to help with the Habitat house. Should she cancel? If so, what would she do instead? She could smoke more cigarettes one right after the other, always outside and brushing her teeth each time so Andy wouldn't know. She could try calling the police again. She could search her address book once more time, to hunt for one of Lizzie's friends she had neglected to call, but that was hopeless. The book was already tattered. She remembered the two long years it had taken her father to die and her mother's endurance; she called up the memory of a long night with an abscessed tooth and the terror that the pain might make her crazy, but none of it compared with what she was going through.

Now it was too late to head over to Woodside, even though hammering nails was one of the few things that gave her relief. Before turning off the computer, she checked the email on her school account. Going back to Burnside in the fall had been excruciating, but it did fill her days and some weekends when she was on duty. Today three students had questions about the research data-bases and the headmaster wondered if she'd serve on the new emergency preparedness committee. Responding took only about twenty minutes. She still had a whole morning ahead. She logged on to Salon.com and read some scathing stuff about Bush. She played ten games of solitaire because she won the first and that seemed too easy so she decided she had to win two in a row, but when she felt nearly cross-eyed she quit, wondering if the program could tell if you were winning too often or too easily and adjust accordingly. She went back into the Salon archives to see if her old essays were still there. Before—everything from now on would be measured in terms of before and after, she thought—she used to write essays.

It had started after her divorce when she wrote scathing things about her selfish ex-husband Brad, who had money to take his new girlfriend to France, but could not make child support payments that month. She'd gotten a ton of email for that one. Then she stole Linda's story about her ex-husband and his temper and people liked that too. The editor asked her to keep sending stuff. After Cate's death she had dared to write about how it feels to lose someone who had slept with your husband. Last winter she'd written about women's bathrooms. Most women these days wore pants and unlike men, these pants ended up down around their ankles. So there were your clothes, crumpled on the floor, where there was undoubtedly old pee, plus whatever kinds of dirt came in on your shoes, and what could you do about it? She'd thought it was kind of rambling, but her mailbox had filled with messages from people who had laughed and loved it and told her she ought to write more. She read those old essays now as though they'd been written by a stranger and could not imagine putting two well-formed sentences in a row.

Sneaking into Claire and Andy's house was easy. Jack knew every inch of the place, and Nina was useless as a guard dog. She loved company and she knew him. Inside he saw books and magazines stacked by chairs and piled on tables in a friendly-looking mess, as if Andy and

Claire each started articles and then passed them to each other. He noticed some new furniture. In the pantry, twelve cans of tennis balls were lined up next to the wine glasses. Though he considered himself an athlete, he'd never played tennis. Now Jack wished he did; it would have been an easy way to be with people. Not much talking, but good companionship.

He stood for quite a while in front of a wall of family pictures, all matted and framed in stainless steel. He had taken many of them. Claire had started this wall many years ago. He liked the care she'd taken. All the frames were the same size and everything hung straight despite the slanting floor and uneven ceiling that made the images at each end appear to be tipping. He found himself smiling at a picture from Halloween; the twins must have been three. They looked sweet in matching cat costumes, but Cate looked hysterical. She was supposed to be a crow, an unsubtle reference to Maud. She had dressed all in black and strapped on a huge pair of feathered wings that she'd found in one of the Old Home Days tag sales. One wing drooped. The other tilted skyward. She had not been able to breathe well through the cardboard beak she'd made, and she'd pulled it off and let it rest against her forehead. For the photo she'd thrown her arms around the kids, tipped her beaky forehead towards the camera and begun to laugh. Jack could remember watching Claire take the picture, wondering if any camera could really capture Cate's antics. It had.

He lingered over the pictures of Lizzie, braces on and braces off, skinny, then stronger, then very strong and confident in a picture taken during a regatta, and in that moment he wished he had some kind of religion because it would have felt good to pray for her safety. He tried to make the numbers work. What was the probability that two families, living so near each other, consisting of seven people could loose four to death in just three years? It seemed impossible. Lizzie had to be okay or they would have heard something. She ought to call, though. It wasn't like her to worry other people. One of the Lizzie pictures hung slightly crooked and he straightened it. He imagined Claire taking it down to have a closer look and then putting it back, only to take it down again and again.

He would have liked to cleaned the kitchen. If he emptied the dish drainer, swept the crumbs off the counter top, washed the coffee pot, and piled all the mail into a basket, there would be a dramatic difference from very little work. Jack liked to clean his own kitchen for the satisfaction. It was like lining up your tools. But, of course, he couldn't touch a thing. Nina was staring at him. The phone rang and he startled. This was stupid. If he wanted to spend time in his old friend's house he only needed to accept an invitation one of these days or knock on their door any time.

But standing there Jack realized he needed something else. He needed to take something. Not anything of value, exactly. Just something to wrap his hand around. Something that would not be missed. He reached into the fruit bowl and took a ripe green pear and bit right into it. The juice ran down his chin and he wiped it away with the back of his hand. It tasted better than any pear he'd ever eaten and he finished it, standing there with Nina watching his every move.

## *October*

Jess, Mary and April Higgins were in line at the post office on a Saturday morning when April suddenly said, "For Halloween I want to be a willow tree," and Jess said, "Mommy already made you a clown costume."

"But now I want to be a willow tree," April answered.

Mary said, "I'm sure I could figure out how to make a willow tree costume, but you are a very funny, sweet clown."

"I could sleep in the clown costume," April said.

"You could be a willow tree next year," Jess said, a little annoyed at Mary for giving in so easily. April began pacing around the post office, picking mailing envelopes off the display shelves. Jess said, "April, leave those alone." April ignored her. Jess made her way to the front of the line and asked Mary to please get April away from the envelopes which had been neatly placed, but were now stuffed back on the rack in a disordered mess.

They were sending yet another set of family photos to Mary's mother who had not come to their wedding or acknowledged April's birth. Jess was sick of mailing photos and sending birthday cards to a woman who hated her guts, and she was in a bad mood even before she got to the front of the line. When she got up to the counter and presented the package, clearly marked fragile, Maud Crowe stamped it as hard as she could.

"Whoa," said Jess, "Can't you read?" Mary patted Jess's arm to calm her, and Jess shrugged it away.

"That's three dollars and forty-six cents," said Maud. Jess began writing a check.

"We don't accept checks for less than five dollars," Maud said.

"Then give me a book of stamps."

"Can we get the ones with birds on them?" asked April. Maud ignored her and pulled out ones with the Stars and Stripes.

"We asked for the birds," Jess said tightly.

"Wait, I think I have the cash," said Mary. "Wonderful weather, don't you think?" Mary hated conflict and could feel Jess warming up to a good fight.

"Unnatural, if you ask me," Maud said, pushing the stamps across the counter to Jess and making a face that looked like a crumpled brown paper bag. Mary dug through her pockets and found three singles, and then she began searching for enough change. Sticky coins came forth with the remains of sucking candies and little specks of tobacco. Mary smoked guiltily and brought her butts home to put in the garbage. Jess began digging in her pockets as well. When the total reached three dollars and thirty-five cents, and Jess said she'd go out and look for coins under the car seat, a person in line behind her handed her a dime and a penny.

Maud shot a poisonous look. Why was it that people stepped forward to help people like Jess and Mary? When Maud could bear to think about them and what it meant for them to be married, and the things they did together, things that married people did or had to do as part of their marital duties, she felt disgust rise and spread heat through her body, like those hot flashes that had tortured her for years. Last summer when that bear had made its lumbering way through Cooper Hill pawing through everyone's trash, Maud had been the first to see the damage, because she always took an early morning walk. The whole street had been disgusting, but the mess outside Mary and Jess's house was the worst of all with soiled sanitary napkins everywhere. Maud guessed that women living together probably synchronized their periods over time. This bloody display, this evidence of seepage and foul odors and the things that happened between a woman's thighs, had forced her to acknowledge the touching with hands and possible mouths, the indecency of it all and her heart had closed. Maud had once tried praying for their souls, but she never could summon any real concern. In fact, if their souls were saved and they ended up in heaven, she thought she'd rather be in hell. They left at last and drove away in their awful foreign car with all the stickers on it. It needed a muffler. One would think they'd at least fix that and not call attention to themselves.

As all these new people moved to Cooper Hill, Maud had tried to accept the changes, but one incident after another had soured her. First she had tussled with Cate Walker. Now nobody dared to say a bad thing about a woman who had tragically died along with her two young children, but if anybody ever asked Maud, she'd have a thing or two to say about that woman. First of all, she might have been a midwife, but she also assisted with abortions. That woman's health clinic where she'd worked and Andy Spencer still worked killed innocent unborn babies every day of the week. How anybody could bear to work in such a place astonished her. And, Cate had not been a careful person. She drove too fast. She came to the post office without her wallet. She forgot to return her library books. She didn't even take good care of her teeth. Maud knew because she'd gone to the same dental hygienist who talked about everyone in town. She'd also neglected to get the twins to the dentist early on, and they both had had cavities in their baby teeth. But all that could have been chalked up to having a busy life, and Maud would not have given it a second thought if Cate had not had an affair with Andy Spencer right under Jack Walker's nose. Everybody knew, it seemed, except Jack. It was before Andy married Claire. He'd lived alone in town and Cate came to him. It was easy for a midwife to be out at all hours. Cate had been smart enough not to bring her car. They'd driven to Andy's in his car, but Maud had seen them coming and going. And she had always liked Jack. He was from a good family and even though he didn't go to church, he helped build the booths for Old Home Days and brought in a bushel of tomatoes for the market stand. Unlike Cate, who had refused to participate and once told her God was just myth dreamed up by people who didn't want to think for themselves.

Back when she would picket the clinic, it was all she could do to stop herself from screaming "whore" when Cate arrived for work. Imagine that: her group had been told to step back out of the way of the patients. Paid police officers had ordered her around like some common criminal when a slut who helped to murder children stayed safe inside the clinic and had the gall to peer out the window with a disgusted look on her face. Maud and her small group kept the required distance, but one afternoon when Cate came out, Maud followed her to her car. Maud, who had once made the long drive to welcome Cate and Jack to town and invite them to church, stood between Cate and her car. Cate had said, "Maud, this is ridiculous. I need to leave now," and Maud had stood her ground.

Very calmly, as if she was talking to some crazy person, Cate said, "Maud, I am going to push past you now and get into my car."

To this day Maud cannot say what came over her, but in a flash she thrust her arm forward and slapped Cate Walker right across the face. Everyone saw her do it.

Cate held her hand to her face for just an instant. Then she glared at Maud and showed just what kind of person she really was. "You old cunt. Get out of my way or I'll call the police." That was horrifying, but worse was her group's reaction. They banned her from future demonstrations. The very group she had formed had cast her out like a leper. Maud had had some hard times, but when she thought of her current problems, she could trace them right back to that day.

And now, one of those very same women came up to the Post Office counter with six large envelopes. It had been years since they'd had a real conversation, and Maud knew Eleanor's husband had died. "How good to see you," she said. "I was so sorry to hear about Bill. How are you managing?"

"The way we all do," Eleanor said. "You know how it is."

"Well, I've been alone so long now. It's different for you."

"I keep myself busy."

Maud felt the strain. The conversation had no momentum at all. "I stay busy, too," she said. "There's always the church. So much to do there, and this work. I am so happy to have it, though it gets harder all the time." She had used her *you know what I mean* voice.

"Because of your arthritis?" Eleanor asked.

"Oh no. That hardly bothers me at all these days. I had my hip replaced a few years ago. What's hard is all these new people. I used to come to work and know every single person who came in. Now, there's no telling what kind of person will walk up to the counter." She tipped her head towards the parking lot, but Eleanor didn't seem to understand.

"Like those two women who just left. This town is certainly changing, if you know what I mean."

"You mean Mary and Jess?" Eleanor asked. Maud nodded. To her shock, Eleanor said, "They are just the sweetest couple and their little girl is an angel. I hired Jess to come help me with Bomber, remember him? Well, after Bill died I thought I was going to have to get rid of him, and I really didn't want to. It would have been the last thing Bill wanted, but Bomber missed him so. He wouldn't go for a walk and he started having accidents in the house. It was terrible, then someone told me abut Jess and I have to say that woman is a magician when it comes to dogs. I think they understand everything she says. She just told Bomber what he had to do if he wanted to stay in his house and keep on eating mashed potatoes whenever he wanted them, and now he minds me like a lamb."

Maud noticed that people in the line behind Eleanor were getting restless. The deep sighs didn't seem to faze Eleanor. "I was just so grateful that I invited her over for dinner one night, and she said, 'I have a family,' and I said, 'Please bring them along.' Well, I do admit I was just a little surprised when they showed up, but I got over it right away. They are like any other family, only better, because there's no man to start burping after dinner or yawning because the women are talking too much. April is a joy, too, and they are planning on another little one, only this time they are going to adopt, unless it's too expensive. In that case Jess will try."

"I didn't think people like that were allowed to adopt," said Maud, momentarily forgetting about the other customers.

"There are all kinds of restrictions. It's a real shame," said Eleanor. "It costs a fortune to go overseas and lots of countries won't let them adopt, either, but they can get a child from Social Services. I've been reading the profiles and it breaks your heart. You could just sit and cry all day. People like Jess and Mary are raising the children no one else wants, and they are wonderful mothers."

Maud had finished weighing the envelopes and she had heard enough. That last sentence sounded a little smug and preachy, and Maud had not asked for a lesson in tolerance, especially from Eleanor who had turned against her over one rash mistake. She quickly took Eleanor's money and said, "My, my, it is getting busy in here today. I do have to get back to my work."

"Of course," said Eleanor.

"It is hard for people who have never worked to understand," said Maud. "I imagine Bill left you pretty well-off."

"Well, it has been good catching up," said Eleanor.

"I'm always here on Saturdays," Maud said suspecting that from now on Eleanor would avoid ever coming to the post office on a Saturday.

With intention but without much premeditation, she then placed two of Eleanor's envelopes on the shelf right under the counter, next to her tote bag. Maud had begun stealing mail one week after Cate's death. Cate had gone to a medical conference earlier that fateful winter and sent a letter to Jack while she was there. Something had held it up. It happens. When Maud saw the tattered envelope with Jack's name on the front she gasped and then decided it would be just too cruel to deliver it. Her principles would not allow her to read the letter, but having it in her possession made her feel both kind and powerful. She'd never planned to make it a habit, but every once in a while, she felt compelled to snatch this one little bit of life from people who had so much of it.

She rarely took outgoing mail, but Eleanor had asked for it. Denying someone a personal letter by taking incoming mail pleased her more. Usually her confiscation served as punishment, though sometimes not. Like a wealthy woman who shoplifts from time to time, Maud enjoyed the thrill it gave her to tuck a piece of personal mail into her bag, knowing that no soul in Cooper Hill or beyond would ever suspect her of such a thing. At home later she added the envelope to her file; she had it all arranged by date, and when she locked the file drawer she turned the key hard and then patted the outside. *There, there,* she said to herself.

Jack made his first mistake when he went to visit Amanda Sloane's house on the day of Halloween. The smell of burnt coffee stung his nose as soon as he entered, and he turned the coffee maker off. That done, he took some time to look around. Unlike most people who lovingly restored their homes and then filled them with antiques, Amanda had gutted her place and opened it up to light and air. Everything was a slightly different shade of white. The painted kitchen floor had just the barest hint of blue. He found it calming, perfect for a therapist who took in pain and angst all day long. On her dining room table, she had a plate of sand filled with seashells. On her windowsills, jars of beach glass filtered the light. And, of course, there was that piano in the living room.

Jack had brought his camera. Looking at the wall of prints at Claire and Andy's had reminded him of the pleasure he'd once taken in photography. In fact, taking pictures was somewhat like walking around in people's houses when they weren't there. A camera gave you permission to stare, when you took the picture, and then afterwards when you could look without guilt or self-consciousness straight into someone's face—right into a life if the picture was well-composed. Cate used to beg him to put the camera down. She thought he hid behind it. That fall when they were walking the beach with the kids, he'd taken tons of pictures. Back then he still used film, and Cate had complained that he never really appreciated any experience until after he'd processed the film in his darkroom. "If anything bad happens to the film, it's like the day never happened," she complained. He'd denied it, but as usual, she'd hit on part of a truth.

He was standing there, camera in hand, focusing on the beach glass when he heard rustling in the yard. Mary Higgins was out there cutting thin branches from a willow tree. Jack watched her until she left with an armful of branches, and then quickly let himself out. He could easily have been seen through Amanda's uncovered windows, and he knew how his behavior would be judged by others. There would be surprise, then outrage, and finally pity. Because of what had happened. People would make allowances. He hated that. He'd have to move if he was ever discovered. He had to get out of there and keep himself from doing this again. It was a crazy thing to be doing, senseless really, ridiculous. In his haste he neglected to pull the door hard enough, and shortly after he left the wind blew it open.

When Amanda got home and saw the open door she froze and imagined every terrible thing that could have happened. Born in the city, she had come reluctantly to the practice of not locking her doors and windows when she went out and before she went to bed. Once she locked herself out. Once a package got wet on her front steps when it could have been placed on the porch, had the porch door not been locked. It had taken a while, but finally she'd made herself relax. Arguments that anyone who really wanted to get in would just break a window had helped convince her

All that fragile conviction disappeared when she saw that open door. Anyone could be inside, waiting. She called the police and they searched the house, and with their heavy boots covered any small trace Jack might have left. Even after they assured her that everything seemed to be in order, Amanda didn't feel at ease. She sniffed and caught the scent of wood smoke and a hint of moth balls. She didn't heat with wood, and she stored her sweaters in a cedar chest. It didn't matter what the police had said, someone had been there. That night she burned sage to cleanse the house, and the next morning she called a locksmith. She never again left without locking both the front and back doors and compulsively checking again to make sure. She'd get in her car and feel compelled to go back. As soon as she knew the doors were securely locked, she'd worry about the coffee pot and the clothes dryer, go in to check and then need to lock everything all over again.

"If anyone is watching me, they must think I've gone crazy. Really. But I can't help it. I can't pull out of the driveway without going back to the house at least once and usually more. Maybe I should move," Amanda said to her friends on Halloween night as they were stuffing bags for the trick-or-treaters who would be there soon. She was there in the warm glow of Linda and Tom's house, along with Claire and Andy and also Peter and Melanie Stokarski. Melanie, who had taken early retirement from the university where she'd started the women's studies program, had developed an outdoor program for women. She was just back from her trip to Alaska, new muscles coiled her upper arms, her nose was peeling and her lips blistered a little.

Melanie, who liked her friends to call her Mel, listened to Amanda closely. "That kind of fear can paralyze you, you know."

"Or keep me safe," Amanda answered.

"From what?"

"From whoever broke into my house."

"You ought to come on one of my trips sometime. After some white water, a few nights in a tent, and a little rock climbing, the women say nothing can scare them."

"Not my style," Amanda said, looking astonished that Mel could even suggest such a thing.

"I don't know," said Claire, "I thought I had my share of camping in my twenties, but I'd love to be on the river. It looks so calm in the morning."

"We could do that," Mel said. "Some morning when the guys are playing tennis. You, me, Linda and Amanda could all go. I've got two canoes."

"Not me," said Amanda.

"I can't swim," said Linda.

"I might want to sometime," said Claire, "some pretty spring morning, maybe."

"The river is high in the spring. It would be better to try this fall, before it gets too cold." Claire liked Mel a lot, but she couldn't go on a river trip just now. She wouldn't go anywhere until she heard from Lizzie.

"Whenever, just let me know," Mel said, gently.

Over the years Cooper Hill had become a destination for Halloween. Everyone decorated, some families added sound systems and blasted eerie ghost noises into the darkness, and people came out of the hills so their children could walk from one house to another in safety. Tom and Linda had bought enough candy to fill two-hundred bags, and they were worried that they didn't have enough. They had lined the porch rail with tiny jack-o'-lanterns and put huge carved pumpkins on the steps next to pots of purple mums. They hung a skeleton from the porch roof and used black yarn to make a giant spider web above the door.

Tom came into the kitchen wearing a huge gorilla mask. He had a collection and offered a rubber Dracula face to Andy, who was surveying the wine rack.

"What are we eating?" he asked Linda.

"I made tempeh with an apricot glaze and basmati rice with almonds."

Tom looked disappointed. He unwrapped a miniature dark chocolate Hershey bar and Linda scowled,

"Before dinner?"

It's good for me," he said. "Antioxidants."

"I really have been thinking about moving," Amanda said, as if Mel had never tried to change the subject. "Even before someone broke into my house."

"No one broke into your house," Linda said. "The police went through every room, nothing was taken. It was the wind."

"Well even if you're right, this town is starting to feel weird. I hate going to the post office if Maud Crowe is there; just thinking about Jack Walker makes me sad, and he's the only single man in town—at least the only one worth thinking about. Sometimes I wish I was gay. All the new people moving in are lesbians. I could have a great love life if I loved women."

Claire smiled and took the glass of red wine Andy offered her.

"I figured we could drink red now and white with dinner," he said. The doorbell rang and the first group of urchins straggled to the door, tripping on costumes. Tom answered, and a little ballerina took one look at his mask and started to cry.

April and her moms were in the next group. April wore brown tights and the willow branches rose from her shoulders, fastened on with brown elastic.

"I was at the post office the day April decided to be a willow tree," Amanda said. "Jess wanted her to stick with the clown costume Mary had already made, but it looks like she won. Now that was a day when Maud was in rare form. You wouldn't believe the look she gave Jess and Mary. I think she hates the whole world."

"She's had a hard life," Mel said. "She lost her husband when she was in her forties. Heart attack, with no warning signs at all. It would have been awful no matter what, but then it got worse when she found out his insurance policy had lapsed, and she had three kids and no money. At least she'd had them young and they were almost grown. She started working at the post office, and they all got after-school jobs and they made it through. She got them through high school and college and told them they could do anything and they did. One's in California, one's in the Army, and I think she has a daughter in New Jersey. They never come to see her."

"I didn't know all that," said Claire, who had not lived in Cooper Hill as long as Linda or Mel. Mel had actually been there longer than anyone. She'd come in 1971 and lived on a commune. "I took her for a bitter old woman who had never been married or had children. Still, if I was her kid, I'm not sure I'd make an effort to visit."

"Well, she's never been pleasant. She's the first one to complain or criticize if someone doesn't take care of their lawn or paints their house a color she doesn't like, which is anything other than white or gray. It was worse when the hippies moved into the house next door."

"When were the hippies there?" Claire asked.

"Before the Rastafarians and after the guy with the pit bulls," Mel said.

"I remember when the organic gardeners moved in and made that compost pile that drew rats into town," Claire said. "We had them in our barn and then in the house. Poor Lizzie woke up one morning and found one in her room."

Andy froze. Claire had not made such casual mention of Lizzie in a long time.

Sounding just a little shrill, Claire continued, "And then, of course, we had to take the barn down, which was a good thing because now we have windows facing south. Jack and Cate helped while Lizzie watched the twins, and we felt like pioneers or something, only we couldn't do it all. We stripped most of the barn board and sold it to Burnside. They used it to make one of their new buildings look two-hundred years old."

"It's a shame to lose an old barn," Tom said.

"Not after you find out it's infested with rats," Andy said, shuddering at the memory. Linda started putting food on the table. Claire made a salad. Andy filled all the wine glasses again. The bell rang and to everyone's surprise, Maud stood at the door with one little ghost in hand and another hiding behind her.

"Maud, hello," Linda said, "Are these your grandchildren?"

Maud shook her head. "Their mother had to work tonight, and their father is away on business," she said. "I know them from church. This is Sally and behind me is her sister Jill." She gently nudged the shy one forward. After they had taken their bags, Maud reminded them to say thank-you, and once they had done that, each offered a small hand to Maud's old calloused hands as she gently guided them down the stairs.

"Wow, that was strange," Amanda said, "do you think we conjured her?"

"I've never been very nice to her. Maybe I should be better." Claire said. "One year we were stacking the vegetable display at Old Home Days and I wanted to take a break, so I asked some boy to help her. He was about fourteen and just hanging around. Well, Maud didn't approve. She said, 'Really, Claire, this needs to be done well,' and what did I do? I turned to her and said, 'Give me a break Maud, a monkey could do this.' I was annoyed, you know. There are people and Maud is one of them, who just make too much of everything. And I really didn't mean it to come out like it did. Of course she was offended, and she never asked me to help at Old Homes Days again, which is fine with me because it's a church event after all. But, I don't know; seeing her like that with those two little kids makes me think we could all try harder."

"I think Jack likes her," Linda said. "I've seen him talking to her. She's as crusty with him as she is with everybody else and it makes him feel normal."

"Well," said Andy, who had said very little all evening, "I don't think anyone can really be normal after something like that happens. To lose everything all at once like that—I don't think I could ever get over it."

"Well, it would certainly be hard if people never stopped reminding you and never treated you like a normal person," Amanda said. "Maybe it's everybody else who can't get over it."

"What's a normal person?" asked Tom, who had taken his mask off so he could eat.

"You want a clinical description or just what I think?" Amanda asked.

"Both."

"I guess it's about balance. Bad things happen and grief is appropriate, but at a certain point a person has to start living. Normal for Jack would be if he started going out again, preferably with me." Amanda poured another glass of wine. Andy and Claire had eaten quickly and now they were answering the door so that Tom could finish his dinner.

"Dream away," said Claire, over her shoulder. "Jack's a one-woman man, and the woman was Cate. You never met her. I knew her before I even knew Andy."

Andy touched her arm, an intimate message cautioning her to stop. She ignored him.

"Actually, I knew her when she was sleeping with Andy, but I hadn't met *him* yet. No, that's not true. I went out to dinner with them once, so they could eat in a restaurant without being *seen* together. It didn't work, of course. She was practically sitting in his lap. They kept sharing food and then, every once in a while one of them would say something to me and not even wait for an answer. Andy doesn't even remember the dinner."

Linda said, "Claire, every time you get drunk you tell this story."

"I never heard it," said Amanda. "Did Cate sleep with Andy before she married Jack?"

"No, during, and then she and Andy both had an attack of conscience and broke it off, and Cate gave me to Andy. Instant family for the forty-year-old doctor who had avoided marriage, and was finally ready to commit. I tell you, it's all timing. Romance has nothing to do with it."

"But why?" said Amanda. "I always heard that they were this perfect couple. See, this is why I should move. This is the most incestuous place. Every time I meet someone and learn his history, he's all tied up with friends and friends of friends. You sleep with one person around here and it's like you've had sex with the whole valley. I thought you guys spent all kinds of time together. Wasn't it weird?"

"First of all, they *were* a good couple," Claire replied. "Cate and Andy sort of drifted into it from working so closely together, you know, the doctor-nurse thing. Plus, living out there so far away from everything was starting to make Cate crazy. And Jack changed. First he wanted to be a prep school teacher forever and live in school housing and let Big Daddy Burnside take care of him, and then he turned into Paul Bunyan. He's got tons of money. There was never any need for him to own three shirts and grow his own food, and cut all his own wood, but he got caught up, and Cate would get home and all he could talk about was seed catalogues. Of course, Cate couldn't say anything because leaving Burnside and moving out there had been her idea, only she had pictured something more like a horse farm with lots of hired help." Claire paused just long enough to pour another glass of wine.

Andy said, "Claire, this may not be a good idea." She ignored him.

"Anyway, Jack never knew, and after a while Andy and I forgot about it. Then they had the twins and Lizzie loved being with them. After I divorced her dad she was starving for family. And, as you all can see, Andy and I are perfectly matched. He is steady and I am boring. I tell the same stories over and over again, and I drink too much." Claire was swaying a little by now. "The thing is, even if Cate had been single, she and Andy wouldn't have stayed together. She was so intense she would have worn him out. Cate was fun, beautiful, smart and careless, like Daisy Buchanan. And I'll tell you one thing, and this is one thing I haven't said before: those children would never have gone into the water if Jack had been there. He would have taken one look at the ice and known it was rotten."

"Claire, that's an awful thing to say," Andy said.

"About Cate or Jack?" Claire asked. "Jack could have gone with them. I'll bet he thinks about it every day." She walked out to sit on the porch. Andy followed. Linda and Tom stood silent.

"That doesn't mean his life should stop forever," Amanda said, groping.

"Survivor guilt can be very powerful, but people can recover."

"His life isn't stopped," Tom said. "He tutors kids and gives piano lessons, he walks around town and talks to some people; he never did talk much. He gets up in the morning and eats and gets himself dressed. It's not like he sits around drooling with a body filled with drugs to keep him calm."

Linda shot a warning look Tom's way, afraid that Claire, who could not put one foot in front of the other these days without antidepressants, had heard him. It was okay. Claire and Andy had settled into the porch rockers, and they were holding hands.

Linda said. "Maybe I should have asked him over tonight, but we all tried for years. He always said no, and it made me feel terrible, as if I was too shallow to understand his pain. What can be worse than telling someone in pain to get over it?"

"Ignoring him could be worse," Amanda said. "One of these days I'm going to ask him over and see what happens. Should I invite you guys and Claire and Andy?"

"I think it's impossible for him to be with us," Tom said. "We were all there that day. Maybe he would have gone with Cate and the kids if we weren't coming over." He pushed his plate away and put the gorilla mask back on.

Linda said, "Give it up, Tom. I think things have quieted down."

Tom went to count the bags. They had just seventeen left. The younger children had gone to bed, and now the streets of Cooper Hill filled with kids too old for trick-or-treating, but hanging on for just one more year to candy and costumes, to mystery and the sound of their footsteps moving through dried leaves, to the smell of wood smoke and this last ritual of childhood. Shredded moving clouds parted for a moment and moonlight filled Claire's lap.

"Tomorrow will be colder," Claire said. Andy agreed.

They sat on the porch without coats, remembering the last time Lizzie dressed up for Halloween. Cate had been dead for seven months. Lizzie had shaved her head and worn a sheet and knocked on doors as Gandhi. What un-haunted thirteen-year-old girl shaves her head? She could have worn a bathing cap or pulled a nylon stocking over her hair. Why hadn't they known then that something had gone terribly wrong?

## *November*

Linda sat at her desk in her third-floor office and could not remember the password to her eBay PayPal account. She tried Greylock's name forward and backwards and variations on her initials and Tom's, the problem being that she had a Yahoo mail account, an

Amazon account and a variety of others, and had heeded the warnings not to write down the passwords and leave them near the computer, nor use the same password over and over. She wanted to bid on two items and watch three others and could not do so without her password.

Relax, she told herself. Keep scanning the site as though remembering the password doesn't matter and the combination will come to you. Combination—yesterday she had not been able to remember her locker combination when she went to the gym. It has to be stress, she thought. She and Tom had taken on too much. Too many details, too much striving for the perfect this or that. But using good taste to ferret out distinctive items from all the mediocre crap on the market had made their business, had made them close to wealthy, and most of the time they had fun. She was looking for just the right wine rack for the kitchen in a house over in Woodside they would soon put on the market.

She and Tom had a small real estate agency. When looking at homes, before they bought theirs in Cooper Hill, they'd been appalled at the way agents presented properties. Their photos showed cords dangling, stained furniture and unkempt yards. For one house, a bedroom picture featured a space heater right next to the bed. Why not advertise a bad furnace, they'd thought. When they opened their agency, they let clients know that they would not show a house until it was ready. This often meant a simple pot of flowers on the steps or fresh paint on the front door. Sometimes ugly lamps had to be replaced. Linda would search out accessories that made all the difference, and in the days before the Internet, she scoured thrift shops or barns filled with antiques and displayed a talent for finding inexpensive items that pulled everything together. For this service they got a ten percent commission, well worth it since people always got their asking price, and during the nineties sometimes got more when buyers got into bidding wars.

For a while Linda and Tom also bought very old houses in complete disrepair and restored them. It had been exhausting and expensive, and the profit margins had been small once the subcont ractors had been paid. When real estate prices over in Woodside began to climb, they discovered an easier and better way to make money. Buy a reasonable house in good condition that had been disfigured by bad taste. Tear up the wall-to-wall and you usually found hardwood underneath. Pull down the layers of ugly window treatments and wash the windows. Paint all dining rooms Benjamin Moore Barley with linen-white trim. Scrape the swans off the bathroom walls and apply paint in very pale gray with just a hint of blue. They had found family rooms with weathered shingles on the inside walls and lobster traps hanging as decoration. They had found cheap paneling covering plaster walls. They had decided that all the knotty pine kitchen cabinets in the world resided in homes in Woodside built in the forties and fifties. These were not the very old Capes and that you found in Cooper Hill. Woodside had been an industrial mill town, attracting working class families for generations until the mills closed. Now there were no jobs for people with high school educations and no woods since all the lumber had gone into the houses, but young professionals were moving in and their taste had been cultivated by the Pottery Barn catalog.

These new houses she and Tom had bought in Woodside were very interesting to Linda. For years they had been hidden behind the old tap and dye factory. The east-facing windows had been blocked by brick stained black by age. The western windows faced the mountain. There had been talk and speculation for years that someone would buy the abandoned factory and make it into condos, but it never happened, and every year more water got in and rotted everything, making the place a hazard. Finally it was torn down, and for the first time, the little row of sweet houses behind it had sun glinting off their windows. Tom and Linda had bought two as they became available, a bungalow and a simple Victorian farmhouse. Each had been occupied by a different widow. Out went the lace curtains and brocade drapes and the overstuffed chairs smelling slightly of urine. In came Tom and Linda's crew. They could transform a house in less than a month. Have it back on the market and sold before the first mortgage payment was due. But everything had to be just right. And in Linda's mind, this particular house would not be right until she'd found that wine rack and a set of decent light fixtures for the front porch. Linda decided to play a game of solitaire or two or more. When she won, the password would reveal itself to her.

Meanwhile, Jack was walking past the house, and he heard water gushing in the basement. From the third floor, Linda could not have heard it, and Jack could not have known that she was home for the day (her car was at the dealer getting a new timing chain). Jack let himself in through the bulkhead and turned off the water valve to the washer. The pressurized hose to the washing machine had split. Until it was repaired, water would flow continuously. Jack knew of people who had gone on vacation without knowing this could happen and come home to wreckage. Now he had some choices. He could go to the hardware store and buy a new hose and install it, or leave a note for Linda and Tom knowing that gratitude would erase any unease about his intrusion. If Amanda had not been scheduled for a piano lesson, he would have gone to the store. He almost had time for both, except that Amanda went crazy if he was thirty seconds late.

Jack was standing at the kitchen counter writing a note when Linda came downstairs looking for aspirin. Dozens of frenzied games of solitaire, one right after the other with no passwords appearing, had given her a migraine. Jack heard her before she saw him. A little bit of sweat trickled down below his armpits and his throat went dry, but his words came out soft and friendly and Linda didn't startle at all.

"I could hear the water running in your basement," he said. "I didn't think you were home, so I turned the valve off. I know you keep stuff down there. I'd have called the fire department or the police, but a lot could have been ruined before they got here."

Linda thought, what a wonderful neighbor, and offered Jack a cup of coffee. "I need some," she said. "Sometimes a really strong cup of coffee is the best thing for a migraine."

"You get them often?"

"Maybe every two weeks."

Linda restrained herself from babbling. In one or two breathless sentences she felt like telling him about the passwords and her locker combination and her night sweats and the business, which was going so well she didn't think she and Tom would ever retire, and Tom, who thought she could keep up this pace forever, and her sisters and brothers who kept visiting and calling, some needing money and others just wanting to talk, as if she had not escaped her big messy family and decided not to have children on purpose. But of course you couldn't unload your own problems on someone like Jack. She pressed her thumbs against her forehead.

"You ought to try massage," he said. "Sarah up the street is a massage therapist."

"I have. About the coffee?"

"No, thank you; I've already had too much for one day."

"I don't know how to thank you for turning off the water. We would have lost thousands of dollars worth of rugs."

"No problem, anytime," Jack said, and then Linda decided to take a chance.

"Jack, what are you doing on Thanksgiving?" she asked, but before waiting for an answer added, "Tom and I are thinking of having some people over. Most of us don't have any family nearby, and it's awful to travel on Thanksgiving, so we thought it would be nice to have a big neighborhood gathering. You'd know everybody."

She saw him hesitate. Maybe if her senses had not been heightened by the migraine she would have missed it, but there was a definite quiver on the left side of his mouth. Such a gorgeous man; age had only carved flattering lines around his eyes.

"Will you at least think about it?" she said.

"Cate's parents usually come."

Linda could think of nothing worse.

"They need to visit the graves," Jack continued. "They come at Thanksgiving, Christmas, Cate's birthday and the twin's birthday."

"Every year?" Linda asked, astonished.

"Cate was their only child."

Linda had such a huge family, a family that would have absorbed such a loss and then spread it out in little bearable pieces among all the brothers and sisters, aunts, uncles and cousins. Jack had to carry his own pain and Cate's parents' too. Poor man—Cate's parents would never let him move on. Their daughter would be erased if he did.

"Well, just let me know if there is any change of plans, Jack.

You are always welcome, always."

Jack nodded and turned to let himself out. "When you go to the store, just ask for washing machine hose. It screws right on. You can turn the water on after you attach it," he said. "The valve is where the hose goes into the drain pipe."

The day had been rainy, but now the sky was clearing and unfiltered winter sun came through the yard and blessed his lovely face with light. At the moment it happened, Linda's migraine vanished and all the necessary numbers and letters appeared as if they'd always been there.

Jack headed over to Amanda's house, hoping that she had practiced since her last lesson. He'd explained many times that she was practicing and perfecting her mistakes and would continue to do so unless she played the scales and learned the keys and, most of all, paid attention to her fingering. Intuitive when teaching U.S. history to a little boy like Eric, Jack became a believer in process when it came to music. An hour of practice for a minute of mastery. The rules come first. No shortcuts. It all sounded good until a woman like Amanda Sloane decided at age forty-five that she wanted to play piano. Her imagination leapt to what-might-be long before her ability had developed at all, which is why she had bought a shiny black Steinway baby grand before she could play "Twinkle Twinkle Little Star."

"Spite. I bought it to spite my ex-husband," she said.

"How does it spite him?" Jack had asked. He had a stack of music books, which she asked him to put down by pointing at them and the table.

"Because it is a perfect choice, and I did it on impulse, with a lot of money that he considered his own. With Hunter there was no such thing as an impulse purchase—not even over a bag of potato chips. It took us two years to pick out a sofa, another year to find a dining room table. When I left we were still eating off a set of tin camping plates because Hunter could not make a final decision on china."

Without asking, Amanda had poured him a glass of cold,

expensive white wine and motioned for him to take a seat. She said, "When I bought this place, I hired a decorator to choose every last item in the house—even the piano. I interviewed her for fifteen minutes and wrote a check. Hunter would have been appalled."

Jack said, "I'm surprised you didn't want to do it yourself, after all those years of compromise."

"I would have made a mess of things," she said. "I can't bring things together in a pleasing way. It's like my walking music: Wagner, Lou Reed, the Unites States Army Marching Band. I'm all over the place."

"But you want to play slow, sad music?"

"I want to play Samuel Barber's Adagio for strings, but on the piano," she said, surprising him for the second time. The first had been an eighteen-foot wall, filled floor to ceiling with CDs.

"Why that particular piece of music?" Her answer almost sent him to the floor. "Because three people I loved, including my father, worked for Cantor Fitzgerald and died on September 11, and when I think about that day I just hear that music over and over again."

"Have you played the piano before?" It was the only thing he could say.

"As a kid, but I never practiced, never even wanted lessons. I wanted to dance, so my mother took me for lessons and pulled me out of dancing school after the first recital. She said I was so clumsy I should learn to play the piano, so I'd have something to do at parties while other people danced."

"Was she always like that?" Jack asked, realizing it was the first conversation he'd had in years when nobody asked him how he was *doing*, with that pained look.

"Is. She *is* always like that, which is part of the reason I am here in godforsaken Cooper Hill, Vermont. She hates the country. She'll never visit."

"Even though your dad is gone?"

"She's already busy with her charities and the parties that go with them. I think she likes being a 9/11 widow. It does offer a bit of cachet."

After that, Jack took a seat on the piano bench next to Amanda with the short hair and tough talk. She began to play and it was awful. She'd found simple arrangements of favorite arias and Broadway musicals, and she pounded away with her foot on the pedal the whole time, making the same mistakes over and over. Jack seriously considered turning her down, until she turned to him with a goofy grin. She was proud of herself; he couldn't believe it.

So he'd said, "If you learned how to use the notated fingering, your hands would be in the right place. It would take a lot less effort to get to the right notes."

Before she began her lessons, Amanda had played all the time. She had played badly and happily. Since Jack began to teach her, the whole endeavor had become a chore, which challenged his whole identity as a teacher. Each week he left Amanda's house with a heavy heart, and each time he came back he sought some kind of clue, wondering what he could latch onto within her that would bring both joy and a respect for discipline.

And now as he approached her door for yet another probably frustrating lesson, the lock startled him, "When did you start locking your door?" Jack asked after he'd rung the unfamiliar doorbell.

"I think someone was in here a few weeks ago," she said. "I came home and the door was wide open."

"Was anything taken?"

"Not a thing and the police came and they found no evidence of a break in, but that was after they walked around in their boots destroying any evidence that might have been here."

"You called the police?" Jack asked, smooth as could be, and terrified.

"Of course, wouldn't you if you came home and found your door wide open? Anyway, even if it was the wind, I feel better now."

"Well, that's a good thing," he said, resenting the locks and thinking about how he had just come to the rescue at Linda's house.

"How's it been this week?" he asked, looking at the piano.

"Not great, my back's been bothering me and sitting makes it worse."

"That's because you get so tense and stiff. Show me how you sit." Amanda moved towards the piano and he saw that she was favoring her right side.

"It looks as though your knee is bothering you," he said.

"It's all connected. I hurt my knee in high school, playing field hockey and limping pulls my back out."

"Where did you go to high school?"

"Miss Halls."

"I went to Burnside."

"I think we had dances with the boys from Burnside."

"I remember some."

"We wouldn't have met. I'm about nine years after you."

"So, other than field hockey, what else did you do for sports?" he asked.

"Basketball in the winter, track in spring."

"Cate played field hockey." The name just popped out. Amanda didn't make a big deal of it, thank God.

"Did she have injuries?"

"Not from field hockey, but her back went out a lot from carrying the twins around, especially when they were toddlers." There, now he'd mentioned *them*. "They'd be almost nine now," he said, testing. Amanda did not reach for him or do anything to make him uncomfortable.

"So, is it worth having a lesson if I didn't practice?" Amanda asked.

"Sure, sometimes a time out actually helps. Start with the C Minor scale." Amanda looked at him blankly. He knew she hated this.

"I should just learn to play by ear," she said.

"Why don't you?"

"Because I can't. I have not one bit of intuition. I have learned every thing I know by following the rules, but it's harder when you're older. C Minor, G Major, none of this means anything to me."

"It doesn't have to," Jack said. "Just do it over and over so your hands know where to go and then the next time you try Chopin it will sound like something."

Like a dutiful child, Amanda turned back to the lovely piano and began grinding away at the scales, head bent and shoulders hunched in concentration, and Jack felt sad; he'd broken the deal. She'd been gentle with him, and he had not reciprocated. Amanda must have felt the same because she stopped playing and said, "What was Cate like? I'm the only person around here who never met her and everyone seems to have an opinion."

"What were your friends who died on 9/11 like?" he countered.

"I asked first," Amanda said and she waited quietly.

"Cate was exciting and unpredictable."

"And beautiful?"

"Yes, very. She had red hair, long and curly, green eyes and pale skin, like someone from a Celtic fairytale."

"And smart?"

"In a practical way; she didn't care to analyze things."

"Did she play the piano?"

"Sometimes."

"Well?"

"She didn't really bother with anything if she couldn't do it well."

"What kinds of music did she like?"

"Big symphonies."

"Who was her favorite composer?"

"Beethoven and Wagner, a little Rossini sometimes."

Then Amanda said, "I like Verdi a lot, but Rossini is too jumpy and fast. It makes me think of monkeys masturbating." She'd caught him completely off guard and he started laughing, and as the image developed, he saw many monkeys working away at themselves furiously along with the music, their little pinched faces gazing off into the middle distance. Nothing had made him laugh that much in years. He raised his hands over the keys and scooted over. Then, without any sheet music or hesitation he played the Overture to the *Barber of Seville*.

And Amanda said, "See what I mean?"

*Thanksgiving*

*Bare trees and frozen ground made Cooper Hill into a sepia-toned village, relieved only by one house painted bright blue with a sunshine-yellow door and another in a colonial green. Slate roofs against lowering skies. A few frozen pumpkins still in the fields. Brittle corn stalks. Cows frosting their muzzles with their steamy breaths. Wood smoke spiraling from chimneys, sending fragrance into the air, while people scrape their windshields in a cloud of exhaust fumes from their warming cars. Time for red wine, for apple pies, for a little tawny port and pears at four on a Sunday afternoon, while something garlicky roasts. Time for hunters, so that nobody walks the conservation land, except on Sundays. Time to read, now that the tyranny of good weather has ended. People who knit buy yarn. People who garden look at the frozen ground and imagined the bulbs they got in, just in time, poking through in the spring. Football fans settle into comfy sofas, clicker in hand. People who heat with wood eye the woodpile, calculating. The five o'clock dog walkers now walk in the dark and enjoy looking into lit windows as they wait for their dogs to do what they are there for.*

On Thanksgiving Day, those who had stayed in Cooper Hill went for walks while the turkey roasted. Maud Crowe's kitchen light was on, but no cars crowded her narrow driveway. One could not look into her parlor. Heavy insulated drapes covered her front windows. Inside her closed-up, very warm house, she thought about all the things people said while on line at the Post Office. They talked like people in taxis, oblivious to the existence of anyone who might be listening. In this way she had learned that Linda and Tom had given up on the idea of a neighborhood party and instead decided to host some of Linda's huge family. They were planning for twenty-two at the table. Amanda Sloane would put aside her feelings for her mother and drive down to Connecticut for the day. Her brother and sister would be there to dilute the poison. Those were the very words Maud had overheard, and she couldn't get over it. Imagine referring to your own mother as poison. Oh, the arrogance of youth. Mary, Jess, and April Higgins would be attending a service of Thanksgiving at the Unitarian Church and then working at the soup kitchen over in Woodside. Andy Spenser and Claire

Westfield would have been welcome at Linda and Tom Brickman's but Claire would not leave the house in case Lizzie called. Jack had received a surprise call from Cate's parents just a week before Thanksgiving. They were getting too old, they said, for such a long drive through so much traffic. For the first time, they asked him to come to them, and he reluctantly agreed.

Good Jack Walker: a fine sad man. For years and years Maud had been tempted to tell him about Cate and Andy. Cate had betrayed him like a common slut. She did not deserve her place in the town's memory. There should not be a tree on the common planted in her honor. The hospital should not have a nursing-school scholarship in her name. Maud thought the world had become so hungry for heroes that people could no longer distinguish selfless acts of heroism from unfortunate accidents.

At noon on Thanksgiving Day, Maud put a small chicken and a sweet potato in the oven to bake and took the frozen pumpkin pie from the freezer and placed it on the counter to thaw. More than once she looked from the kitchen into her big dining room where her family had once gathered around the long cherry table. They had used the formal dining room on the best of days, and the children had sometimes been sent from that same table, to go to bed without supper when they misbehaved. Once her son had been hauled up by his shirt collar and dragged to the bathroom to have his mouth washed with soap after saying something vulgar during meal. At this table on the most terrible night of her life, she had sat her children down to tell them their father had died. Years later her son had chosen that spot to tell her he was joining the Army. Rebecca and Paul had announced their engagement one Christmas Eve. Right after they'd said grace.

When she had first learned that Rebecca was pregnant, Maud purchased a high-chair and a crib so all would be comfortable when they came to visit. Rebecca and Paul had brought baby Anna just once, before she was old enough to use the high-chair, and they stayed for just three days. Maud had planned for a week. After that, they moved to North Carolina and stayed for nearly three years. Maud had been to see them just once during that time. She had not felt welcome.

Things had happened when the children were small. Maud remembered them dimly. She always had a quick temper and a nasty tongue, but what mother didn't lose patience from time to time? Edward's death had been so sudden, and she had felt old and weary at the time, but now realized that she'd been just forty-two which wasn't old at all. Forty-two and fending for herself. Maud's own mother and father did not have a penny to spare, and though her parents offered, she really couldn't move in with three children. Stupid friends had said, "You're an attractive woman, Maud, why don't you marry again?" as if men were just hanging around on street corners looking for women with three children. Three children—two of them boys, hungry every minute of the day and growing out of shoes practically while she watched.

She had raised her children in the Church; they had all learned their Catechism and gone to Confession on Saturday afternoons. She had urged them to hold themselves in the image of Christ, to think pure thoughts and be worthy of His love in thought and deed. She knew Rebecca rolled up her skirt of her school uniform, after she rounded the corner. She had smelled cigarettes on her breath. With all her strength she had fought the persistence of sin and evil to instill strong character and determination. Television time had been limited. She'd checked their homework every night. In Cooper Hill, she held her head high in the face of pitying glances. She knew what she stood for, and her successful children—all straight A students and both sons alter boys—made her proud of them and herself. At night she would pray for their souls and most especially pray for Rebecca so that she might keep her virtue intact.

Her life had little room for joy, not when the curtains must be starched and the boy's white shirts ironed, when a pound of hamburger meat had to stretch for four, and everything required vigilance. But that did not explain why she had called her nine-year-old son liver lips because his new braces made his mouth flap in a way she just could not stand. There was a morning when she'd slapped Rebecca up the side of her head because she'd been sitting there, looking crooked and it had made her furious. God's perfection spoiled by laziness. She never could explain her rages. They passed quickly and left her with remorse.

She thought she would be different as a grandmother. Being a grandmother transformed women; she just knew it. When Anna was a little past three, Paul was transferred again, this time to New Jersey and they drove up for Easter. Maud had been elated. First she went shopping for an Easter outfit for Anna to wear to church. She found a dress in pink cotton, a tiny straw hat with flowers, and a Navy blue coat, just in case it was chilly. She bought white tights and black patent leather Mary Janes. Then she went to work on the Easter basket. Chocolate bunnies, marshmallow peeps, and a sugar egg with a picture of Jesus inside, gum drops and jelly beans, of course, and purple plastic straw to set off all the colors—she put them all in a basket festooned with ribbons and set it on the dining room table.

Then she went shopping for food. She bought a ham and pineapple rings, fluffy dinner rolls, two cans of baked beans because the homemade ones weren't really worth the trouble. For the night before Easter, she made a huge macaroni and cheese casserole. For Easter morning breakfast, she had hot cross buns and eggs and three kinds of juice because she didn't know what Anna liked best. She dragged Rebecca's old playpen from the attic so Anna would have a safe place to be while she and Rebecca cooked, and she aired the crib mattress and lowered it so Anna could not climb out. Feeling like she still knew a thing or two about young children, she'd awaited their arrival, pacing, peering out the window every few minutes until they finally pulled into the driveway on the night before Easter about two hours later than expected.

They did not want dinner. They had stopped on the road. The traffic had been terrible. They did not need the crib. Anna slept in their bed.

"But she might wake and try to come downstairs. She could fall," Maud said.

"We're exhausted. If you don't mind, Mom, I think we'll just settle her down and go to sleep ourselves," Rebecca said. Disappointed, Maud didn't let on and said, "Go and rest. I'll wake you in plenty of time for church." And then Rebecca and Paul had slipped in these looks at one another, and an awkward silence followed until Rebecca broke it by saying they didn't go to church and hadn't planned on it. Shocked,

Maud had still managed to contain herself, and she told Rebecca not to worry, not to worry at all. She had bought Anna an Easter outfit, and as for Rebecca and Paul, their regular clothes would do just fine. It was a shame really, but people went to church these days in just about anything, jeans, and shorts in the summer. Really, it didn't matter. What mattered was being there in the presence of the Lord on His day of Resurrection.

Rebecca had stiffened, "I don't think you understand, Mother; we don't go to church at all, and we aren't planning to subject Anna to its dogma. If she chooses on her own later on, so be it."

"But how can she choose if she doesn't have the love of God," Maud has asked. Paul had intervened, "This is a long conversation, Maud, and we're exhausted. Let it be for now."

"But what about Easter Sunday?" Maud had told all her friends she'd be there with Anna and her daughter and her son-in-law.

On Easter morning, Maud learned that Paul didn't eat eggs and Rebecca ate nothing made with white flour. They all had oatmeal, and Maud could think of nothing less festive. They didn't go to church that Easter Sunday, nor did they give Anna her Easter basket, since she wasn't allowed to eat sugar. All that was left was the lovely little dress and dinner. Paul and Rebecca went for a walk, leaving Anna with Maud for a while. When Maud put Anna on the potty, she said she didn't need to go. Then after she'd been buttoned into her new dress, looking adorable, Anna asked for a diaper.

"A diaper, but why?

"So I can go poo."

"But I put you on the potty."

"But I need a diaper."

Maud had never heard of such a thing. She pulled on the white tights and tied a ribbon in Anna's hair and just as she was finishing the loopy bow, Anna soiled herself and began to cry. Maud tried to be patient, but this was ridiculous. She kneeled in front of her granddaughter and held her little upper arms between her thumb and forefingers and said, "Stop that crying right this minute, Anna. You are acting like a baby. Only babies soil themselves like this. You are a bad and willful girl; that's what you are, a spoiled little girl who has just ruined her Easter outfit. God is watching you and He is not happy. Not at all. Now, I am going to take off all your nice new clothes and clean you up, but then you are going to get into a diaper, like the baby you are, and go to the bed for a time out."

Anna was sobbing now; fear filled her dark blue eyes. The sweet smell of the roasting ham, combined with the mess in Anna's pants was sickening. Maud took pity and pulled the child in close. "Poor dear little girl, come to grandma; grandma loves you. God loves you, too. I will teach you to be good."

Anna arched her back and pulled away, screaming and at that moment Paul and Rebecca returned and rushed to hold Anna. Then those long looks again, and Rebecca saying, "See, I told you we shouldn't come."

Maud just hated that, and the awful words poured from her mouth like poison. "Don't you two look at me that way; don't you dare. Oh I know. I did everything wrong and I don't know a thing about babies, and you are doing everything right. Every single little thing. So let me tell you this—watch out. Just watch out. Because there is no magic formula. Anna might grow up to be the smartest, strongest woman in town, or she could become a little slut, like you were, Rebecca, when you were a girl. And watch out Paul. Don't take too much time off or call in sick, no matter how bad you feel, because you might lose your job and fail to make an insurance payment and that would leave Rebecca in the unfortunate position of needing to come to me for help, and I'm sure that very thought of that could keep you up for many nights to come."

She had raised her voice. Rebecca covered Anna's ears. Paul began to gather their things. It took a surprisingly short time for them to clean Anna and pack up. When they were changing her clothes they found bruises on her upper arms, Maud's thumb prints to be exact. Rebecca cried then and Paul packed the car. Maud looked over the heads of her daughter and granddaughter, who were crouched together with Rebecca's mouth on one of the bruises, kissing it away.

Time passed. Efforts were made. Maud sent gifts and paid for ballet lessons. She traveled to New Jersey once or twice for stilted visits with a grandchild who did not know her, but after she stopped driving, the journey became too much. It required a bus, a train, another bus, and then she had to wait for Paul to come get her at the station. They never came to her. Anna could not sleep in the car. Paul could not get enough time off. The traffic from New Jersey to Vermont was awful. Then they had another child, this time a boy.

Excuses, excuses. Maud pretended to believe them. She sent cards and gifts on birthdays and they dutifully remembered hers, but her grandchildren did not know her. In her younger son's case it was easier to understand, California being so far away. Her older son, the one who had needed braces, had not married. He came back sometimes, but not this year. He was in the Army Reserve and been deployed to Iraq for the third time. At his age it seemed ridiculous, but Maud was proud of his sense of duty.

One could dismiss Christmas; it had become so crass, but Thanksgiving was a cruel holiday for an old woman living alone, especially one who worked in such a public place as the Post Office where everyone was talking about the long lines at the market and saying, *My oh my, I just don't know where I am going to put all these people!* It actually appeared that some children—but not her Rebecca—honored their parents.

Children had all the power in the world to hurt. Maud had had a moment of warmth for Claire Westfield the other day, watching her peer deeply into her post office box for any small message from her missing daughter. Her thoughts turned to April, who would not be having a proper Thanksgiving meal. What bitter accusations might she throw at her mothers some day? Then she thought of Jack Walker's sweet babies in heaven. They'd be approaching that age when kids need new soccer shoes every season. Maud could imagine them getting older and hating the isolation of their place in the woods, begging their parents to take them to the mall, itching for their driver's licenses, and undoing in a frenzy of adolescent indulgence, their carefully controlled childhoods.

It consoled Maud to understand the real role of children on the planet. While mothers cooed and nurtured, children grew to assume their place in the world, and a big portion of that rested upon displacing the generation that had come before. Among animals, this inbred understanding was not complicated by the idea of love. The idea that worked was necessity. As long as need existed, the generations could live in peace, but if a grandmother was not needed for advice or child care, if a child's support was not required in old age, the bonds broke. Someday April would eye the furniture in her family home with thoughts to its worth. Lizzie would either return, in need, or find her own way and never look back. Anna would rebel against Rebecca, and Rebecca would remember Maud and regret the holidays that she did not visit.

After checking on the chicken, Maud went into the parlor and slowly lowered herself into her favorite chair. Her knees pained her this time of year. She folded her hands in her lap and bowed her head and tried to pray. She wanted to offer thanks for reasonable health, sufficient food, and healthy children. She wanted to find a place of peace, but questions intruded. Had she been chosen to suffer, like Job, for some future reward once her faith had been proven? If so, how could she prove it? Or had God, at some point, decided to punish her, and if so, for what? Was she a selfish fool for feeling punished, considering what she had and what so many others lacked, and not just in the realm of the material? She had her faith. Despite all that had happened, it had never faltered. Wasn't that something? But her loneliness—her loneliness felt like punishment.

She had been a good child. She had been a faithful wife. After Edward died, she'd done everything for her children. Most of all she'd instilled confidence. You can do anything, she'd told them. The impossible just takes longer. Study. Be the best. You are the best. She had blessed them with confidence and cursed herself into a lonely old age as they went off to prove themselves. People like her friend Eleanor had not had such high ambitions for her children, and where were they? Over in Woodside working at the hospital, and down the road at the Burnside school working for the physical plant and getting good benefits. They'd be with Eleanor today, baking pies and peeling potatoes and taking turns comforting tired children. College, a shining dream, but nobody had told her that once your children go away, they never come back, at least never for long, and a village like Cooper Hill no longer has anything to offer them.

Her head became heavy and she let it fall to rest upon her chest, but after a short nap, her agitated mind pulled her out of the chair and into her study where she found the key that locked the drawer to her desk. Inside the lower drawer all the letters she had stolen were filed by date, and the first, Cate's letter to Jack, had a special folder all to itself. She had never opened it or any other. She could only go so far. But here it was, nearly four years old, and it occurred to her that now this letter might make an exquisite gift to Jack. Enough time had passed. The raw grief had ended. She could simply put it into his post office box, and when he questioned it, she'd say, "Occasionally these things happen. Letters get lost. And found." The she'd invite him over for tea so he could calm himself before opening it. Then she'd watch him walk up the street with a full heart. Some of the other letters looked interesting, but not like this one. Truly, a letter from the grave. The concept of atonement swelled inside of her. She smoothed the wrinkled envelope and imagined Jack's joy, then she set the table in the kitchen and sat down to eat, alone but radiant with the expectation of what she planned to do.

At Burnside on the Wednesday morning before the Thanksgiving break, the library was quiet, and for this Claire felt grateful. She emptied the bin of returned books and checked the computer to see who had late returns. She checked the acquisitions list, and she looked at the clock too often. Soon, in fact right after lunch, the students would leave for the break, and what a relief it would be to have a few days without bobbing ponytails and straight white teeth to remind her of Lizzie. She had that Friday off, so there would be four-and-a-half days when she could live her life in Cooper Hill. Not that her worry would stop, but the comparisons might. Each female student gave her pause, looking as innocent and carefree as Lizzie always had. What might she be up to at night in the dorm, long after the house parents had gone to bed? What had Lizzie been up to this time last year? Working there was almost unbearable. Claire lifted an armload of returned books to shelve and knocked over her coffee cup. "Shit," she cried out, as she watched the light-brown stain spread across the counter and drip onto the rug. Had any students been around to witness this display, she might have lost her job. She ran to the bathroom for paper towels and dealt with the mess while the library director looked on with something worse than her usual sour face, and Claire knew she was an object of pity.

By nine on Thanksgiving Day, Andy finally began worrying along with Claire. He too had expected a call, just a simple acknowledgment of the day and confirmation that Lizzie was okay. At this point Claire said either Lizzie hated her beyond repair or something terrible had happened. She was lying in some hospital bed in a coma, having been found on the street without any identification.

Andy tried to say the right things. He told Claire with today's kind of news her picture would be all over the place if that was the case, but saying this implied something even worse, and Claire's terror had become contagious as they both recalled stories of serial killers and bodies found buried in suburban back yards where nobody had ever suspected a thing about that nice auto mechanic. Early in the day Claire had kept herself busy by cooking. A turkey, calling up all memories of holidays past, would have been awful. Instead she made little Cornish hens stuffed with apricots and wild rice and burnished with a port wine glaze. She braised Brussels sprouts, and poached pears in white wine, but most of it did not get eaten and the remains of the little birds sat on a plate in the refrigerator, picked over and scrawny looking. Though Andy thought they had started drinking too much lately, he did not choose Thanksgiving to bring it up, and by the time they went to bed, they'd consumed two bottles of wine in addition to their five o'clock martinis. Now he just played tennis once or twice a week indoors. When spring came this drinking and the heavy meals would have to end if he hoped to play four or five times a week outdoors in the heat and sun.

It surprised him that he could think ahead to spring and tennis and the vigor it brought while Claire was suffering so. Claire resented his ability to live. She thought it was because Lizzie wasn't his real daughter, and he always argued that this wasn't so, but maybe it was. Having never felt the pull of progeny, he couldn't know. He'd delighted in every bit of his life with Lizzie, but that thing that compelled many of his friends to dream of babies and pass out cigars after their children's birth had eluded him. He had never felt lacking. In fact, given the problems caused by over-population, he'd felt a little smug.

When he went to pee before bed, he looked down at his slightly drooping penis, source of pleasure but not life, and touched himself gently, like you might pat a good loyal dog. So far no problems there. Most men his age were consumed by fluctuating PSAs or various inflammations that pulled them from their seats at the movies at annoying intervals and kept them up throughout the night. Tucking himself into his briefs he then flushed, flossed, brushed, rinsed, and had a good scratch before folding himself into bed and curling around Claire. He felt like making love to her. He thought it might actually help. But she'd refuse and count it as another sign that he did not care about Lizzie as much as she did, and they'd been down that path today and too many days before. He felt unfairly judged. He had to hold himself together for Claire and whatever horrible news that might come their way, and she took it as not caring. Where would they be if he gave in to despair?

Claire had no capacity to comfort him and he understood that, and he held himself together with work and tennis and wine and reading. Touching her warm body, releasing her even if she sobbed during orgasm would not be a bad thing. He was a doctor. He affirmed life wherever he found it, and he loved Lizzie and he loved Claire and he knew that he'd lose Claire if they lost Lizzie for good. Andy did not feel thankful at the end of this Thanksgiving—he felt frightened and he wanted to be held. But instead, he patted Claire's back and turned over.

## *December*

Jack returned from his Thanksgiving with Cate's parents in a black mood. "When are you going to go back to teaching? When did you last visit the graves; have you cut back the lilac? Are you still living in that shabby apartment? Why? Piano lessons and tutoring are not enough, Jack," they lectured, "not with someone of your abilities. Cate would not want it this way"...and on and on until he came very close to saying, "I don't give a flying fuck what Cate would or would not have wanted. Whatever she wanted only lasted until she saw the next thing she wanted. Want. Was that her first word or what?" They meant well. That's what they said. But how come they didn't go off on cruises like other people their age? Why could they not leave him alone?

He tried, when he got back to Cooper Hill, to resume his normal pattern, but Eric had the flu and his mother cancelled their session. One of his tires went flat while the car just sat there in front of the house. It could have been one of the Bensen boys or just dryness and age; he'd been meaning to replace that tire. No matter the reason, getting the jack out and finding the donut under all the junk he stored in the trunk had taken most of a morning, and by the time he'd driven over to the garage and bought a new tire, he'd lost all interest in grocery shopping, so he had to eat the leftovers Cate's parent had insisted he bring home. The long car trip had soured the turkey, and he spent a long night retching and a day recovering.

He missed a visit to Claire and Andy's because Claire's car was in the driveway on a day when she was usually out. He thought he ought to wait a while before going to Tom and Linda's again. Amanda's locked door irked him. It felt personal. Such a hefty lock she'd chosen, just like something a city person would use. Let her leave the coffee pot on again and burn the house down, he thought. Let one of her washer hoses spring a leak; she probably doesn't even know the washer has a hose. Let her pound away on the beautiful piano until she got carpal tunnel for all he cared.

Cooper Hill, the place he'd longed for while he was with Cate's parents, made him feel restless. The days were short now as the solstice approached. People stayed indoors, and he could not rely on a walk for the human contact he wanted, the kind that carried no obligations. He did not have enough to do. A truth about himself slowly emerged from his circle of thought. He had never been a self-starter. He would have stayed in school forever unless Cate had pushed him to find something, and then he would have stayed at Burnside. For all he resented her pushing and prodding, he had no energy to do anything much on his own, and having so much money complicated the issue: he didn't *have* to do anything at all.

At four one afternoon, just as the sun was fading, Jack decided to take a drive over to Woodside. Over in Woodside people decorated with lights and huge plastic Santas on the rooftops, as opposed to Cooper Hill where wreathes and simple window candles were all you could expect. He thought he might take some pictures. There was something interesting to him about the big old three-decker houses, where families had once lived with generations stacked on top of each other. Now mostly rentals, they had fallen into disrepair. On the outskirts of Woodside, humble subdivisions had sprouted as farmers sold off their land. These were populated with ranch houses and here the Christmas decorations spilled out to the front lawns. He wondered how people who lived from one paycheck to another could afford the electric bills, which must have been huge.

Photography had been important to him once. Before meeting Cate, he'd traveled back roads from coast to coast taking pictures of America off the highway. He'd liked old gas stations and rugged mountain people, cowboys and the cluttered backyards of suburbia. Cate had not approved, calling the enterprise invasive and beside the point. He'd pulled out big glossy photography books containing the Farm Security Administration photographs by Dorothea Lang and Walker Evans, and even older pictures of New York tenements taken by Jacob Reis.

"And what good did they do?" Cate had asked. "Has poverty ended? Who buys these books, and why? Each one costs a fortune. These photographers turned tragedy into art. I can see the skill, but have you ever noticed that no photojournalists get to point their cameras into the ugly side of the super rich? No, the rich are protected. They are insulated from everything, including the real needs of the people in these books of yours."

For a while he'd continued, but she'd pretty much ruined it for him. Still, having a camera in hand gave him some reason for being in one place rather than another. Back when people still used film, he'd sometimes go out with an unloaded camera and enjoy looking at the world through the frame of his 35 millimeter lens. It had a way of tidying things.

But really, what was the point of using a camera to demonstrate the bad taste and unwise spending habits among the working poor in Woodside? He took a detour and drove through Burnside, so named because that part of town had suffered a terrible fire more than a hundred years ago, leaving black fertile soil that could grow anything. Farmers became rich there. Those who loved the academy deeded their homes and land to the school. Those who resented it sold their property for great sums, since Burnside always needed faculty housing and also had to make sure no unseemly developments ruined the pristine town. In just a couple of weeks the place would be desolate. The students took exams and left, and then on the morning after the faculty Christmas party, the entire faculty left too, to see parents or go to their real homes—the ones they bought for summers and retirement. It had always struck him as odd that the school people described themselves as family and complained that they never had enough time to relax together, but when the chance came, they fled because Burnside was not the "real world."

They were right about that. The real word could never be so beautiful. A layer of snow covered the quadrangle and light from the Georgian buildings spilled out into the blue-gray night. He had to stop to let a group of students pass. Their teeth were white and straight, their skin clear and rosy—not a pimple to be seen. They walked and bobbed their heads in laugher like frisky colts. Trailing them he saw Trip Skye, the ancient track coach who still inspired his team to victory more seasons than not. He wore the uniform—khaki pants, tweed jacket, and woolen scarf. None of the boys or men ever wore overcoats. They rushed between buildings wearing not enough clothing, but looking vigorous and wonderful. And Jack had been one of them, as a student and later as a member of the faculty. Oh, what innocence! He drove down to the end of the lane and turned around. Over by one of the dorms, two golden retrievers tumbled in the snow. A brown lab approached them to join the play. He thought Conway would have loved living here. He could no longer remember why going over to Woodside had seemed like a good idea, and so he headed home.

Back at his apartment, his landlord had not turned down the heat, and Jack had to open a window in order to sleep. He could hear the furnace clicking on and off. The loud fan poured hot dry air past him and out the window. He rested on the small raft of his bed, thinking of all the people who were dying because of oil and found yet another reason to despair. Cate would have hated the war in Iraq every bit as much as he did. In fact, her energy would have led them to protest rallies, kids in tow, like people in the sixties. She'd be writing letters to the editor and probably getting herself arrested.

To protest or not? For Cate there would be no alternative. For Jack the alternative was living as simply as possible. Cate would argue that that was selfish. He would say it was all they could do. Get off the grid. Stop consuming. She would say, "Look at Vietnam," and he would say that it wasn't the protests that ended that war; it was all the boys in body bags who turned middle-class opinion against the war. Round and round. Point-counterpoint. This was the substance of their marriage, and he had not minded. It was nice to know someone so well that you could fill in both sides of a conversation.

Jack had spent many nights doing this until exhaustion overwhelmed him, but on this particular night, Hannah's freckled face popped up in his mind to interrupt. He tutored her, along with Eric, but whereas Eric could read way above his grade level and had trouble remembering facts, Hannah remembered all she heard or saw, but stumbled over simple words until her throat clenched and tears filled her eyes. *I need to read Mr. Walker,* she had said to Jack during their last session. He'd wanted to cry.

Hannah lived in Cooper Hill with her mother, a massage

therapist, and her mother's boyfriend of the moment. He'd never heard any mention of a dad. He bartered reading lessons for massage, though he'd only had one massage. The first had released too much. Sarah had touched a place at the base of his spine that made him tremble and cry. She'd told him not to hold back, but all the will power in the world would not have helped him hold in what she brought forth. The woman had magic hands. The stiff neck he'd had went away over night, but he didn't want to feel that vulnerable again. Anyway, he liked Hannah; he didn't need any compensation for helping her out.

He figured her mother and teacher had tried all the usual things. He'd need something new, a story written just for her, or the beginning of a story that she could write, as well. He thought about those dogs romping over at Burnside and he remembered Conway, and the fragments of a story began to form. He'd make her laugh. He'd write about a disobedient dog that always ended up doing the right thing by doing the wrong thing. Should it rhyme or not, he wondered? How much word repetition would be needed? All the stories he'd read to Molly and Zeke came back to him, but he could not discern a pattern, except that the characters had to be charming. Well, with Conway as a model, that would be no problem. He would also use Nina, Claire and Andy's recalcitrant hound. When he let himself into Claire and Andy's, he always let Nina out in her yard and he loved watching her sprint. Had she not injured her leg as a puppy, she would have easily jumped the fence. A hound and a Newfoundland would made great best friends. Nina would be all energy and nose, eager to run full-out even if it meant she wouldn't be home for hours, and Conway would be more interested in dinner than adventure and always worried about her family.

At Claire's invitation, Amanda swam three mornings a week in the pool at Burnside, and afterwards she showered with the other women and marveled at them all. One had had a mastectomy. Another bore the scars of a double hip replacement. A woman who had lost eighty pounds massaged the loose flesh on her thighs and belly and joked that she had once filled all this skin, enough to make a whole other person, she said, grabbing a handful. In a gluttonous haze of steam and endless hot water, they swapped shampoo and conditioner and talked about life while their bodies turned pink. Even Claire, relaxed from her long swim, yielded to the atmosphere of the shower room. She lifted her face to the streaming water as if she was submitting to some ancient rite, but she had lost too much weight. The sight of her sagging bottom and bony hips alarmed Amanda.

All the women were married, except for Amanda, and her single state presented an irresistible challenge. Everyone knew someone who would be perfect for her, and after months of polite refusal, Amanda finally gave in and accepted a blind date. She had never believed it would come to this, but she had to face the facts. In Cooper Hill and nearby Woodside and even over in Randall, there was no way to meet a man unless you went to a bar. Linda and Tom had met back in New York. Claire had met Andy through Cate. Most of Amanda's clients were single women who'd been discarded at middle age for someone younger, and if there was any lesson to be learned from them it was stay away from the university professors, men with such enormous capacities for love that monogamy was out of the question, or any man recently divorced.

So, the lawyer this woman Judy kept talking about sounded pretty good. He had been happily married to a woman who died of leukemia, but this had happened years ago. A man who had been happily married was better than one who was divorced and bitter. He had kids, but they were grown and on their own. Grown children were better than little ones. Amanda thought she would like to have a child, but older men fathered kids all the time. Why not? What was one night anyway? At home she'd just bang on the piano and think about Jack Walker, whom she hadn't completely given up on, no matter what Claire said. Still, making progress there could take a long time, if it ever happened. So she gave Judy her number.

William Dwight called a day later. She proposed that they meet at a restaurant, and he agreed. Figuring out what to wear consumed her for the rest of the week. Amanda had an entire black and grey wardrobe from when she lived in the city, and she had what she called her therapist clothes, flowing soft skirts and tunic tops in the colors of earth and sky. Around here you could wear practically anything. People showed up at fine restaurants in jeans, but she wanted to look nicer than that, but not too nice. She didn't want to seem over-eager. But he was a lawyer, after all, and older; she should just forget about the skin tight black pants and velvet jacket with rivets. Fine. Then what?

In her white bedroom she flung clothing around and looked at the piles that would have made anyone walking in think two different women lived there. The sleeveless black dress was way too New York. The Eileen Fisher outfit that Linda had talked her into had baggy cropped pants and a blouse that kept slipping off her shoulders. The Talbot's suit her mother had sent made her look like a librarian. In the end her choice was not perfect, but she could live with it, and on that Saturday night she wore leather boots, a long black knit skirt, a purple sleeveless sweater, and a long silk scarf with reds and purples and some gold. It wasn't quite right, but Amanda could not have described what she wanted if she had a private dressmaker. Really, these days she would have happily lived in her running clothes.

William was waiting at the table when she got there, and though the restaurant was dark, she could not miss the delicate metal hooks that substituted for his hands. He helped her with her coat and she felt the metal against her skin. He handed her a menu and signaled for the waiter, and made her comfortable by explaining it all in the first few minutes. From his elbows down, his arms were made of titanium; when he was a child they had been plastic, but the technology got better all the time. He'd been born this way. His parents had been great and done everything right. End of subject. Nothing more to say about that. And really, there wasn't. William Dwight had been well-loved all his life. That was obvious. He possessed not a shred of self pity.

He had a thriving law practice and had fathered two children. He was wearing a perfectly tailored black suit and a starched white shirt. She could see no nose hairs or tufts sprouting from his ears. He asked her many questions about herself and seemed genuinely interested in her answers. He handled a knife and fork without difficulty. His hands and arms should not have mattered one bit to Amanda.

Later that night when she was alone, she told herself that, again and again. Beyond a doubt, William Dwight was a good kisser, and he could probably do other wonderful things with his tongue. He might even have certain attachments for his hands, some digits made of rubber instead of metal, and she was sure he could find ways to please her, if it came to that. But it wouldn't because what Amanda needed was the feeling of strong arms around her, arms dusted in summer by golden hairs; long, strong athletic arms to quiet her nervous jerky self, and William did not have those. She didn't like herself a lot for knowing this and wondered how she'd handle a patient in this situation, and what it all came down to was honesty. William didn't need favors or pity. Some woman smarter than her would have no problem with William's arms or lack thereof. But she would, and seeing him again wouldn't change that. He'd said he'd call. She doubted it. The man had great manners, but she was sure he'd felt her stiffen when he pulled her closer.

Before getting into bed, Amanda decided to play the piano a little. She pushed the exercise book out of the way and found a little Chopin waltz she'd taught herself. In two bars, she got her fingers tangled. She forgot to take her foot off the pedal, and she paid no attention to the rests. It didn't matter. She loved the lilting tune and played it very slowly and badly, as usual. Jack would have stopped her again and again, until fear of making another mistake erased all pleasure and made it worse. Sometimes in the middle of a lesson, he'd stop her and signal where she ought to start again, and the whole page of notes would scramble and make no sense at all. On this night she just let herself be and watched with wonderment as her nimble pink hands, filled with blood and covered in skin, moved across the keys.

At five o'clock on a Tuesday night, Jess and Mary Higgins were sitting at their kitchen table making Solstice decorations for the Tree of Light they would decorate on December 21. Mary called April for the third time, "We're gluing the stars on now; don't you want to help?" April ignored her for the third time and continued to read aloud from *The Night Before Christmas*, the book she had taken from the library, despite her mothers' protests. April had learned to read early, and this book had come with a CD, so she had memorized long portions. She was sitting in an overstuffed chair with her legs folded under, and she had stuffed her red pajamas with toilet paper to make herself look like Santa Claus.

April got all the way through, for the second time and only set the book down to announce that they had to go shopping soon because she needed a Christmas present for her piano teacher. "A box of handkerchiefs would be nice," she said.

Jess turned to Mary, "Where does she get these ideas?"

Mary shrugged, "Nobody has given hankies for a gift since my mother was in school," she said.

"Well then, we certainly know April didn't learn it from her." They had just had another set of family portraits taken. You could get them cheap this time of year and Mary was planning to frame them and send them off in time for a Christmas arrival.

"Nina is going to start barking any minute," said April, who was now looking out the window and down the street. "The paperboy is coming."

"The paperboy doesn't deliver at night," Jess said.

"But he's walking down the street." said April. "Here he comes." Sure enough, Jess heard Nina, and Andy shouting, "Nina! No! Stop! No pulling." Even with the windows tight shut and the furnace whooshing, he was easy to hear and so was Claire whose higher voice also carried. Jess looked out and felt like a failed dog trainer. Under the streetlight Nina's eyes gleamed like a wolf's and her teeth were bared. She strained and lurched against the leash, head down, feral-looking, and Claire and Andy were doing everything wrong.

"Wow, look at Nina. I think she's bigger. I think next Halloween she should dress up as a reindeer." said April.

"Pets don't dress up," said Jess.

"They do," said April. "My friend dressed her dog up as a princess, but that's dumb because a dog could never look like a princess."

"You are a little girl who looked like a willow tree," said Mary. She still felt proud of the costume.

"Not really. Hannah down the street said I looked like a weed. She said her mother said all people should get massages. Can I get one?"

"You do not need a massage," said Jess.

"Then can I have a mouse for my Solstice present?" April asked.

"A mouse, why?" asked Mary.

"So he cannot be stirring anything when Santa comes."

"Honey, we celebrate Solstice, not Christmas. We get presents before Christmas, remember? We don't believe in Santa."

"But how does Santa know that? He brings presents to good girls and boys. I'm good."

"Where did you learn so much about Santa Claus?" Asked Mary.

"Everywhere." April sometimes talked to Jess and Mary as if they were children. "His picture is in all the stores and in books. Plus my best friend at swim class told me he comes to her house every year."

"Not everybody believes in Santa Claus," said Jess.

"But he ate cheese and crackers and left crumbs on the rug," said April. "I don't think it matters whether you believe in him or not."

After April went to bed, Mary and Jess talked about it. Still troubled by her failure with Claire and Andy as dog owners, Jess argued that they had to stand firm. Mary thought they ought to get a few things for Christmas morning. It had not been her idea to give up Christmas in the first place. Having a very smart child, they agreed, was a problem, a good problem, but challenging. Until this year they'd been able to shelter April, but now she was in the world, reading, taking classes, and it would only get worse when she went to school. Still, Jess argued, they didn't have to give in. Jewish families made their children understand about Christmas.

"Yeah," said Mary, "but my Jewish friends still wished they had Christmas. Some put up trees. And Hanukkah itself is a holiday celebrated by millions, so Jews are still part of something. Let's face it. How many people make a big deal about the Solstice? April will have a hard enough time as the kid with two mommies; why do we have to make things even more difficult for her?"

Jess shrugged and looked at Mary's sweet face in the lamplight.

All their plans had sounded so noble when they were only plans. They agreed on most things. What Christmas had become disgusted them equally. But cutting this magic out of April's life without having another belief system in place troubled them. There was a group of Pagans nearby who celebrated the Solstice by dancing around in the woods wearing old brown blankets, but this didn't work for either of them.

"Should we give up Solstice?" Jess asked.

"No," said Mary. That was their holiday. They'd created it before April. The candles and music and quiet exchange of handmade gifts felt exactly right.

"What if we did Solstice and then took a trip, maybe April would forget about Christmas."

"Some kids might, not April; she'd be counting the days and wondering how Santa would find her."

"If we cave in on Christmas," said Jess, "then I think we should do all the holidays, add Hanukkah and Kwanzaa, find out if the Buddhists do anything this time of year."

"We could still do all handmade presents," added Mary, "and make sure we did the adopt-a-family program over in Woodside. That would work."

"That was so depressing last year," Jess said, remembering the sad list they'd been given for their adopted family. A hairbrush, lip gloss, video games, bubble bath, a dog toy, and Tickle Me Elmo, a bathrobe size eighteen, winter jackets for three boys and two girls aged four, six, eleven, twelve and fourteen. Buying for someone you did not know, who was poor and fat and had five kids, had been nothing but sad. Still, on the day they dropped off the package, along with cranberry sauce, a bag of oranges, a bag of stuffing mix, and a coupon for a turkey, and seeing the entire church basement filled with similar bounty had felt good, although neither Jess nor Mary had imagined there were that many poor people in Woodside.

"It was okay," said Mary. "I'm glad we did it. I wish we could do more."

"What we should do is get moving on adopting another kid,"

said Jess. Mary agreed. It was now about nine o'clock. Jess went to turn off the porch light and saw Jack walking, alone as usual. She thought that he might be able to see her there at the door and waved just in case. He did not return the gesture.

With his usual care, Andy placed the electric candles in each window and, because they were light and tippy, he taped each one to the windowsill. He also ran the extension cords neatly behind the furniture so Nina would not tangle herself in them. When he had finished, he hung a fresh green wreath on the front door and installed a flood lamp on the lawn to illuminate it. He came back in and heard Claire on the phone with Linda. He wasn't all that surprised to hear her say, "I should probably have stayed with Brad. I would not have been the first woman to look away from the truth in order to protect her family. I should have gotten pregnant again. I should have pretended to believe all his lies, because eventually spinning lie after lie would have worn him down, and then he would have given up that bitch he was seeing, and we would have picked up our life together as if nothing had happened."

Claire remained silent for a long time, and Andy imagined that Linda was talking her out of this crazy idea. Of late, Claire had been blaming everything that happened to Lizzie on the divorce that led to Andy and then Cate and Jack and the kids, who according to Claire, drew her in and then taught her that any awful thing can happen at any time.

"I let my pride ruin Lizzie's childhood," she now said to Linda. "I just took her from the only home she'd ever known, feeling brave, humming *I Am Woman* and *These Boots Are Made for Walking* and *You Don't Own Me*, all Fuck You Brad, and packed whatever I could stuff into my Honda Civic and brought Lizzie to Vermont because there was a massage school, and I had visions of working just three hours a day at fifty-dollars an hour. And how stupid was that? It took about fifty hours to find one client and no one has a once-a-week massage.

"I should have stood up for Lizzie and seen a vicious lawyer who would make him give us enough money," she told Linda. "We lived in hovels. It was awful."

Andy had of course heard this story before. Claire had found herself engaged in some sort of good person contest in which she was trying to prove she was better than the other woman. She kept expecting Brad to want her back and eventually he did, but by then it was too late.

Again Linda talked for a long time. Claire poked around in her bag, found a cigarette and glared at Andy, daring him to say anything. He heard her say, "Sometimes." He heard her say, "Most times," and then, "We were better when Lizzie was young and we were doing things as a family. He took her to every orthodontist visit, you know. We went skiing."

He heard her say, "She could be dead."

Linda had to be some kind of saint to endure this conversation week after week, mostly on Sunday afternoons, thought Andy. He knew that she'd now be finding some way to comfort Claire. Thank God. He didn't seem able to any longer. When Claire got off the phone, he asked her if she wanted to go find a tree.

"How can you do this? How can you?" She pleaded. Andy looked perplexed.

"How can you act like everything is okay and Lizzie is on her way home from college for the holidays?"

"How am I supposed to act?"

"Like you care, like you hurt, like you miss her."

"You know I do."

"I can't feel it."

"Because I don't cry and walk around town in the middle of the night?"

"Because you never talk about it. If it was you and Cate going through this, you'd talk about it plenty. When we used to go there, I was amazed at all the things you had to say to each other."

"Claire, we talked about work. We talked about women with breast lumps big as eggs who hadn't been to a doctor because they didn't have insurance. We talked about the state and the regulations that made mountains of paperwork none of us could manage. I love you;

you have no reason to be jealous of Cate."

"Except my daughter thinks she was perfect. My daughter, Andy, not yours. Yes, you did fine. You were a great stepfather, but you didn't plan her and hope for her and watch her grow. You didn't carry her inside your body and you weren't there when she was born and you cannot know how I feel. You can't even imagine it."

Claire caught her breath. She looked terrified. The words coming out of her mouth were hateful and she knew it. He stood there, taking it. It was all he could do. He could absorb her grief like the transformer on the pole outside their house. He wished he could take all her fury and package it and send it off somewhere, hurl it far into some desert landscape where it would become just a small scar on chalky earth.

The next day Andy went to his office early to catch up before the day began and the red light on his phone was on. The woman who cared for Claire's mother during the day had called him to break the news that Claire's mom was in a bad way. She had not wanted to say this to Claire over the phone, but she told Andy that they better plan a trip soon. Andy set the phone down and looked out the window at the steely sky that meant snow later. He picked up the phone again, to call Claire and then stopped himself. He would wait until he could hold her hand, and maybe it really wasn't as bad as it sounded. They had been at this place before and rushed down to see Florence, only to have her recover. It seemed that everything in Florence's old body had wasted except for her strong heart. As a doctor, he new it couldn't be long, but he didn't know how much more Claire could take, and so he held this news the whole day long while he examined patients and wrote up charts and harbored the ridiculous thought that if Florence would just let go and die, Lizzie would come back well and strong, as if there existed some formula for the number of human lives that could co-exist on the planet at one time.

God, he was tired. Worrying about Claire and Lizzie, and his patients and the future of the clinic struggling along in the face of drastic funding cuts and the war in Iraq was wearing him down. Just listening to the morning news deflated him. Yesterday the local station had run one of those feel-good stories about a food drive for the families of soldiers overseas. But he had not felt good knowing that the Army pay was not enough to sustain those families. Billions were going into the war while he treated people with no health insurance. A nostalgic feeling overcame him then as he remembered that that was exactly the kind of thing Cate would think about. She had armored herself against self-pity by keeping personal problems in perspective.

It had frustrated Jack and annoyed Claire who thought Cate was often pompous and a kill-joy and—her favorite word—disingenuous. "With all that money and absolutely no concern about the cost of college for the kids or heating the house or keeping her car running, it's easy to preach simplicity and organic foods and the Green Party." Claire had wagered that one year as a poor single parent would have sent Cate Walker to the nearest Wal-Mart for the cheapest clothing she could buy, and she'd never think twice about child labor in third world countries.

At six Andy remembered that he was supposed to play tennis with his buddy Peter. Why not? It would put him home at eight with plenty of time to talk to Claire and maybe clear his head, too. Sweat and concentration would be good for him. Peter had won the last two times they played, but he would not win tonight. His resolve worked. Andy won in straight sets.

Light snow was falling outside as he drove home, the kind that blows across the road and barely sticks. He opened the car window and took a deep cold breath and understood why some people plunged into snow after a sauna. From his long hot shower at the club, his body felt warm right down to his bones, and the cold air made him think about a shot of vodka in a frozen glass. Then it made him think of red wine. The road turned, the trees disappeared, and the view opened to wide windswept fields. In the distance he could see three coyotes running. Claire would say no, they had to be dogs, but these skinny creatures were more wolf than dog, and he would have liked to think they were wolves, but no wolves had been spotted around here for years. He loved this drive from Woodside to Cooper Hill. He loved this part of the state and had been drawn here after medical school, even though the pay at the county hospital was far less than he would have earned in one of the pricey suburbs outside of Boston. He had not listened to a weather report all day and hoped the snow would continue falling. Big storms often began with this kind of powder, and it was just the right temperature, hovering in the low 20s.

He slowed for the turn into Cooper Hill. Linda and Tom's house was lit on all three floors, and they had electric candles in every window. The chandelier over their dining room table twinkled and cars lined their driveway and up and down the street. It was two days before Christmas, and Linda's huge family had arrived for what would be days of celebration. He and Claire had been invited, and he had thought she might be willing to go, but now they would probably head to Long Island, weaving their way through the impossible labyrinth of highways. Jesus, he wished they'd moved Florence up here when she got sick, but she'd been so stubborn. He slowed again and made the turn into his driveway. He could see Claire in the kitchen with her back to the door and all her attention focused on the stove. This was a good sign. Some days she didn't care about food or cooking. On others she chose complicated wonderful recipes and filled the house with the fragrance of garlic and rosemary. Andy stomped the snow off his shoes and put on his doctor's face, the one he used when he had both good news and bad news for a patient. Your cancer will be cured, but you will lose your right breast; your child is okay, but he's allergic to peanuts and will have to be careful for the rest of his life. No news of Lizzie, no news is good news, but your mother is dying.

*Christmas Eve*

*All is quiet in Cooper Hill, except at Linda and Tom's where the relatives are drunk and singing. Linda cooked real food—no tofu tonight—but she watches Tom like a hawk. He still manages to pull long strips of crispy skin from the turkey and fold them into his mouth while carving. Nobody suspects that Linda and Tom are worried about the little houses they bought and renovated over in Woodside that have not sold. The market has grown soft as an old Halloween pumpkin and just as rotten. They have been "flipping" houses for years and never before held three mortgages at once. The profit margin on these houses is not large. Volume and speed are what works, but not this time. The houses are empty and forlorn-looking. Linda believes that empty houses revert to an old worn-down appearance. These houses she'd painted and decorated remind her of the ladies in New York who sold tickets at the movies. They would get all dressed up for the job and apply too much makeup. They always seemed to have painted upper lips that arched way over their lip-lines, and they fooled no one with their girlish ruffled blouses and crimped hair.*

*Greylock is upstairs in a far bedroom breathing lightly as though something hurts inside, and if it wasn't Christmas Eve, Linda would have called the vet—maybe. Their vet either prescribes horribly expensive new-age therapies like acupuncture or advises them to put Greylock down, because really, he is an ancient cat. Ancient or not, Greylock occasionally rallies and just the other day tossed a catnip toy around like a kitten. Perhaps it wore him out.*

*Tom makes sure everyone has a full glass as he clears plates and stacks clean ones for dessert. In crowds, he is most comfortable when he has a job. As always he surveys Linda's huge family with amazement. The sisters and brothers have produced their own children, none, apparently daunted by the idea as Linda had been. Progeny are hanging on the arms of chairs, slouching on the floor, and the youngest are chasing each other perilously around the coffee table. Big as their house is, it is shrunken now. No normal home could hold all this life. Tom worries about the septic system, which surely must be on the brink of overflowing, and he hopes that none of the women have flushed anything personal. Tom worries that the space heaters they have placed upstairs in the guest bedrooms will overburden their wiring. And Tom worries a little about the houses in Woodside, but not for too long. He does not get as anxious as Linda does about money. They can cover; they have enough.*

*Linda looks across the room at Tom and smiles as if to say, "Didn't we make the right choices?" As they have grown older, each has been waiting for regret. Their friends are enjoying grandchildren now while they nurture one huge cat. Are they lonely? Do they worry about who will care for them in old age? No, really they don't. What they have is what they call their Linda and*

*Tomness, undiluted. They still sometimes hold hands, they have wonderful sex when they have it, and the main reason why they can weather a bad economy, as this one appears to be, is that they aren't paying off old orthodontist bills or college loans. When they talk, as all couples do, about their friends and other people they know, the litany of pain caused by children seems endless. Just look at Andy and Claire and Maud Crowe.*

*Linda's nieces, who range in age from nine to twenty-eight, are sleek female creatures with the family's hazel eyes. They constantly sweep their hair from their eyes. They arch their slender backs and stretch, like cats. In anticipation of the annual after-Christmas shopping trip with Linda, they almost purr. Linda enjoys them completely and is always pleased to see them go. The nephews are more direct, "Aunt Linda, when you are ready for a new car, you ought to give me that Lexus. I could pay you something for it."*

*Later, when all the beds are full and the futons have been rolled out and the sleeping bags clutter the living room floor, Linda and Tom creep to their third-floor bedroom and make love while barely moving and without making a single sound. They each find this necessary restraint erotic. It is the best thing about Christmas Eve and one reason, among many, why they go through this ritual every year, even though once everyone is gone they will swear never to do it again and talk at length about spending the whole week between Christmas and New Years in the Caribbean.*

*Across town and earlier in the evening, Eric Darling had an asthma attack, but it wasn't a bad one and his inhaler worked okay. Now he's almost asleep. It is hard to get to sleep on Christmas Eve, and even though he knows he can't have everything single thing he wants, he is hoping very much for certain things. He has been good and his last report card was great. It's all because of Mr. Walker. Not only does Eric now know the answers a lot of the time, he also feels okay about asking questions and speaking out, and sometimes one kid will have an answer and Eric thinks maybe it is part of the answer but not the whole idea the teacher is trying to get at, and he will say so. Most of the time he can do this without coughing or feeling his throat get tight, because besides teaching him history Mr. Walker also makes him go outside, even though the doctor said cold air can cause asthma. Mr. Walker doesn't believe it. He says fresh air is good, and one time they jogged together, and sometimes they kick a soccer ball, and Eric's father has said he can go out for soccer next year, and if he needs more medications, then that's just what they'll do. His mother is not so sure, but between Mr. Walker and his dad, Eric can't believe she could stop him. So, he is hoping there will be a soccer ball under the tree in the morning, and a bike and a baseball glove, because in the spring his dad is going to teach him how to pitch.*

*Eric knows there is no Santa Claus, so right before finally letting the weight of his eyelids drop, he worries about hurting his parent's feeling, just in case there is no soccer ball. It was easier when you could just think Santa ran out of room on the sleigh.*

*April Higgins, having already enjoyed Solstice and Hanukkah, also has a hard time falling asleep. She knows Santa will come to her house. She put out cookies and milk and carrots for the reindeer. She drew a picture with Round John Virgin in the corner and put it on the mantle. She has brushed her teeth and smoothed her worn list and gone to bed the first time her moms asked, and she is sure that the bike will be there in the morning, even though all her Solstice and Hanukkah gifts had been handmade. A bike is the kind of thing Santa Claus brings.*

*After lengthy debate Jess and Mary agreed on a bright green bike with training wheels and the shopping and hiding of it had been surprisingly joyful. Once they knew for certain that April had fallen asleep, they brought it out and put it under their tree of light, along with a few smaller packages. On Christmas Day they would bake cookies to bring to the fire station and the police station, and then they would go to a Lesbian Gay Bisexual and Transgender potluck at the Unitarian Church. After years of ignoring Christmas, they are surprised tonight to find out how good it feels to be part of a world-wide celebration, and with all the bad news and a particularly bloody week in Iraq, they've decided to accept joy wherever they find it.*

*Andy is sleeping and Claire is pretending to sleep. She will not get up tonight and pace the house or walk the streets. In the morning, she will give Andy a case of tennis balls and a grey cashmere sweater and then they will drive to Long Island. She will leave her cell phone number and her mother's number on the message machine in case Lizzie calls the house. She listens to Andy's calm breathing, interrupted from time to time by a small snort. She'd been furious at first to learn that he'd kept the news of her mother to himself for a whole day, and then in the middle of screaming at him, she let it go. The anger just dissipated like a harmless gas floating up and away. She's spent months being angry at Andy, and she's sick of it. Andy's chest rises and falls beside her with steady rhythm. He sleeps on his back with his hands clasped across his chest and gives himself up to sleep with the most wonderful trust, and what overwhelms Claire on this silent night is a sudden understanding that here is her future. She and Andy together. It is she and Andy who will decide whether or not to get another dog after Nina. She and Andy will figure out the details of retirement and assisted care, if it ever comes to that. One of them will tend the other in the last minutes of life, and Lizzie, wherever she happens to be, might or might not be there. This fine good man opened his heart and gave her and Lizzie everything it contained. Without a lot of words. Not necessarily accompanied by bouquets of flowers. Just straight up I'm there when you need me and okay by myself if you need time alone kind of love. Claire sits up and looks down into Andy's sleeping face, barely visible in the moonlight. She touches his hair line, glad that he's finally cut it short around his bald spot, and then she kisses his chest. Andy flutters his eyes and wakes; he reaches for her and hears the church bells chime twelve times as Christmas Eve becomes Christmas morning with Claire and Andy wrapped around each other. Like big old seals, she thinks, remembering some she once saw resting on warm rocks by the sea with an occasional flipper spread across the back of another.*

*Amanda Sloane is on a night flight to Paris where she will meet up with three good friends from Brown. She had to recover from that date with William and think about Hunter, who'd been calling lately, and reevaluate the whole move to Cooper Hill. The quaint town she and Hunter had once visited together didn't look so good close up. She had not met any men, and there weren't many single women in town to befriend. The satisfaction she'd gained from impulsively buying the house had faded. Spite for Hunter seems quite stupid actually, and she now thinks she should have bought him out of their condo in*

*Boston. Jack Walker continues to interest her, but maybe that's only because he's so impossible. Learning to play the piano has been a bust. And she can't find anyone to do her hair right. The color is looking dead and the ends are brittle. A few weeks ago one of her clients, who had become a sort of friend even though she usually stayed clear of making friends with patients asked her if she'd like to go dancing. Music, movement. That sounded good, and then she ended up at a Grange hall lined up for a contra dance, with fiddles sawing away old repetitive music that made her head ache. And the men! The woman who brought her said there would be lots of men, and there were, but they all had scraggly beards and smelled of wood smoke, and not a single one used deodorant. By the time an hour had passed, she thought she might faint from the barnyard smell. In fact, some of their heavy boots probably held traces of manure.*

*She has splurged on a first-class seat on Air France. They serve good wine with dinner. She asks for and promptly receives another pillow—down-filled. She pushes her roomy seat back into a full recline and sleeps soundly at 35,000 feet, looking forward to Christmas in the City of Lights, strong coffee and croissants, fabulous food and the company of like-minded friends, who all think she'd been crazy to move to Cooper Hill. At least she'll have amusing stories.*

*Maud has retired early after putting Jack's letter from Cate into a box and wrapping it. Beneath her small table-top, there are presents from her children and grandchildren. There will be a sweater and slippers, some candy, and recent photographs of the grandchildren. They send the same gifts every year. Her son in Iraq wrote a nice long letter telling her not to worry. As an aging reservist in charge of getting supplies to the troops, he is not in danger. In the morning after breakfast she will open her gifts, then she will go to church and after that she will take a walk to Jack's house and give him the letter.*

*The only thing bothering her as she dozes off is her garbage can, which is trapped in snow and full of ice and a dead squirrel. She hates squirrels because they steal food from the bird feeders, and from spring until late fall she traps them in a Have-a-Heart Trap and then drowns them in a plastic garbage pail filled with water. She likes the reusable traps. All she has to do is fish it out, bring it to the edge of the woods and spill out the dead rodent—that's really all they are, those squirrels, rodents with bushy tails. The problem is that the unseasonably warm weather around Thanksgiving tricked her and she kept on trapping, and then it got really cold. Now the trap is half submerged and stuck. She hates thinking that it will be there until spring, that during January thaw, the ice will still be too thick to release the cage, but the squirrel might begin to rot and possibly smell. There could be maggots. Over the years, if the squirrels had any brains at all, they would have seen what happened in her yard and stayed away. She'd thought putting the dead ones by the woods might have served as a warning, but it didn't work. What she'll have to do, and soon, is get out there with an axe and chop away at the ice.*

*Jack is tossing in his bed and twisting the sheets all around him. He is dreaming that Molly is grown and married with children, and he is a grandfather, entrusted for the day with the care of his little granddaughter. They are somewhere with cars, small bumper cars, and she wants to ride in one and it seems safe enough. There are plenty of children doing it. But as things can happen in dreams, she suddenly pulls her car away from the others, and now she is on a busy road in a tiny blue car. A green bus with a flat front approaches her and she swerves. Jack feels as though he could reach out and pick her and the car up and out of harm's way. He is big, and the scene appears in miniature, and then it doesn't, and he watches the little blue car pass beneath the protective railing on a bridge and plunge over. Next he is picking up the blue car, and the remains of his granddaughter look like a can of diced tomatoes. He scoops them from the car, and they run through his hands. Jack nearly wakes. He wants to wake up and end this dream. Somehow he knows he is sleeping, but sleep drags him under, and now he is in Molly's house, and she is on her way home to see her child, and it would be better if she never knew what happened. It would be a gift if she never had to confront such grief. She approaches the door and then walks down the hall to the child's room, and Jack lifts a gun and points it to the back of her head.*

*And that is when he finally wakes up for real, sweating. His heart is beating hard into his dark room and he sits up to make sure he's awake and the cool air hits his sweaty body and makes him shiver.*

*He pulls a blanket around him and goes out on the porch. The storm two days ago left about eight inches of new white powder. The wind has come up, and it is blowing into drifts across the common. The crèche is lit, but sparse this year as some of the village bad boys stole all the figures. Joseph and Mary were found behind a barn, along with a couple of sheep, but the baby Jesus had to be replaced with a doll, and the camel and cattle were never found. There's a Menorah out there, too. The lights are still on at Linda and Tom's, and Jack is tempted to get dressed and go over. He knows he'd be welcome. But the dream lingers. He would not want to bring it into anyone's home. Going back to bed doesn't seem possible, so Jack goes inside and sits at his kitchen table to work on a story for Hannah, the little girl he tutors who is having such a hard time learning to read. He has made numerous false starts. He has tried to insert the adventures of Nina and Conway into an alphabet book and gotten stuck in the middle. He has tried to make a rhyming story, but not liked the result. The shape of it is all right there in his mind: one lanky long-nosed hound looking for and finding trouble, and one lumbering, timid Newfie, following Nina's lead and coming to the rescue. The trouble should never be very serious or scary, and the resolution should be obvious to the child reader before Conway figures it out. Easier said than done.*

Christmas Day

Maud called her children after opening their presents. Her daughter sent a red sweater, identical to the one she'd received last year. Her son sent a box of candy and a music box and a small tabletop tree with the lights attached. She said thank you. Done for another year. Then Maud was drawn to her file drawer where she sifted through her real treasure, the mail she'd acquired over the years. She flipped her fingers along the tops of the envelopes and enjoyed the little fluttering sound. She closed her eyes and pictured words of love and anger and apology rising and dissipating like mist.

An hour later Maud slowly made her way up the street to deliver her package to Jack, and she refused to stay while he opened it. Box in hand, Jack watched her making small fearful steps down the street, then he opened the card and learned that the box contained a letter from Cate, somehow lost at the post office years ago. His dream of the night before came back to him along with a feeling of dread. His hand began shaking. The butter cookie he'd eaten earlier had left a greasy taste in his mouth. He put the box on the table and decided to go for a walk.

On the common, in front of the church, people were singing carols. He watched for a while and decided to stay. He'd sung with an *a cappella* group at Burnside. The harmonies came back to him, and he joined in on *Oh Come All Ye Faithful*, adding high notes with his clear tenor voice so that people turned to listen. After three more carols, people began to drift away. Turkeys needed basting; there were potatoes to peel. Finally the choir members closed their hymn books and went into the church.

Back at his place, Cate's letter awaited him. He made a cup of coffee and poured a shot of fine old whiskey into the steaming cup. He pulled off his shoes and his damp socks and found his slippers. He turned off the phone, even though it seldom rang.

And only then did he sit down to read. When he finished, Jack's honest laughter filled his small apartment. The laughter poured from him like sound waves made visible in a physics lab. He could see them vibrating, hitting the walls and ceiling and regrouping into different shapes and colors. He could feel his laughter purging some dark thing that had coiled inside him. If only Maud knew. Maybe she did. Perhaps she had steamed open the envelope. He would not put it past her. But no, he examined it carefully and satisfied himself that no one has tampered with the thin airmail letter, the kind that folds up on itself.

Cate had sent it from South Africa where she had gone to attend an international conference on women's health. She had been taken on a tour and seen poverty that blew her away. And in this letter she had proposed that they move once again, this time to a place that needed her more than the clinic in Woodside ever could. She laid out her arguments passionately. It really did not matter where they lived. These people had nothing. A clinic here would make her feel like she was doing something that mattered. And Jack would like it there, and the kids would see another culture. It would be good for all of them.

Beautiful, restless, persuasive Cate. Someone had once told her she could sell shoes to amputees. They probably would have gone. Jack had always been willing to follow anyone who had ideas, and on this Christmas day he realized that when you got past the raw grief, what he missed most about Cate and the twins was that they gave him something meaningful to do every minute of the day. How strange to be a person without ambition. He liked to blame this on his money, but lots of people with money found passions. There were men who loved their work and others who lived to go fishing. Not him. Even as a child, he'd complain of boredom, and his mother would say, "Well, go work on your models or read a book or play the piano" whatever, and he'd just go do it.

Then his parents sent him to Burnside, a perfect place where every day was scheduled with classes in the morning, sports in the afternoon, time only for a quick shower and a change of clothes before dinner, club meeting from 6:45 to 8:00, followed by study hours. In college and graduate school he'd floundered. His life had been all starts and stops punctuated by more degrees. Earning those gave him markers, but they didn't add up to much. The move back to Burnside had suited him fine. He had the same schedule he'd had as a student combined with grading papers and preparing for the next day's classes. At every commencement some speaker urged the students to go forward and take risks, but in truth, a Burnside education muffled students from any risk at all. They took the classes that would earn high grades so they could get into certain colleges, and all along they were taught by men and women who had sheltered themselves from the world by living on that safe and lovely campus where the busy schedule dictated every moment of their lives and silenced anything remotely risky.

He read Cate's letter again, more slowly than the first time. Now he was hungry, and he got up to find those cookies April had brought earlier that day. On the way back to his chair, he stopped at the hallway mirror and looked at a face that needed a shave and a raggedy head of hair that needed cutting. He rubbed his abdomen and found it soft. The muscles formed by chopping wood and working in his garden had grown slack, and his face looked pale. No wonder his parents nagged. He felt like a piece of bread in an unplugged toaster, going down, popping up, still bread. He knew all the words for what he was, yet Cate had loved him, and that was something. That was really something. Had she lived, they'd probably be in South Africa now, living contentedly until the next adventure came along.

New Year's Eve

Worn out from Christmas, Linda and Tom forgot about New Year's Eve and went to bed early. Exhausted from their long trip and the emotional ups and downs, Claire and Andy stared at the TV, waiting for the ball at Times Square to drop, but by eleven fifteen, they fell asleep on the sofa. Peter and Mel made their way to the common where a small group of contra dancers had left the Grange Hall and gathered to observe the last minutes of the old year. Peter hoisted a foil wrapped basketball over a tree limb. Jack had seen all this from his porch and come down to join in. He held a stop-watch. While the church bells rang, Peter lowered the ball so that it struck the ground at midnight—exactly. A musician played *Auld Lang Syne* on a penny whistle.

# *Part Two: Cooper Hill, 2005*

## *January*

Amanda Sloane stood in line at the post office and coughed; she folded forward and gasped before the next set of spasms began. People stared. It's just a cold, she told them, careful to cover her mouth before the tickling erupted again into more coughing. Maud scowled. Mothers pulled their children in close.

Jack, who was last in line, thought Amanda didn't look well. Her eyes had a glassy sheen and her skin looked clammy. He wondered if anyone was taking care of her and thought about that door lock of hers, how she'd have to get up out of bed to let someone in. He didn't feel angry as he had before, just sad that things had turned out this way. Since Amanda got the lock and blabbered to everyone about *Things That Can Happen*, even in small towns, almost everyone had gone out to buy lock sets for their doors. Eric, the boy he tutored, had a big lock on his house and so did April's. Only Sarah Gray, the massage therapist, left her door unlocked these days, and when he went to tutor Hannah, all he had to do was step inside and yell that he'd arrived.

It was nice. It was how things were supposed to be in a place like Cooper Hill. Of course, he knew that in places like Cooper Hill a trusted friend should not go prowling around, uninvited.

When Amanda was done at the counter, Jack decided to postpone his own business and walk her home. He told her he'd bring some soup, if she would leave the door unlocked and promise to get in bed.

"I've been living on canned soup and crackers," she said

"That stuff is all salt."

"Whisky helps the cough," she said. "But I'm all out."

"I'll bring some brandy then," he said. "Some lemons, too."

"That would be so nice," said Amanda, sounding scratchy, as though she was about to start coughing all over again and looking like a sick little girl.

When Jack returned he found a locked door, and he heard the

shower running. Damn. She just let the door swing behind her, he thought. He should have seen her into the house. With that fever, she probably couldn't keep anything in her head for long. He tried the back door, no luck. Well, he'd just wait a while until Amanda got out of the shower. Time passed. He went around the side of the house and saw that the bathroom had filled with steam. More time passed, and all the hot water was used up and the steam went away. The bathroom had a high window. He couldn't see in, but he knew something was wrong. Cold water running, no sign of Amanda. He pushed at a window or two, but they would not budge. He called and rang the bell and made enough of a commotion to draw a neighbor's attention.

"You better call someone," she said. "A woman shouldn't be living alone, young, or old like me—it doesn't matter." Jack asked her to call the police. She hesitated a moment, like a city person afraid to get involved, but then she went inside.

In Cooper Hill, the fire department responded to emergencies with an all-volunteer force, so it took a while for help to arrive. Jack told them what he knew, and they battered in the front door and found Amanda naked and cold on the bathroom floor. The EMTs said she probably slipped or passed out and banged her head and shoulder on the way down. An ambulance arrived. All the neighbors came out in time to see Amanda's flannel-wrapped body on the stretcher.

Jack left the soup pot on the steps and set out for the hospital over in Woodside. Amanda's cap of black hair had looked so dark against her white face and the blankets. He felt sick; he felt death hovering around him again; it made him furious, but Amanda turned out to be okay. She had a concussion, a light case of pneumonia, and she'd wrenched her back. She would not ski this winter, but she would recover with the help of antibiotics, muscle relaxants, and massage. Jack stayed at the hospital until her cheeks turned pink, and when she asked him, he agreed to find a carpenter and locksmith to fix the door. When she came home from the hospital two days later, she gave him a key and asked him what had happened to the soup.

In the third week of January, the expected thaw brought Maud Crowe out to the place in her yard where the garbage can holding the dead squirrel was frozen fast in a snow bank. She'd caught the flu from Amanda. Though recovered, she still felt weak, but she could not miss this opportunity. The sun felt warm on her face. It had melted the top layer of the snow, but the ice held beneath. She made her way slowly over the slick treacherous surface, occasionally crashing through the crust and plunging knee-deep into powder. Snow filled her right boot, and she shivered but pressed on. The can was not set in the driveway with the other garbage cans, but in the back of the yard near the shed and the compost pile. Crossing the crested snow, she used the shovel she'd brought along like a cane, but it occasionally broke through the surface, too, and then she stumbled and had to brace her feet in order to pull it free. By the time she reached the can, sweat covered her body, and her knees were shaking.

The top of the can held a dome of frozen snow, but she had come prepared with the shovel and a trowel. Holding onto the handle, she pushed the snow off the top of the can and lifted the lid. Her heart sunk when she saws the cage containing the squirrel still locked in ice. Some melted water swirled at the surface, but the milky ice below had not been affected by the January sunshine and three warm days. Still she had to try. Bending over the can, she held the shovel high, intending to plunge it down in one hard motion and possibly break through. But she lost her balance and fell hard, breaking her hip, her right arm, and her collarbone.

Maud liked her privacy. Thirty years ago, she and her husband had planted arbor vitae around the yard. It now created a dense eight-foot fence along the perimeter. She called out a time or two, but knew it was hopeless. Lying there with the sun on her face and the cold seeping into her broken body, she felt peaceful. If she didn't try to move, the pain wasn't too bad. She closed her eyes, and the last thing she remembered was Jack's bashful thank you. He never said what news the letter held and she had not trespassed, but it had changed something in him. He walked more lightly after Christmas, and he'd gone and gotten himself a decent haircut. Such a good man. Maud hoped with all her heart that he'd find his way.

Later, people would speculate about how long she had been lying there in the snow. Ed Stone, the guy who plowed everyone's driveway, had found her. He'd been taking advantage of the thaw to do some clean-up on driveways where slush had turned to ice and then back to slush. He got to Maud's house around four-fifteen, just as the light was fading, but noted that just a month ago it would have been totally dark by then. He remembered this clearly when the police questioned him. He'd called them after he went to investigate the dark shape in Maud's backyard, and he almost missed it, but from the end of the driveway he'd been able to look deep into the yard from the high cab of his truck. He also slipped and stumbled, but he weighed more, and most of his footsteps crashed through the crust, giving him purchase. She had already succumbed to death in the cold, a gentle death that comes with sleep.

Maud had lived in town all her life, and the church was packed for her service, despite the fact that most people found her unpleasant. This was simply the way things were done. Her late husband had been a member of the Select Board and served on the Finance Committee. She had worked at the Post Office. Everyone knew her. In the steamy warmth, people coughed through the 23rd Psalm, the Lord's Prayer, and the Benediction. The soloist, who sang *Amazing Grace*, wavered on the high notes because she had a sore throat. At least one person in three crunched wads of tissue, and with all the nose-blowing and eye-watering, a stranger would have thought the community was overwhelmed with grief.

As it turned out, everyone who was not already sick at or before the funeral got sick later. It had been a fine service, as far as those things go, but Maud would have been so shamed to know that walking to the church and from the church most people were talking about the frozen squirrel in the garbage can, in a Have a Heart Trap, of all things. How many had she killed? So sad. She hadn't even made a dent in the squirrel population.

Of course her children were there, and they too became subjects of gossip, since they'd not been back in a long time. People didn't have much to say to or about the son in uniform, except for the fact that as a reservist he really wasn't in great shape, and he looked much too old for soldiering. The son from California didn't merit much comment either, but Rebecca, who really didn't live that far away and had those adorable children Maud hardly ever saw, caused lots of speculation. She looked sad, but not sad enough, considering she'd lost her mother. Mothers, you only get one, people said. She should be ashamed of herself, and how long will it be before she puts the house on the market? Well, not until she strips the place. Because she was old and had lived in town forever and been widowed as a young woman, it was easy to feel that an institution had died. But because of the squirrel, people also had the uneasy feeling that something evil had lived among them. Few lingered after the service. Those who did spend a little time in the church basement, drinking coffee and eating a sheet cake, came down with the flu in hours.

Jack was one of the few who stayed well, and people needed help. Now he had keys to all the houses he had once snuck into. People could approach him. News of Cate's letter had spread, and everyone said it was like a benediction, freeing him to live in the world again. He made eye contact. He smiled, or as Claire said to Andy, "He looks like he grew a spine at last. That Cate Walker has power beyond the grave." When Eric was much better, but still not ready to go to school, his mother had to get back to work, and she asked Jack to check in on him throughout the day. As soon as Eric felt well enough, Jack took him down to the basement and began showing him how to move his new soccer ball around. Claire and Andy were called away because Claire's mother was in crisis yet again, and they asked Jack if he could take care of Nina. Tom and Linda decided they needed some sun. After recovering from the flu, they went to the Caribbean for a week and asked Jack if he would look after the house and Greylock. It was perilous to leave a house alone at a time when pipes could freeze or furnaces might suddenly die, and Greylock needed care. He now only ate once a day and slept the rest of the time on a heating pad covered with washable fleece, because he sometimes didn't even try to make it to the kitty box. Linda and Tom had agreed that they needed this vacation and that afterwards they would figure out what to do about the houses over in Woodside that had not sold and, of course, Greylock, who sometimes gazed at them through filmy eyes as if he didn't even know who they were.

Jack liked talking to the inscrutable cat. This cat knew his secret and acted like it. Jack would turn the key in the lock and hear that deep sound cats make when they bring a bird or rodent to the door. Jack would check the water bowl first and then kneel next to Greylock for a chat, and more often than not, Greylock would choose this moment to release the most fowl excrement anyone could imagine, and of course Jack had to clean up.

"Old boy, it's time for you to go," he'd say, as he tucked clean flannel over the heating pad, gently moving the huge cat from side to side like a nurse giving a bed-ridden patient a bath. "You know it. I know it. Tom knows it. Even Linda knows it, but she pretends she doesn't. Look at this house you live in. Even your tiny brain ought to understand that this is not a place for shitting wherever you please."

Greylock would stare as if listening, lick a paw and then release a stream of urine on the clean bedding. "Ah," Jack would say, "You didn't much like my visits, did you? Well, I'll tell you something, I feel bad about those. They aren't going to happen anymore. You're a cat. In your life you must have done things you weren't supposed to do. In fact, if you're a normal cat, you made an art of stealing food and shitting in flower beds and killing song birds, so don't look so haughty."

Greylock would narrow his eyes. "The difference between you and me," said Jack, "is that you never felt sorry for a minute. If you could, you'd go out and kill some innocent creature right this minute."

Jack enjoyed this patter. It was only a way to fill the silence. Linda and Tom's house felt emptier when he came in with a key than it had when he snuck in and felt their life only temporarily interrupted. There was no chicken thawing on the counter nor fruit that needed to be eaten that day. They had cleaned the refrigerator before they left. No vases filled with fresh flowers graced the table. He checked the thermostat and went upstairs to make sure the pipes that ran along the side of the house to the upstairs bathroom had not frozen. He could have pulled out all their drawers, sifted through the mail, even pulled back their sheets to see if there were sex stains on the mattress cover—but he'd lost interest.

At Claire and Andy's house, Nina greeted him with a soulful head tilt and then craned her long neck to peer around him. After all this time, she still expected Conway, and Jack remembered that day when he and Cate had gone with Claire, Andy, and Lizzie to find a dog. They wanted a shelter dog and had a puppy in mind, but Nina had brought her beautiful brown-eyed face to the front of the wire cage, and when Claire pressed her hands against the wire, Nina licked her fingers to seal the deal. Nina, who had a nasty case of heartworm then, a bad hind leg that still gave her trouble, and a scar on her face that suggested former abuse became one of those great dogs, a hound-shepherd mix with a mind of her own and an intricate vocabulary of howls and moans. She really had inspired the children's story he was still trying to write for Hannah Gray. She would follow that long nose of hers into all sorts of trouble. Back when she and Conway both roamed the land, it was always Nina who found and then rolled in the dead skunk. Conway followed, and then both smelly dogs got locked out of the house for the afternoon, Nina acting as though she'd been doused in perfume and Conway looking confused.

That wall of pictures on Claire and Andy's kitchen wall still fascinated him, because of the images that were there and the ones that were not. He wondered if anywhere in the house, tucked away because it didn't need to be seen often, but not thrown away, Andy might have hidden one picture of him and Cate together.

Of course Jack knew. He wasn't stupid. It had just made sense to ignore the affair. If you ignore such a thing, the people having the affair have to become liars, and if they have any decency in them, which both Andy and Cate had, they would hate being liars and eventually end the thing or confess so that they could be together out in the open. Jack had had no desire to rush either one of those conclusions by having some kind of showdown. Also, as soon as a man knows his wife is fucking someone else and he tells her, he has to do something about it, and there just aren't that many choices. Stop it now. Get out of here. I am leaving you. What good is "Stop it" if your wife is laying there in bed next to you and longing for the other person? What good is "Get out" if you are then all alone, and the fucking is still going on, only you are cut out of her life all together. No good at all.

So, like many other things in his life, he had let it run its course, and then knowing it had burnt itself out made it easy for the two families to be friends. He'd always liked Andy. Andy had seen Jack and Cate through three failed inseminations and two early miscarriages. He could understand why they'd grown close, and it wasn't in him to judge anybody.

So, yes, this house of Claire and Andy's was many layered. First it was Andy's, then a place where Cate went to be with him, then home to Andy, Claire, and Lizzie, and sometimes—but not often enough—a place where Lizzie's dad came to visit. Jack would never ever understand how Brad had neglected Lizzie for all those years. Her eleventh birthday came to mind. She'd been helping Cate with the twins while they all stacked firewood, but she'd told everyone she had to leave early because her dad was coming to take her out to dinner. Around two, Lizzie began to anxiously eye the clock, even though he wasn't expected until four. At three she'd convinced Claire and Andy to head for home so she'd have time for a shower. According to Andy, she'd showered and spent a long time drying her hair and deciding what to wear, but she'd been ready at four, still hopeful at four-thirty, teary by five and insisting that nobody use the phone for any reason because surely he'd call. At five-thirty she'd been stoic, but by six the tears began to fall, big gulping sobs that caused Claire to say, "Never again." Never would Claire or Lizzie believe a thing Brad said. At seven, they returned to Jack and Cate's. Lizzie gave the twins a bath and read to them for an hour.

Nina stretched her languid self across the full length of the sofa and going for a walk didn't seem urgent, so Jack climbed the stairs to peek into Lizzie's room. Molly would have had a room like it after a while, with its mixture of old stuffed animals and rock star posters. At the time of the accident, she still slept with Zeke. All four of them had shared a family bed until the twins were three, and then, without any coaxing, Zeke and Molly said they wanted to sleep in their own room, but they hadn't wanted to be separated. Sometimes he and Cate would look in on them late and night and find them curled into each other like they'd been in the womb, Molly with her head at Zeke's feet.

Jack didn't spend too much time at the doorway to Lizzie's room. It made him sad, such an unlikely place for a healthy young girl to stash liquor bottles and drink all by herself. Claire said Lizzie had hidden one bottle in an old Barbie case, of all things, a small pink quilted suitcase that once held Barbie's wardrobe. He wondered if Zeke and Molly would ever have been tempted to drink or try drugs, and as much as he liked thinking no, he knew too much about adolescent life. Good kids from loving families did every kind of self-destructive thing you could think of. Claire and Andy had been over it a thousand times, deconstructing every detail of Lizzie's life, wondering what they might have done differently. They needed to place the blame somewhere. But Jack knew and had tried to tell them that they would never locate a moment, a real or imagined slight, a time of inattention, or a villain.

The sound of Nina's toenails on the wooden floors and a deep woof pulled him from this reverie. He headed back downstairs, and she was pacing by the back door and looking out the low windows that faced the yard. Claire and Andy's neighbor had a cat that had climbed to the top of the fence that bordered the yard. With its ears flattened, it looked straight in the window at Nina and hissed. Nina whined to go out, but Jack could not open the door because Nina had had surgery for her bad leg and could not run or jump for at least six weeks. He rattled her leash, and she came to him. Without the distraction of a cat or the paperboy, Nina did okay on the leash. They headed up the street, and Jack passed Jess who complimented him on how well he controlled her.

"That's because you're not a cat or the paperboy," he told her.

"Have you dealt with that yet?" She asked.

"No, tomorrow morning will be the test, I guess."

"What if we walk together?" Jess asked. "I'd like to see how Nina behaves when she isn't taking advantage of Claire and Andy."

Jack declined. He knew Nina would behave herself with Jess around. Jess had that natural authority common to all dog trainers. He thought maybe certain people just possessed this quality. Some became animal trainers, some went into the Army, and the ones with mean spirits went to work for the Registry of Motor Vehicles.

Jess understood. Like everyone in town, she had noticed a difference in Jack. You could have a conversation with him now. He didn't look all coiled up like a dog that'd been beaten and was just waiting for the next person to turn on him. He had promised to teach April how to ride her bike, and she and Mary had talked at length, first about the importance of having good male role models in April's life and then about the wisdom of letting April be alone with any man, even a good person like Jack Walker, given that priests and Boy Scout leaders kept coming up on charges of abuse.

As usual Mary had been more protective than Jess, but in the end she'd said, "If we can't trust Jack Walker, then the world's completely fucked." Still, before the first lesson, they gave him a list of things he should and should not do so that April would come away from the lesson with her self-esteem and bones intact. If she fell, he was not supposed to tell her not to cry. If she begged him not to let go, he shouldn't try to trick her, and if she succeeded, he shouldn't make too much of it or April might think that he was surprised that she could learn so easily.

Jack brought Nina to the common where she did what she had to do, and on the way back, he struck up a conversation with Cate. That lost letter had opened a channel of sorts, an ongoing dialog in which Jack took both parts:

"Oh Caty girl," he said, "You would have loved that one. You would be filled with opinions on the matter."

And Cate said, "Jess and Mary make a good argument against same-sex marriage, don't you think? Not because of religion or politics but because women talk too much and process everything to death. Sometimes that mute male energy that just stops it all can be a relief."

"Well, Cate, you just try telling them that."

"Oh, I wouldn't even try. I wouldn't be able to get a word in edgewise anyway. Poor April. I wonder if she ever gets to do anything spontaneously."

"Not likely," said Jack. "But April's got a mind of her own. She'll be one hell of a teenager."

Jack and Nina passed Maud's empty house. He told Cate about the squirrels. These days, he told Cate about most everything in his life. When he cooked his simple dinners, he named the ingredients as if giving a cooking lesson. Cate had been an awful cook. He didn't shy away from talking about the accident, either. "People say all kinds of things about me, you know; everyone's a therapist these days. They think I have survivor guilt, but that's not it. You know what I have Cate? Survivor envy. Now that doesn't mean I go around wishing I was dead. If that was the case I could have taken care of it long ago. No, I just envy your oblivion. The police said it all happened in a flash, and death in icy water is fast. Maybe you had a few seconds of horror when you heard the ice breaking beneath you. Maybe you didn't even know what it was at first. Ice crackles and crunches all the time when the weather changes. You would have seen the kids go in first and that had to be awful, but it was over. For you it is over, and for me it's like a movie playing in some impossible to get at part of my brain. Maud Crowe tried once to tell me that we'd all be together in heaven. What a wonderful myth. I tutor this little girl Hannah who is having an awful time learning to read, and her mother, who is a massage therapist, keeps suggesting that I burn sage and put out bowls of water to collect all my negativity so I can find the healing white light. Yeah, I thought you'd enjoy that. She's okay, one of the last remaining hippies, walks around in those long floppy skirts, smells of dope in the morning, lets her dog run free all over town. Maud Crowe hated her of course."

As he passed by Linda and Tom's place he told Cate about Greylock and about his four months of trespassing. "I like to tell myself I didn't do any harm, but Amanda would not have had those locks on her doors if I hadn't failed to close her door tightly one afternoon. And Linda thinks she's losing her mind because she can't remember cleaning up after Greylock one morning, and of course she didn't. Worst of all I guess is that almost everyone has locked doors now. It changes the way the village feels. I never intended anything like that. You know, it was just one step more than walking around at dusk, looking in windows. I was trying to find out how people lived their lives."

Jack stopped muttering for a moment to take that in. "Hey Cate; that's it. I just surprised myself, tripping over the answer, just like that, because honestly, if I'd been caught, and anyone had asked me just what the hell I was doing, I would not have had an answer. Not then. I would have stared blankly until they took me away."

Nobody was out to see Jack Walker walking along having a complete conversation with himself, and Nina seemed to like the sound of his voice. Every once in a while she looked over her shoulder at him and playfully tried to grab the leash. Nina liked to pretend that she was walking him.

He continued, "You would have been better at this than me. You would have grieved and then moved on. But you always had so much to do. South Africa! How I laughed when I read that. That's the real problem now Miss Cate; what am I to do without you leading me along?"

And then he imagined Cate's answer to that. She'd say, "Jack, that's the most maudlin thing I've ever heard. Don't blame your inertia on me or get romantic about me and our children being dead while you live your tormented life. Get over yourself. You sound more and more like some rich lazy teenage boy who is just so bored with life that he can't stop himself from sneaking into the other boy's room and taking things, even though there's nothing in the whole world he needs. Go jerk off and then find something to do." Ah, his mother had said much the same thing, without the reference to self-abuse. Cate had made that speech, or something like it so many times, but she never ended nasty. After she'd scolded him, she'd reach out and touch his face. "Jack Walker, you are kind, handsome and very wealthy. You make it possible for me to work at the clinic and it might as well be for free when you figure my hourly pay. You make big donations every year. You are a wonderful father; why don't you go bake some bread?"

Often he would do just that.

With the end of his soliloquy, Jack and Nina were back at the house. He brought her in, fed her, and filled a bowl with fresh water. "Now, no running around the house. I'll be back early in the morning, but I don't want you bounding around from window to window on that bad leg just because you see a cat or squirrel, you hear me?"

Nina cocked her head as if she were listening, and Jack let himself out.

## *February*

"Chasing trucks or the paperboy is a hard behavior to correct," said Jess. She was working with Andy, who was stronger than Claire and not likely to get pulled to his knees, which had recently happened to Claire for the third time, this time on ice. It was a miracle that she hadn't broken anything. She'd threatened to get rid of Nina, an impossibility to Andy, so now he was taking lessons alone. Jess had decided that Nina needed one person in charge. In a wolf pack, there could not be two leaders.

"What you need to realize is that in her mind she succeeds every time. She barks and lunges, and the paperboy rides away. The only way to correct this one is to let her know that you don't like it, because after food, which you supply, she wants your approval."

"I don't think she really cares if I approve," Andy said. "If I scold her she walks away. When I try to rub her stomach, she lifts one leg slightly as if she's doing me a favor. Our friend's dogs roll over in ecstasy. Not Nina."

"What kind of dogs do they have?"

"Golden retrievers mostly or Labs."

"Well, breeding is everything where dogs are concerned. Nina is a hound-shepherd mix. She's more independent, but that doesn't mean she shouldn't respect you."

Jess stood back so she could see how Andy was working with Nina. He had her pulled up tight to his side, but she wasn't really heeling; he had her reeled in like a fish. "Andy, relax your shoulders. Loosen up on the leash. Walking on a loose leash is a reward for Nina; one because it pleases you, and two because it's more comfortable for her. Have we talked about the gentle leader?"

"We tried it once. She hated it."

"It's really more comfortable than having her neck jerked around, and she can't use all that power in her shoulders against you. Next time I'm bringing one."

"Can Claire come next time?" Andy asked.

"It's better that she doesn't. The two of you end up arguing about who is doing it right, and Nina just goes her merry way."

As always, Andy marveled at Jess's authority. She made him feel like he was twelve years old.

Jess walked with Andy back to the house where Claire was sitting in a chair, staring at the TV and crying. The room was filled with the smell of cigarette smoke, a bad sign since Claire rarely smoked in the house. At the end of Christmas break, she'd asked for a leave from her job; being at Burnside had become unbearable, and it seemed that they went to her mother's every couple of weeks now. Florence rarely even knew they were there. She drifted in and out of a morphine-induced sleep, and when she woke asked questions about things that happened thirty or more years ago.

"Where's the Motorola?" she asked last time, referring to the first TV she'd ever owned.

Claire and Andy played along. "They took it out for repairs, Mom."

"Oh, I hope it came with a good guarantee."

"They come with warrantees, not guarantees," Claire said.

"How true," Florence had answered, suddenly looking shrewd, "There are no guarantees."

Thinking Florence had died; Andy placed his hands on Claire's shoulders and looked at the image on television. Bright yellow police tape defined an ordinary looking backyard where people were carefully excavating. He took the remote and turned up the sound.

"Please, no," said Claire. "I can't listen to any more, but I can't stop watching either. They are finding body parts. This guy; he drove a school bus, fixed cars, lived in town all his life, and his backyard is filled with arms and legs and skulls."

Since Lizzie disappeared, Claire had started clipping horrific stories from the local paper and the *Boston Globe.* A boy had come home from college for Thanksgiving vacation and missed the first train. By the time he got to his house, his father had shot the entire family and then put the gun to his own head. A man rushing to the hospital because his wife was in labor ran a red light, and was killed by an oncoming SUV. A perfect-looking, eighteen-month-old infant died at home, in her mother's arms, from a rare genetic disorder that doomed her at birth. A peanut allergic teenager in Canada kissed her boyfriend, who had eaten peanuts earlier that day, and died. Every day Claire also clipped stories of death in Iraq and starvation in Darfur.

"It will take a long time to identify everyone. In some cases it may not be possible."

"How did they find him?"

"A neighbor's dog came home with a hand."

"Claire, you shouldn't be watching this."

"What happens?"

"What do you mean?"

"Are we supposed to call? Send information about Lizzie? Do they have a list of all the missing people? The reporter said some of the bodies have been there for fifteen years and some are more recent. They are going to start digging in his cellar. Someone said he was running out of room or getting careless, and that's why the dog could dig something up."

"This is happening in Iowa," Andy said. "What would Lizzie be doing there?"

"That's a really stupid thing to say. This guy could have picked his victims anywhere. Maybe he traveled, went on vacation and came home with his own special souvenirs."

"I guess we should call the police," said Andy, "just to make sure they have Lizzie in some kind of national database."

"Ask if we should send her dental records," said Claire.

"I will, but honey, but sweetheart," he said, his voice cracking, "please hold on, please. We have no reason to believe Lizzie met up with this monster, and don't forget how smart she is and how strong. She took that self-defense course, remember? She learned all about letting strangers get too close. She learned how to drop a guy with a few simple moves."

"And how do you think she left Cooper Hill?" Claire asked, looking angry now. "In the middle of the night when there's a bus that runs only twice a day? She hitched a ride, that's what our smart, strong girl did, feeling safe because she's lived in this town for years. And what if somebody bought her a soda and spiked it with some drug? After that how good would she be with her self-defense moves? I think we should go there. We should bring her dental records ourselves and make sure someone looks at them."

Andy tried to breath. He looked around the messy kitchen with its photos and fruit bowls and bottles of expensive olive oil. On the counter, he saw a thin letter from Princeton. They'd be wanting to know if Lizzie was enrolling in the fall. Getting in had been one of the happiest days in her life. Jack Walker had gone there, so had Jack's father, brother, and two uncles. Undoubtedly his recommendation had helped, but at this moment Jack's presence in their lives felt like a curse.

"I need to go there," Claire said. "If you won't go, I'll call Mel."

"Let's call the police and then decide. It will be a horrible scene there, and these guys have to do their work. If every worried family shows up there will be mayhem."

"If every worried mother and father shows up, I need to be there even more." Claire was now smoking her sixth cigarette.

"You know, there's a good chance that Lizzie never met this guy. Someday, when you're not expecting anything, we're going to find out she's been at some farm or commune or something," Andy said.

"That what the parents and friends thought about the people in this guy's yard, Andy. Andy, just once be with me. This isn't me imaging the worst. This *is* the worst. This is the worst of the worst, like a movie. This is why they make movies about sick people. Because it really does happen. It really does. It did, in that town, for how many years? Oh, Andy, what if she was tortured? What if she suffered for days and days?"

Andy lifted her from the chair and held her against him. Her body sagged. When he'd come in, she'd been crying softly. Now terror had made it impossible for her to cry. She'd gone limp. He wondered if she'd fainted. He bent his knees a little and scooped her into his arms like a bride and carried her to the bedroom. She didn't fight. He got a sleeping pill and put it under her tongue. She didn't resist. The phone rang just as he was pulling the covers up to her chin.

Florence again. Tonight she wanted to tell them about the horse at her window. It had grey bangs and a spotted coat and it was hitched to a shiny black wagon. It was looking right in her window and shaking its mane. "You should bring Lizzie here to see it," she said.

"We'll bring her soon," Andy said. So far they had spared Florence.

"Young girls always love horses; she will love this one."

The woman who cared for Florence took the phone. "Yesterday there was a little girl at the window, and the day before she traveled to Greece and swam in bright blue water. It's what they do when they're getting ready to leave. You better come down again soon if you want to see her one last time," she said.

Andy thanked her for the call, took a sleeping pill himself and settled in next to Claire wondering how they would possibly get through the next few days or possibly weeks. How long would it take to sort through all that evidence?

Ten days passed with Claire calling the Iowa police every day and getting no information at all. She never left the house. She didn't get dressed in the morning. Andy led her to the shower like a child and sponged the pale and flaccid skin of a woman who once worked out four times a week, a least. Andy went to work like a robot and picked up food on the way home. He was about to carry Claire to the car and head to Iowa as she'd wanted to do in the first place.

Mel, Amanda, Linda, and a few other members of the book group met at Linda's house to talk about the situation. This time there was no elegant dinner, just a bag of taco chips and some dip. It seemed that their years together had to add up to more than great meals and conversation. If they couldn't find a way to help at a time like this, they were just a group of women with a little too much leisure time on their hands.

"There's no use in telling her not to worry," said Linda. "That would be ridiculous. She has every right to worry. This whole thing has not been like Lizzie at all."

"What about Jack? Has he talked to her? They were always so close," Mel said.

"Jack Walker is the last person Claire wants to talk to. There he is, the living embodiment of the worst that can happen. No, nobody wants to belong to his club," said Amanda.

"She's smoking and drinking too much, and we can't just sit here talking and do nothing," Linda said. "Andy looks like a ghost. I see him walking Nina, and even that crazy dog seems to know something awful is going on. She walks with her head down."

Everyone was quiet for a while. Linda poured some wine. "We all drink too much," she said. "No wonder Lizzie started; what did she see all her life?"

"That's crazy," said Amanda. "Social drinking is not the same. None of us drink alone or in the morning."

"Not yet," said Mel, who'd been quiet for a while. "I just thought of something I might be able to do, maybe. I know a woman out at the University of Iowa. She took one of my trips a year ago; she said it changed her life. I'm going to give her a call. Maybe she knows somebody on the police force. Any information would help, don't you think? Even a timeline. They just keep telling Claire the investigation will take time, and they can't give out any details at this point."

"The police won't tell her anything."

"It's a small town. She could have an uncle in the department. Look, how many secrets do we have around here?"

"Then what?" asked Amanda. "What if you find out something awful?"

"I can't worry about that now. Something has to be better than nothing."

Mel made her call and got the information she sought easily. But before she could call Claire to tell her that all the found bodies were male, mostly young boys, and before Andy could settle his schedule and make time for a trip to Iowa, Brad called to let him know that Lizzie had turned up at his home in Pennsylvania an hour ago. She looked worn out, and she was asleep now. She claimed to have written many letters to her mother and Andy, and then just given up. She had not wanted him to call, but of course that was out of the question. No, he did not think they should race down there. He'd call again when he knew more; he'd take care of things. For now, they should try to rest themselves. Of course he'd been riveted to the news about the serial killer as well, with all the same fears. In fact, Lizzie had made her way to him because she knew how worried everyone would be.

Dumbfounded, Andy said, "But why didn't she call here? One simple phone call would have pulled us from this hell!"

"You'll have to ask her," Brad said. "I don't think she's been thinking straight for quite some time."

"Why did she go to you?" Sounding wiser and more thoughtful than Andy had ever given him credit for, Brad said, "There are times when some distance can be a good thing. Didn't you ever have an aunt or uncle you could confide in? Look, this is not the time to get into my history with Lizzie. She is safe. I will take care of her, and I suspect she'll be ready to talk to her mother in a day or so."

At her second therapy session with Sophie Weis, Claire wanted to talk about what would happen when Lizzie came home. After all these months of worry, she should be nothing but happy, but anger and fear were getting in the way. Lizzie would come home, and Claire could not picture their reunion. They had parted in anger. They had not communicated for months, and Lizzie had gone to the one person Claire resented above all others. So what kind of relationship were they going to have, and was she expected to open her arms as if none of this had happened?

She'd talked with Amanda some, as a friend, but Amanda could not be her therapist, which was too bad because Claire trusted her. It was Amanda who'd suggested she find a professional, and Claire had resisted at first. She'd made it through the worst without needing a therapist, she'd argued, but she was wearing Andy out. She knew that. Attentive as always, he tried, but Claire could see that he had nothing new he could say, and his worn out advice about taking things one day at a time was beginning to irritate her. He deserved to be mad as hell. He'd been a better father than Brad ever dreamed of being. Lizzie had hurt him, too, but try as she might Claire could not provoke Andy to anger. She could tell Linda had also reached her limit, so had everyone in the book group. Now that they all knew Lizzie was okay, nobody understood Claire's need to keep chewing at it.

Sophie had an office in her home that overlooked a meandering stream. The sofa where Claire was invited to sit filled a pretty alcove. Claire liked the setting, but before she sat down she noticed that some of the wood around the alcove windows was rotting. She wondered why Sophie didn't take care of it. She should have been able to with what she charged, she thought, and then in a split second realized that was exactly the kind of thing her mother would say. If someone borrowed twenty-five dollars and neglected to pay it back, Claire's mother would be figuring the size of the debt, with compound interest, thirty years later.

Claire settled in and saw the tissue box, waiting. She guessed Sophie expected her to cry this time. Last time she'd come close, but Claire felt like saying, fuck you world. Losing a best friend in a tragic accident—a best friend who once had an affair with your husband—and then finding out that your daughter is an alcoholic and blames you, and then having her run off with such fury in her face and going to Brad of all people would make anyone angry, so why couldn't she just *be* mad?

Claire began at the part that seemed easy—Lizzie and the letter from Princeton. "I can't imagine she'd give up a chance like that," she said, "but she might. She might make that furious face again and pretend going to Princeton was all my idea, which it definitely was not."

"How did she choose it?"

"I work at the Burnside School. I took a job there years ago for the free tuition people get for their kids. Lizzie thrived in the place, but it was always hard. First, she was a day student among all the boarders, second, it isn't easy to be around so many rich kids. They were all talking about Harvard, Princeton, and Yale. In her junior year the college advisor put Princeton on the list. She said they had plenty of financial aid, and Lizzie stood a good chance of being a recruited athlete, which she was. When she goes she'll row there, if she goes."

"And if she doesn't, how will you feel?

"Awful."

"And"

"Angry."

"Because?"

"I never had a chance like that. Never. Also, you should have seen her when we went to visit. She took one look and fell in love and decided to apply early admission. I've pushed Lizzie in lots of ways, but this was not one of them. This was her decision, and I'm afraid Brad is undermining it as we speak, or she's lost confidence, or she might turn it down to spite me."

"And Brad is?"

"My first husband, Lizzie's father; I think I told you that last time." Suddenly Claire realized how much territory she'd have to cover just to get Sophie Weis up-to-speed. And did she even care, this stranger in a very expensive sea green silk pants suit who was being paid to listen to her?

"You think she would hurt herself to spite you?"

"Hasn't she done that already? She says I wasn't there for her when Cate died. You do remember the story about Cate Walker and the twins?" Sophie nodded patiently and Claire felt a little guilty for being so sarcastic.

She continued, "God, she's not a child; can't she understand how I was feeling? I don't think Lizzie ever gives me the benefit of the doubt. She stands in judgment of every thing I do. And then she runs to Brad's after the way he treated her all those years. I can't understand how she can bear to be near him, let alone in his house with his latest girlfriend."

"Who else won't give you a chance?" That question stopped Claire. She took a look at the clock. Sophie would cut her off at fifty minutes no matter what.

"My mom," she said very quietly so that Sophie had to ask again.

"My mom and my dad when I married Brad, then Brad when I thought we could get some counseling and maybe stay together, also the administration at Burnside that brushed right past my application when I applied to be the director of the library. I'm still just staff. Even Andy, who says he loves me, and in his way I guess he does, but I feel like a sound and practical choice. "

"What does that mean?" Sophie asked.

Claire reviewed the speech she'd just made and thought she sounded like a whiny over-tired kid, but just the same, Andy had been given to her, by Cate, when Cate felt good and ready to give him up. And Andy had accepted her gift. He was ready. Sure. He wanted to be married and he loved Lizzie and he loved her. Sure. But Claire could never get over the suspicion that being with her allowed for proximity to Cate. Look at all those weekends spent on THE LAND, with both men admiring Cate, who did everything well, if she felt like it. "But you know what kind of person she really was?" she told Sophie. "She sort of strolled around the garden while the rest of us were pulling weeds, and then when it was time to eat she produced a huge basket of flowers for the table, and that made the whole meal special."

Sophie asked, "Cate was your best friend?"

"Cate was friendly to everyone. I arrived in town as a single mom. I think she thought of me as a stray. She kind of adopted me and Lizzie."

"Do you miss her?"

"I think I miss my mother."

"When did she die?" Sophie asked.

"She didn't die, but she's been dying for about three years, and now the morphine is giving her hallucinations, so I can't even talk to her."

"Were you always close?" Sophie asked.

"No, not really. At least not after I married Brad. She and my dad couldn't stop talking about how selfish he was, and one night I couldn't stand it any more and I snuck out after they went to bed. I left a note, but it was awful for them. Back then nice girls lived at home until they got married. They did not move in with their boyfriends."

"What did she do?"

"She had my dad call me at work, and he told me to send back my house key. When Brad and I finally got married, they almost didn't come to the wedding; they were still so hurt. Then time went by and Lizzie was born and things settled down, but that didn't mean she didn't watch Brad like a hawk, looking for signs, and she found them, but I wouldn't listen."

"Does she know about Lizzie's disappearance"?

"No. I've kept it from her. If she understood it at all she'd say I had it coming after what I did to her. Also, she's never been very involved in Lizzie's life."

"Does Lizzie know her grandmother is dying?"

"She does and she doesn't. My mother has been dying for so long."

"So, if you could talk to your mother, what would you say?" Claire wondered how they'd managed to get into her mother this way when she'd come intending to talk about Lizzie. They had less than fifteen minutes left in the session, and she wanted to bring their conversation back to Lizzie, but instead she just took the cue and imagined the words she'd say to her mother if she could.

"I think I'd say I'm sorry. Years went by when I made no effort to go see her. Oh, I thought I had good excuses. No money. No time. After my dad died she offered to take me and Lizzie on a cruise. She always wanted to go on one and my Dad didn't, so it would have been a treat and a way for her to go without being alone, but I couldn't imagine going on vacation with my mother."

"Would it have been a good time?"

"I didn't think so then, but I do now. Once she came to stay with me and Andy for a few days. She loves Andy. He's exactly the kind of man she had in mind all along. We had a nice visit. We could have had more of them, but then she got sick."

"How's that been?'

"Hard. We go see her every other weekend. Sometimes she knows us and sometimes she doesn't. She's fired three home care workers. She calls in the middle of the night to say they are trying to kill her, and she asks about Lizzie when she's lucid. I keep making up stories."

"Aren't you exhausted?" Sophie asked.

Suddenly the image of her frail, horse-loving mother, a daughter who nearly drank herself to death and then ran away, a loathsome ex-husband, and good fine Andy who took everything in stride overwhelmed Claire and the predictable tears welled up and spilled down her cheek. She did feel exhausted, as though Sophie had conjured her fatigue and ordered her eyes to close, like a hypnotist. She blew her nose and calmed herself a little and looked up to seek solace, but Sophie had fixed her eyes on a spot over Claire's head, and she had a look of growing horror on her face.

Claire looked up, too. The beam above her head and one of the window frames was covered by mounds of shiny crawling insects. Thousands of carpenter ants had hatched in the sunny warmth of the alcove. They crawled over and around each other until the beams seemed to be writhing. Claire jumped from her seat, and Sophie seemed to forget she was even there. She bounded for the phone book and began searching for exterminators. All the veneer of her professional calm had vanished. Claire wrote a check and placed it on the table. Sophie was on hold, but she pointed to the appointment book,

"Same time next week?"

"I don't know," Claire said. "I'll call," thinking she might or might not. She'd check with Amanda, but it did not seem okay for someone who was guiding you through such tender moments to fall apart at the site of a swarm. All she could think about as she drove back home were those sturdy-looking beams, eaten away inside, looking like lace.

## *March*

On the morning of March third, snow began to fall in steady small flakes that almost looked like rain. The temperature held at twenty-eight degrees, and the weathermen all spoke in a kind of shrill frenzy because this was the Big One. Some apologized for the weather. Some took credit for it. Both types annoyed Linda. The storm had come up from the Carolinas and was now stalled over New England. They had predicted it perfectly. The people who had believed them, which included Tom and Linda, had done their shopping the day before. The stores had been mobbed with people buying bottled water and toilet paper as though there was no DPW that would have the state roads cleared in no time once the snow stopped.

Linda and Tom stood across from each other at their kitchen island. He minced the onions while she chopped the parsley, celery, and carrots. Their knives made a nice sound on the chopping block. Once the vegetables had sweated a bit in oil, Linda added wine, tomatoes, and the lamb shanks she'd already browned. Tom couldn't stop grinning. She had relented because it had been so cold out, and comfort food was needed. However, she was also doubling the vegetables and warning him that this would have to last two days. She'd also found a recipe for barley risotto to serve with the lamb instead of the garlic mashed potatoes swirling with butter that Tom loved. When the heavy Dutch oven could be set on the back burner on simmer, they started on some bread. When the bread was ready for its first rising, Tom made two frothy cups of cappuccino, and then they sat down in the breakfast room with seed catalogs and three gardening magazines. They already had an abundance of tulips that would bloom in the spring, along with the magnolia tree and the lilacs, but every year Tom cleared a little more land so they could expand, and in the existing gardens they left room among the perennials for some annuals. Some years they picked a color scheme, and sometimes a rampant unruly display of color appealed to them more.

Since Tom's cholesterol had become an issue Linda had expanded the vegetable plot. Tom argued that with the cost of the fence, plus all the tools and the compost bin and everything else, they had the most expensive vegetables in New England. They could buy from the stand down the street and help a local farmer and sometimes they did, but there was this: in all his life, Linda's father had never seen how the produce grew that he lovingly displayed in his grocery store. He might have told you tomatoes grew on trees. Linda knew, and she cared enough to pick aphids off by hand before she'd spray a drop of poison on something Tom would eat. The cost of these vegetables was really not an issue at all. They were a testament to her dad's life as a grocer.

In the bright warm colors of their kitchen, it felt like they were living in two amazing realities. Open the door into a cold silent curtain of snow, turn around to Mozart and golden light. Tom and Linda imagined the scents and colors of the garden, the feel of well-composted earth and the sun beating down on bare shoulders, the pleasure of tired muscles at the end of the day and a gin and tonic on the deck. Then at dusk, a final walk-through when the low light intensified all the colors and some of the white flowers looked their best.

Normally, Linda would be alone on March third. She always took the day off. Her father had died on March 3, 1972, and her mother on the same day thirty years later. The day was always dedicated to a kind of luxury her parents had never enjoyed. Even during a storm like this, her father would have made his way to his grocery store, especially on a snowy day when his customers wanted their food delivered. And if his order boys didn't make it in, he'd deliver the big boxes himself, taking the service elevator to the kitchen entrances of luxury apartments on New York's Upper East Side. He once sold a peach to Greta Garbo. Judy Garland died owing him money. In winter, he wore a long underwear top covered by a starched white shirt and over that a red woolen shirt; he got a new one each Christmas. His store had no heat. He packed delicate produce in ice to keep it from freezing—the melting ice being warmer than the air in the store.

It wasn't snowing on the day Linda's father died. He hadn't been ill. The sky had been clear and the temperature around thirty—not bad. He'd actually started for home a little earlier than usual, and he'd hit a huge pot hole on Second Avenue, his route to the Manhattan

Bridge. He pulled over to change the blown-out tire. Because this is just what people did in his situation, he found the jack and slid it under the car. Nobody he knew called for help to change a tire. Nobody he knew kept orange cones in the trunk or flares. While he cranked with ungloved hands—he never remembered his gloves and his hands cracked every winter—a car swerved to pass another car on the right, which was against the law but done all the time, and ran right into him. Linda would never forget that night and her mother's frustration at his lateness until the awful phone call.

To honor her father, who had said he had nothing to sell but quality and service and who had fed his growing family from the stock on his shelves and, according to her mom, let them "eat all the profits," Linda always used the best produce and the finest meats she could find for one of the savory dishes he had loved. When she and Tom sat down to eat, she lit candles and together they remembered Frank and raised a glass.

On a snowy day such as this, her mother would have known no leisure, either—not with all the kids home from school, wanting to go out and play and then coming in and begging for hot chocolate, and wouldn't it be fun to make apple pie? At the end of the day, soggy mittens and wet socks cluttered the kitchen. The hot water would give out with so many kids needing a bath, all the cups would be dirty with the thick scum of cold cocoa staining the bottoms. Linda, the oldest, would often creep downstairs after all the younger kids had gone to bed to watch a TV show with her mom, but usually she'd find her asleep in her chair with a book on her lap. On March third, for her mother, Linda settled into the big chair by the fireplace and read for hours. She read novels her mother would have loved, the kind of intricate stories that made great Betty Davis movies. Sometimes she placed a box of chocolates by her side. She always had forced bulbs on the windowsill. She savored every detail of her life and thanked her mother, who had died gently in her sleep, for everything.

Linda could feel the presence of her mother and father on these cherished days and she felt their approval, too, though from her mother she also felt some sadness. No children. Her mother had taken such joy in each and every one of them, she would not have been able to imagine a life without their clutter. Still, she would smile at how Linda treated her nieces and nephews, and she would not judge.

This March third was almost perfect except for the absence of Greylock, who had waited for them to return from their trip and then died quietly in his sleep on a frigid February night. He was in a box in the garage, frozen solid and awaiting burial in the garden in the spring. Knowing that he might not make it through the winter, she and Tom had chosen a spot below the weeping cherry and dug a hole in the fall, before the earth froze. When snow covered the place, they had considered cremation, but the sight of his soft body curled around itself in peace had made them want to set him into the soft earth that way as they'd planned. Linda often had to fight the urge to go into the garage and uncover the box and look at him one last time.

Tom kept himself occupied most of the afternoon. He'd fed the birds and cleaned off the driveway a time or two, trying to let Linda have the day as if she were alone, but finally, around three he interrupted her reading to ask if she thought they ought to buy Maud's house. Houses in Cooper Hill did not come on the market very often. Maud's was not yet listed. A call to the family could avoid the realtor's fees. But the houses over in Woodside had still not sold and Linda had heard that Maud's family was a greedy lot. They didn't know how much the housing market had fallen in the last year.

Filled with longing for all the life her father had not lived, because he was working so hard at the store and thought the store would make him comfortable in old age, Linda didn't warm to the idea of taking on another property. When her mother put her dad's store on the market, nobody wanted it. Nobody wanted to work twelve hours a day or six days a week. The chain stores were beginning to take over, offering delivery service, at cheaper prices. In the end, Linda's mother had sold the stock on the shelves and the cases to another grocer, and that had been the end of a twenty-seven-year effort.

For many years afterwards, Linda could walk up to 59th Street and stop at other stores and at Rowen's, the bar on the corner where people remembered her dad. He had once been elected honorary mayor of First Avenue. No one remembered him now, and he never had his retirement years at all. Her mother had also died with regrets. She had wanted to retire in Florida. She had bent to the demands of being a grocer's wife, but had not expected a marriage without much companionship, followed by thirty years of widowhood.

Of course this line of thought led straight to Cate Walker and those sweet children, and also to a terrible story that had been in the papers that week about a forty-two-year-old woman, otherwise healthy, who had died of a heart attack on Christmas Eve, leaving her husband with three young children to raise. Heartbroken, he had not been able to take down the tree they had trimmed together. It dried out and drooped and neighbors had offered to take it down for him, but he had turned them away. By March it was brittle and brown and it caught fire just two nights ago. Though he got the children out safely, the house could not be saved. The tree, her clothes, teddy bears, and cookbooks smeared with her fingerprints; photographs and children's drawing on the refrigerator door, letters and photographs—all gone. Now he was a homeless widower with three children. Life seemed filled with missteps and lost opportunities. Had that man kissed his wife goodbye on the morning she died? Had they deferred vacations because the kids needed shoes? When was the last time they'd gone out to dinner?

On a day in which she'd intended to savor all she had, the weight of all she and Tom owned began to settle on Linda thickly, like the snow that had mounded over the cars. Their luxurious house felt cluttered with stuff that would probably end up in a tag sale someday. Accessories over in the Woodside houses chosen to highlight the good point of the homes and conceal the flaws, were getting dusty as the weeks and months passed with nobody to care for them. She asked Tom how much the mortgages on the houses were draining their savings and was shocked to learn that they were costing a little over three thousand dollars a month to maintain, with insurance, taxes, and some necessary heat. She asked how little they could ask for them and come out even.

Tom said, "In spring, everything will start moving again and we'll be fine. Right now the losses are a tax deduction we can use."

"But don't you always lose more than you gain?"

"Basically, but if we get our asking price, we'll make it up."

Tom thought they should be ready to make an offer on Maud's place once the estate was settled. They had to move ahead. It was a buyer's market. He reminded Linda that her mother would have been much better off if her dad had bought the building that housed his store. One reason nobody wanted the place was that rents went up every year. Linda remembered conversations about that. Her mom and dad had struggled over the decision, and in the end, just couldn't imagine that much debt. What would they think of the way she and Tom made their living, flirting with debt as they did?

Tom sat in the fading light, clicker in hand, ready to cruise all the channels, and Linda watched him, wanting to let it go and make him happy. He had managed their business well all these years, and she trusted him. Their house had been paid off long ago when the market was so strong that people called them to see if they had any properties, but Maud's house gave her a funny feeling. They'd never bought one from a person they knew. If they set the price too high, their friends would talk. It all felt too close. This was not how she'd wanted this day to be. It wasn't a day for decisions. She'd lost the serenity of early afternoon.

Then Tom, who could sometimes read her mind or anticipate her thoughts, came up with a wonderful idea. He said, "We can wait on Maud's house and see what happens. Meanwhile, we could offer the smaller house in Woodside to the guy whose place just burned down. He could rent for now with an option to buy once the insurance is settled. We'll just sell to him at cost and have one less place to worry about."

Linda seldom needed a reminder about why she loved this man, but it was nice to have one placed right under her nose like this. She smiled. He did too. The food they'd prepared smelled wonderful. She went to the pantry and chose a nice Zinfandel while Tom got napkins and knives and forks and set the coffee table in front of the sofa. She brought out candles and they ate in front of the fire.

While Eric and April and Hannah played in the snow in the fading light, and Mary and Jess discussed having another child since learning how much adoption would cost, and Claire composed another letter to Lizzie, and Linda and Tom savored their meal, and Jack Walker thought about putting on his snowshoes and hiking through the meadow, and all the other people in town checked the gas and oil in their snow blowers or hoped that Ed Stone would get to them early, air currents high above shifted. Soon the lovely snow turned to a gentle rain.

Later that night the jet stream swooped down and pushed the warm air aside and temperatures fell into the teens. Cooper Hill looked like a giant ice sculpture. The lower tree limbs on the giant pines that bordered Claire and Andy's yard brushed the mounds of ice-covered snow. The few drivers who had ventured out for one reason or another, skidded and fishtailed and avoided accidents only because there were so few cars on the road. This would have been bad enough, but towards morning it warmed again and heavy rain began to fall. It had nowhere to go.

Linda and Tom were awakened by the sound of water rushing into their basement and went down there to find that water was gushing in between the stone walls. Because Tom was always prepared for these kinds of events, he had a package of Quickcrete handy, and he mixed it and began trying to patch the wall, but it was hopeless. With the earth frozen solid below two feet of frozen snow, the water had nowhere to go, and as soon as he patched one area, it began to trickle in at another site. Before long, four inches of icy water covered the cellar floor and threatened to flood the furnace. Tom called the fire department. They would come and pump out your basement at times like this or after a summer thunderstorm, but the dispatcher told him he'd have a while to wait. There had been two chimney fires, and there was a list of people with flooding basements. He turned off the furnace, made a big fire in the living room and hoped the power wouldn't go out next. There were trees down all over.

At about the same time that Tom was trying to patch the wall, Jack got a hysterical call from Amanda Sloane. Her basement was flooding, too, but that wasn't the worst of it. A very wet bedraggled skunk had crept up to her enclosed porch and found its way in, because the porch door would not close with the snow weight on its roof. She'd meant to use the roof rake the day before, but she was still mending and couldn't use her shoulder to push the rake to the roof top. She had plans to rebuild the foundation on the old porch in the spring, but that didn't matter now. The back door was blocked in by snow, and she couldn't use her front door without disturbing the skunk, which was sound asleep. Jack said he'd be right over.

"Do you have a shovel by the back door?" he asked

"No."

"Then I'll bring one with me."

They had resumed the piano lessons in February, and Jack had immediately noticed a difference. Amanda had slowed down and something melancholy and thoughtful had entered her playing. She'd begun practicing in earnest, and now she could play simple pieces slowly with the pedal in the right places and the correct fingering. But on this day she'd reverted to Amanda before the accident. She combed her fingers through her spiky hair and talked non-stop from the minute he arrived. "It must be rabid; otherwise, why would it come up on my porch like that? Skunks are not supposed to like to be around people, unless it wandered up from that house down the street where that weird old couple feeds them, have you ever heard of such a thing, and if we disturb it, it will spray, and I'll never get rid of the smell. I am so tired of fucking winter; I can't tell you how much. I can't drive on these roads, not with clowns in pickup truck riding my bumper and blinking their lights to make me speed up, and I want to scream, 'Fine, I'll speed up and go into the other lane and get us all killed if that's want you want.' So I stay home. I try to be self sufficient, like you're supposed to be if you live in the country. I've got my books, the piano, my computer, movies on demand, pasta and canned goods on the shelf, firewood in case the furnace goes off, and what happens? This disgusting creature hobbles up to my porch and ruins everything. I did not need this, not at all. I should just leave and let nature take over this place."

Jack let her run herself out. The skunk was small. It could be rabid or just hungry. Amanda got some salami, and he went around to the front to see if he could coax it out. He waved the meat around, trying to get the smell in the air, but the skunk didn't move. He creaked the door open a little more, and it looked up for a moment and then tucked its nose under its tail. Amanda signaled furiously from the window, and Jack came in again through the back door.

"I think we should call someone," she said, "What about the police?"

"Why don't we wait awhile?"

"No, the police take forever. I should call, and we can wait, and if it goes away I'll tell the police not to come."

Jack couldn't argue with that logic. Amanda seemed glad to have company and she was terrified of being there alone with the skunk on the porch, so he agreed to stay. After they'd had some coffee, tuna sandwiches, and store-bought but pretty good chocolate chip cookies; a little piano playing and some awkward silences, Linda told Jack about her blind date. It was a sad kind of story, but the way she told it made him laugh. The sound of his own laughter startled him. Amanda wondered if it was too early for a glass of wine. It was four-thirty. Jack said on such a day as this, a glass of wine any time would be alright. Amanda wanted to go into the living room so they did, and he very carefully lowered himself into her white sofa. She'd given him a huge, hand-blown stemmed glass of deep red wine. They both stared at the front door like it was a TV screen. Jack set his glass on the coffee table and went to the window. The skunk had not moved. He returned to the sofa, one of those plush, down-filled kind, and slowly began to tell Amanda about Cate's letter. Something about her blind date story made him want to tell her about it.

"And that's why you've been so different since Christmas."

"Different, how?"

"Well, you don't look so wounded. You talk to people before they talk to you. Everyone has noticed. It's like you came out of some kind of deep freeze. Was it just getting one more chance to hear her voice, even if it was in a letter?"

"No, not really. It was remembering all her crazy energy. I'd relied on it, you know. I didn't have to generate any of my own. She had enough for both of us. I've always been that way. It's probably why we got along."

"And?"

"It was remembering that she loved me and the kids so much, and I remembered her sense of fun. Cate was always ready for fun. I'll bet they were screaming with joy when they went down that hill."

"Have you spent the last three years thinking you don't deserve any joy?"

"You're sounding like a therapist now."

"Well, I am a therapist. Did you ever see anybody after the accident?"

"No. I didn't need anyone to get me talking about survivor guilt or helping me get in touch with my anger. I knew I was angry. Cate could be so careless."

"So you've forgiven her?"

"It's not up to me to forgive her. It was an accident. She could have been hit head on by some crazy drunk driver, with the kids in the car, and I'd still be in the same place today."

"So what are you going to do now?

"I haven't a clue."

"So, why have you been so different?"

Now he could have told Amanda that he'd stopped breaking into people's houses so he didn't feel guilty all the time, but in truth, he had not realized that he was acting that differently. But whether he had radically changed his behavior or not, he did feel different.

For all her jumpiness, Amanda knew how to listen. She watched him as though she had all time in the world until he felt uneasy in the long silence. Finally he said, "I have spent the last three years without any idea of what to do with myself. I tinker. I read. I waste a lot of time. I teach a little. None of it adds up to anything, and I thought it was grief. I thought I was paralyzed by it. Now I know it's just me. It's ironic, because when I taught I spent a lot of time telling kids that they had to be in charge of their learning. They had to take action. Meanwhile, I might as well have been following a training manual. And I was the same as a dad. I just did what was needed and that was enough to fill a day. I don't know why Cate loved me. I must be the most boring person on earth."

Jack had delivered this speech with his chin down. Amanda reached over and put her hands on either side of his head so she could look right into his eyes. She then delivered a speech pretty close to the imagined conversation he'd had with Cate after he'd read the letter:

"Jack Walker, you act like everyone has some kind of mission but you. That's just not so. Most people have to work, so they get up and do whatever it is they have learned to do, and it's a good day if they don't get humiliated in their eight hours, or fight with a co-worker, or think they might just die of boredom. A few people, very few, write music or go to the jungle to heal the sick. The rest can't wait to get home at night, and then they don't know what to do so they watch television, and then they get up the next day and do it all over again. For a man who pretends to be humble, you really want to think you're different from other people, but you aren't. You're just rich and aimless, but at least you're not decadent, so stop beating yourself up."

"Cate used to get impatient with me," he said.

"Cate would not have wanted you any other way," Amanda answered. "She chose you. From everything I've heard, she could have had any man she wanted, but she wanted you."

While he considered Amanda's words, Jack noticed that the house was very warm. She must have her thermostat set at seventy. She was wearing a sleeveless woolen shell. He could see the red scar on her shoulder. He could smell a faint musk from her underarms. One had been shaved, but not the other. She couldn't bend her bad arm to get to it. If she wanted him to, he could shave her. He'd done it for Cate once when she dislocated her shoulder. He took another large sip of wine and thought about how easy it would be to pull her towards him, how long it had been since he held a woman; he knew she would yield. He thought about stroking her nipples through the thin woolen top. He wondered if they were pink or brown, delicate or large like bruised berries. Amanda was not his type in any way. She was shrill and urban and bossy, but she made him feel known, and any man would find her sexy. She watched his face as though she could read everything he thought and began to lean towards him, but at the same moment, a police car pulled up, red and blue lights flashing.

The officer looked as though he'd graduated from the Police Academy about a week ago. His pants held a knife-sharp crease along the front. It was still raining and water dripped off the brim of his hat. Jack went to the back door and called to him so he wouldn't come up the front steps and set off the skunk. The officer's first plan involved trying to coax the skunk off the porch, but a wad of canned dog food failed to tempt it. He poked at the porch windows with a stick, and it roused for a moment and then went back to sleep. All the while Amanda yelled at him not to make it spray, and he told her he'd do his best. It was easy to tell that nothing in his training had prepared him for this. He trudged through the deep snow at the side of the porch to get closer to the spot where the skunk was and tapped again. This time the skunk got to its feet and looked confused, before it collapsed again.

"It looks sickly to me," he said, "I might need a net or a trap." He went back to the car to radio someone, and Amanda lost patience. Without telling Jack what she was planning to do, she opened the door and threw a large piece of salami over the skunk's head and out the door. This got its interest. It raised its head to sniff and then slowly lumbered out the door and down the steps and began eating the salami. The officer was waiting, holding his gun, and he shot the skunk but failed to kill it. Wounded and frightened, the skunk moved as quickly as it could down the driveway. The officer fired again. The sound of shots drew neighbors from their homes, and in no time a small group had formed on the street to watch the officer take yet another shot at the skunk that was still managing to drag his wounded body through the snow.

Amanda was crying. Jack watched in horror as a final shot stopped the skunk. It never sprayed. The officer put on gloves and put the body, which now seemed as small and harmless as a kitten, into a black bag. The crowd dispersed and Jack went to check on Amanda. All thoughts of running his hands over her soft skin had vanished. The first shot had so startled her that she'd dropped her wine and a deep stain marked the white carpet. Amanda poured milk on the stain and Jack went out to the porch to disinfect the spot where the skunk had slept. Before heading home, he also turned over the snow where the skunk's blood had stained it.

It was such a miserable day. The cold rain went right through his jacket. Amanda had said she needed a nap, and he thought about going back and letting himself in and curling next to her, but he could not do that. She had nailed him with such honesty that now a confession stood between him and intimacy. Before he could let her take him into her body, he would have to tell her how he'd prowled around her house, and he'd have to tell her what a coward he'd been when he made up his mind to give Conway away. He could make some sort of peace with the accident. It was an accident after all, but calling Conway to the car when he knew she loved rides and betraying her trust in that way was a premeditated act of cruelty, and for a person who rarely took action, he could not believe that he'd suddenly become decisive at the wrong time and with Conway.

In March the Book Group met and ate a very late dinner because Linda, who was hosting, got locked out of her house after going grocery shopping. For some crazy reason she'd brought her car key and left her house key on its hook. Even the bulkhead door had been locked, so there was no way she could start the meal before Tom got home.

"Remind me why we all started locking our doors," she said to the group that was standing around the stove, helping but mostly pouring wine.

"It was because Amanda thought someone had broken into her house. It spooked all of us," Claire said.

"She really isn't cut out for country life," Linda said.

"This isn't even the country; what would she do if she lived up on the hill?" said Patty Dolan, a sometimes member of the group who lived outside of town on a small farm.

The village of Cooper Hill was nestled against a small

mountain with two acre zoning. The big houses with long dark driveways were there, and though they shared a zip code, the people on the hill never saw the people in the village, and the people on the hill looked out on a night sky uninterrupted by street lights.

"It doesn't matter anyway. She's moving," Linda said.

"Moving!" the group said in unison. "She just got here, and she put so much into the house."

"I just saw her the other day. All she could talk about was that rabid skunk that terrified her two weeks ago, and her phantom prowler, and carpenter ants and the absence of shopping out here," Linda said. "She has a big time crush on Jack Walker, but it's not enough to keep her around."

"Well, I'm glad," Patty said. "She's another Democrat and I am just so tired of being outnumbered here. You all get that dismissing look if I say one little thing about our President. You try to look patient, but you treat me like I'm stupid."

"If the shoe fits," said Claire.

"And what's that supposed to mean?" said Patty whose cheeks had turned a bright pink. "Look, I happen to think Bush is doing a good job. There hasn't been a terrorist attack since 9/11; they caught Saddam. We have to be patient and give this a chance."

"Seven years have passed between the first attack in the Trade Center and 9/11," Claire said. "I don't feel safer at all. These people are patient, and all we're doing is making the whole world hate America. Plus, Saddam had nothing to do with 9/11."

"It's tribal warfare over there, we shouldn't be involved," said Linda, who had been listening to a set of lectures on tape that covered two-thousand years of Middle Eastern history.

"And look at the civilian deaths. It's heartbreaking," added Claire.

"But they're doing that to each other," said Patty.

"With the weapons we've provided and because of the instability we've caused," said Claire."

Patty's cheeks turned pink again. "Listen to yourselves, just listen. So broad minded. So liberal. So well informed. You all sound like you memorized a month of NPR broadcasts. You refuse to even listen to another point of view."

"Patty, read *The New York Times*. Read this week's *New Yorker*. There's so much information there that can't be ignored," Claire said.

"Oh, those publications are all controlled by liberal Jews," Patty said, and right away she knew she'd gone too far. She immediately started back-peddling.

Claire, who had lost all color in her face, drilled her dark eyes into Patty and said, "It's okay, Patty. I know some of your best friends are probably Jews."

Nobody said a word for at least a minute.

Patty wrung her hands and began twirling her thumbs around each other. "It's just that you all get me so worked up. I try to explain that reasonable, thoughtful people who know more than any of us support this war, and you attack me. You've all known me for a long time. You know I'm not anti-Semitic."

Her words just hung there. Nobody knew what to say. The others, who had quietly watched the evening unfold like a one-act play, began to clear the table. Linda concentrated on cleaning her grease-spattered burners. Claire juggled the contents of the refrigerator to make the leftovers fit. Patty swept the floor.

After a while Linda said, "If we can't disagree in a civil way, what hope is there for the Middle East?"

Claire said she had no hope for the Middle East or anywhere else where fundamental extremism flourished. One by one the members of the Cooper Hill Book Club checked their watches or yawned, anything to get out of there. Only on the way home did Claire realize they had not chosen another book or set a time for the next meeting.

On March fourteenth, the anniversary of the accident, Jack usually spent a long time asking the same questions over and over: *What in the world were you thinking? That they'd be kids forever? That you had all the chances in the world to take them sledding, to pull a boot off and shake the snow out? You goddamn fool. All you had to do was say yes, and get yourself up off the couch and out into the afternoon.* He would try to read and fail, remembering how important some book had been to him that day. He couldn't even recall the title. Walking did no good. Sleep refused to come. Only music helped some. Mozart's *Requiem*, Verdi's *Don Carlo* or *Otello*—anything that spoke to timeless agony played loud enough to vibrate through his bones got him through the day by making him know he was not alone in grief. And since the country had engaged in this tragic war, he also watched the news, knowing that every day fathers lost their children, saw their wives' heads blown away, watched the skin burn off the bodies of people who simply went out to the market to forage what they could for dinner. Pain did not belong to him alone. Life continued to assert itself, and no matter what, the sun would come up the next day and there would be 364 days before the next anniversary.

This year he acknowledged the date by spending the morning alone, listening to gentle sad music—the "Four Last Songs" by Straus, but then he needed to be out, and he went to the Post Office and found a thick envelope filled with applications for the grant Cate's parents had funded. The foundation's board had taken a first pass and rated the applications, but final approval rested with him. He usually dreaded this, but not this time. All the hope and good will contained in the applications gave him a great feeling. This year he read each with care and determined that all had merit. How could you rank a women's health clinic in Appalachia against one in Africa? The people writing these applications were so young and completely convinced that they could make a difference. Who was he to dash their belief? And, really, all the stipends were small. Another fifteen thousand dollars would fund them all, and Jack wrote a letter to Cate's parents and a check to the foundation.

Done. Easy. He closed his eyes and saw Cate smiling at him, a wide, white-toothed smile that could light up a room.

# *April*

In early April, Rebecca came to clean out her mother's house and meet with a realtor. Chatty Joan, the hairdresser who couldn't shut up, had grown up with Rebecca and they still kept in touch. In addition to her day job, she maintained a website on eBay for collectibles and begged Rebecca to let her go through the house with her, although Rebecca had protested that she wouldn't find much. But Joan remembered the collection of ceramic chickens and all the salt and pepper shakers shaped as peppers, tomatoes, corn, kittens, and one in particular, a 1950s sports car with two small terriers driving, a white one for the salt and a black one for pepper. Rebecca thought Joan would be nothing but a distraction, but since neither of her brothers could come, she agreed to let her come by. Whatever she carted off would be something Rebecca didn't have to worry about.

From Joan, Rebecca had learned that Jack Walker was a person generally available and willing to help people. He refused any pay and agreed to come by once the dumpster was in place, but arrived earlier than that and walked through the house with Rebecca and Joan while they figured out what to do with her belongings.

Out went the old brown sofa, a TV that must have been made in the 60s, a sagging easy chair, a coffee table with scratch marks from the time Rebecca's brothers had rolled their toy trucks over the top. Into Joan's box went the ceramic animals and the plastic sunburst clock, the crochet doilies that once protected the arms of the chairs, a lamp shaped like a train, a pillow that said "Welcome to Miami," Jello molds in the shape of rocket ships, cookie cutters, a wooden rolling pin, a doll made from a plastic milk jug, and a vase shaped like a woman wearing a gauzy 30s dress, walking a hound. Jack offered to take Maud's rocking chair. It was not an antique, but Rebecca didn't want it, and he could not bear to see it go into the dumpster.

Into one corner they moved the furniture that might fetch something at auction. The cherry dining room table and matching chairs and a few mahogany end tables from the living room went there first.

Organizing the downstairs was pretty straightforward. Upstairs presented more problems for Rebecca, who was not prepared for the sad little display of clothing in her mother's closet. She had not bought anything new in years, but then, she'd had no one to take her shopping.

Bless his heart, Jack helped her go through them and sort what might be of use to someone from what had to go into the dumpster. Knowing her mother well, Rebecca checked all the pockets and came up with almost a hundred dollars in cash. All the while, Joan swept the table tops for fanciful objects but found little until they came to Maud's jewelry box. After locating the engagement ring that Maud stopped wearing when her knuckles swelled from arthritis, Rebecca lost interest, and Joan scooped up handfuls of costume jewelry for her stash. At one point Rebecca got a little suspicious of Joan's sense of bounty, but she gave her old friend her way. If all the junk Joan was putting aside had any value, Rebecca certainly had no time to try to unload it.

A life reduced to trinkets. Maud's house looked like just what it was, a lonely dwelling for a lonely old woman whose children never came back to visit. The large cherry dining room table had called up the most memories. At that table her father had helped her with her homework. At that table their family had said grace and eaten Sunday roasts. Maud had gathered Rebecca and her brothers around that same table, poured hot cocoa and told them their father had died. After that, they seemed to eat in the kitchen all the time. The dining room table became the place where laundry that needed to go upstairs got stacked, along with library books, school books, mail, bills, and newspapers. Except for a day Rebecca would never forget nor forgive.

It concerned a model penis she had fashioned from a pencil, some cotton balls, and a blue balloon, all in an effort to find out what going all the way really felt like. She had friends who had already done it, but she wouldn't dare. In fact, she'd even been too frightened to fully insert her little toy and it had slipped off the bed and fallen to the floor, forgotten after one unsuccessful attempt at penetration. Her mother found it while vacuuming. Maud could have done any number of things, including ignoring it. Instead, when Rebecca and her brothers were called to dinner that night, they came downstairs and found the dining room table nicely set, with a roast chicken in the middle and platters of vegetables all around and a bright blue penis, sticky and covered in dust, sitting right in the middle of Rebecca's dinner plate.

Rebecca had faked ignorance and thrown it in the trash, and held her head high through the meal while her brothers snickered and her mother frowned. That night she'd gone to the movies with her best friend, and in the dark theater she'd cried. Nobody knew that story, not her husband or her closest friends, who thought it was strange that she never went to see her mother.

Maud had criticized her mothering when Anna was just five-months-old. Maud had called her brother "liver lips" when his mouthful of new braces made speech difficult. Maud had lied to her best friend about her children's grades. She had called their father a failure more than once. Maud had been damaged, Rebecca now knew. And she'd had moments of kindness, and Rebecca remembered them. The same woman capable of such things had also bought her a good suit and driven her all over for college interviews. Told the boys she would match every dollar they managed to save for their educations. Checked homework. Encouraged extra-curricular activities, even when she couldn't afford the soccer shoes and figure skates.

This swarm of memories, terrible and lovely, was giving Rebecca a headache. In the kitchen, Rebecca had been surprised to find only five dishes, two bowls, and a few glasses. Maud had not replaced what had been broken. Rebecca felt a small pang and then thought that some broken things could not be replaced, not ever. With evidence of her mother's shriveled life all around her, Rebecca felt pity.

Jack said, "What about this desk?" It was the small one in her bedroom and locked.

'Is it an antique?" Rebecca asked. Joan took a closer look.

"No, I think it's a reproduction, but still about sixty years old. The veneer is cracked in a few places."

Once Rebecca had wanted this desk, but it didn't go with anything in her house. "Could you use it?" Rebecca asked Jack.

"Not really, it's kind of small for me."

"Can you sell it on eBay?" Rebecca asked Joan.

"I could, but I don't like to bother shipping larger things."

"Let's put it in the auction pile," Rebecca said. "It's too nice for the dumpster, but first we need to empty the drawers." She discovered some of them were locked, but found the key in a small leather box in one of the slim top drawers.

"She probably saved every receipt back to when she and my dad bought the house," Rebecca said as she tugged at the heavy drawer. It came free suddenly when a large envelope at the back got unstuck, and Joan gasped as the drawer fell.

All of Maud's stolen mail fell out on the floor. There had to be more than a hundred letters and small packages. For a moments they all just stared, then Rebecca knelt down and began sifting through the pile.

"She must have been crazy," said Rebecca in disbelief. "The squirrels were nothing compared with this."

Jack said, "I'm half-tempted to mash all the mail into a black plastic bag and stuff it into the garbage."

Joan said, "Look, there are bills here and notices from doctors. This package with Jess and Mary's return address feels like a picture frame, but it's broken. You can hear the glass rattle when you shake it. I wonder if people will get their letters right away or if they'll be some kind of investigation first. Oh my, who would have guessed it? You feel so secure when you take something to the post office. I mean, things do get lost and every time a plane goes down mail is lost, but you never think of that, and it's amazing how it works just fine most of the time. A miracle, really. Oh my. Look, here's an invitation to a baby shower. The postmark is four years old. That baby is four years old now. Imagine."

"Joan, you have to stop talking right now," Rebecca said, knowing that Joan couldn't wait to leave and begin making phone calls.

And then Jack saw a number of small blue envelopes. They were addressed to Claire and Andy, with no return address, written in the upright square print Lizzie always used.

"We have to tell the post office right away," Joan said. "I wonder if we should call the police."

"The post office will notify the police," Jack said.

"Tampering with the mail is a federal offense," Rebecca said. Tears filled her throat as she ran her hands over the envelopes. "This is just so mean, mean and awful. How dare she do this? God, what a mess! This will be all over the news, even where we live. How will I explain this to my kids? 'Your grandmother was a sick, mean, old woman,' is what I'll say, and that is why we never went to see her. Shit, I just wanted to sell the house and have everything done and now this."

"I think this is about it for today," Jack said. He offered to pack up the mail and bring it to the post office. Joan gathered her bags and boxes. Rebecca said she'd quit soon and head back to her hotel. She needed to call Paul and talk to her kids and picture her sunny kitchen, and remember the life she had and would still have once she left Cooper Hill for good. There was no reason to ever come back.

The whole collection fit into a sturdy liquor store box and Jack carried it the two blocks to the post office, set the box down inside the doorway and walked away. An hour later the police would be looking for a man of his description, but by then Joan would have the story all over town and they'd call off the search.

Jack took the long way home. He could smell the earth. At the base of south-facing trees, snowdrops were sprouting and the grass was greening up. Linda and Tom were out in the yard by a small weeping cherry, and when he stopped, they asked him to stay just a little while so there would be more people to say goodbye to Greylock. Claire and Andy would be there any minute. Figuring that any cat that lived that long deserved some kind of ceremony and remembering his own strange relationship to the ancient cat, Jack agreed. Tom went to the garage and brought out a tin box. Jack had assumed it was filled with ashes, but it was too big. Linda told him Greylock was in there and had been since he died. They were burying him today so he didn't thaw. Tom had dug a nice deep hole and he settled the tin in neatly. Claire and Andy arrived. Linda shoveled the first dirt and handed the shovel to Jack. He then passed it to Claire, who passed it to Andy. Tom finished up and patted the dirt.

Linda said, "Goodbye Greylock; you were the best cat ever."

Jack liked her simple words. Claire had brought a bottle of champagne. Andy asked Jack if he was going to stay. Being here felt easy. Maybe anything would after his strange day, so he accepted a glass of champagne, and they all drank to Greylock's wonderful life and then Claire and Andy headed home and Jack did, too, feeling guilty that he hadn't said anything to Claire and Andy about the letters, but also knowing this news was not his to deliver. It would all come out soon enough.

Claire couldn't look at a calendar without thinking that the Princeton deadline was right on top of them, and Lizzie had not said what she planned to do. In Pennsylvania, she had found a job on a farm mucking horse stalls, and she took care of three children after school. She was going to AA meetings and staying sober. She had never said so, but Claire thought she detected little signs of homesickness. Lizzie had been asking a lot of questions about Nina, a safe subject, and Claire had gone on at length about their training sessions and her hatred of the paperboy. Lizzie, who had once said she wanted to become a veterinarian, had lots of suggestions. Had the paperboy ever teased Nina, was it a control issue, had they tried a gentle leader? Claire just thanked her for her good ideas and did not mention that Jess had been through all those possibilities.

Claire was tempted to issue one more small reminder about the impending deadline, but Andy talked her out of it.

"She's eighteen. She knows what she has to do."

"She's a recovering addict."

"In which case, a college campus may not be the best place for her."

"Then where will she go?"

"Odd jobs won't hurt her for a while, Claire. She's smart; she'll figure it out."

"But Princeton, with all that financial aid and a forgivable loan—she'll never get another chance like that. It's got to be the most beautiful campus I've ever seen. I can't imagine going to school in a place like that. She wanted to go. I'm afraid she's lost confidence. I just want to tell her she can do it."

Andy moved from where he was standing and folded his arms around Claire. "You're the one who needs the confidence," he said, looking straight into her unguarded face. "I helped some, but most of all, you raised a smart, resilient young woman who got into a little trouble last year. Lizzie won't let that stop her life. She'll get past it and figure out what she wants to do, but I think it's a good thing to take this time. At Burnside all the kids were going to Princeton or Harvard or Yale. Maybe it's not really her. Maybe she's figuring that out. She loves kids and animals, so she's caring for kids and horses. She's finding her own way to be in the world. Leave her be, Claire. Rest. Princeton would be nice, but cosmetology school would be okay if that's what she really wanted, but I don't think you have that to worry about."

"She doesn't even believe in shaving her legs."

"Or combing her hair most of the time."

"But she is beautiful."

"Yes, but she doesn't come close to you."

"Oh, you're just saying that because you sleep with me."

"Not a bad reason," Andy said, pulling her closer. They swayed together for a while.

"Greylock's really gone," Claire said. "I wonder if Linda and Tom will get another cat."

"Tom says no."

"So does Linda, but I don't believe them. You know that big chair in front of the fireplace? It's always been Linda and Greylock curled up together, there. Just wait."

"Do you ever think about Conway?' Andy asked.

"I was just thinking about her five minutes ago. She's nine now, if she's still alive. The giant breeds don't live that long."

"What a dog."

"We should have taken her. Lizzie wanted to so badly."

"I don't know. Maybe, but none of us were thinking straight."

That morning Claire had opened all the windows and a breeze lifted the curtains, but as the sun fell and the air chilled, the house became cool. Still leaning into Andy's big chest, she said she really should go close the windows.

"And we need to take Nina for a walk."

"And I need to start dinner."

"Unless you'd like to eat out."

"You are so bad. Do you ever think that we're eating our retirement?"

They might have stood there for a few moments longer, contemplating dinner, enjoying the quiet of their small town, and feeling safe because they had just found their way through a conversation that could have been a disaster, but the paperboy went riding past the house, and Nina took off like one of those cartoon dogs that jump straight up and churn their legs in mid-air.

"She's going to tear her ACL again, if she keeps doing that," Andy said.

"There doesn't seem to be any way to stop her." Nina had raced to the living room and she had her front paws on the newly painted windowsills.

"No, Nina! Down!" Claire yelled.

Nina moved to another window and didn't stop barking until the paperboy was out of sight. Andy pulled her down and said, "Sit Nina. Stay."

Claire reminded him that Jess had told them to only use one command at a time. Nina made no effort to sit but made her woo-woo sound and then grumbled and went to find her favorite toy.

Jack did not go straight home. It was too lovely to be indoors. He had passed Claire and Andy's in time to hear Nina going nuts and that made him smile. Then he passed Eric's house, and Eric came running out to say he'd been accepted at Burnside for sixth grade, and he was going in the fall, even though there was a second visit day to help him make up his mind, except his mind was already made up, only if it was very hard, he might still need Mr. Walker to give him some extra help sometimes, if that would be okay.

"You're not going to need any help from me," Jack said. "The teachers at Burnside will give you all the help you need, anytime. They live there. They'll ask you to come over for cookies, and you'll just sit right down and feel like you're at home."

"But I'm not gong to live there. Someone told me it's not the same for day students."

"Sometimes that's true," Jack said. "But there aren't that many boarders in the sixth grade. You'll have to make a good effort, but if you get involved, everything will be fine. Tell your mom and dad not to pick you up until after dinner; then you'll get to do everything."

"That's a good hint." Eric said. "What if I don't like the dinner?"

"You will like it. Burnside is very proud of its food, and they have great desserts."

"What if I don't know who to sit with?"

"No problem; they assign seats and every few weeks everyone switches, so you get to meet kids who aren't in your classes. Are you going to play soccer?'

"If I make the team."

"You may make JV, or you can play on thirds, but in the spring I want you to think about crew."

"Really? I never did that before."

"Nobody has. That's what makes it so great. Everyone is a beginner at the same time."

"Do you have to be strong? I'm not very strong, you know."

"Some of the good rowers are very strong, but those are the seniors. Just give it a try. If you listen and cooperate, you don't need to be strong."

"I'll bet my mother won't let me. She thinks the river is dangerous, because she never learned to swim."

"When the time comes, I'll talk to her if you like."

"In winter I think I'll try out for the play. I've never been in a play. And I want to take Arabic or maybe Chinese, plus astronomy. They have a great telescope there and a planetarium."

It seemed that Eric might have stayed there forever, sounding like the Burnside admissions video, but his mom called him to dinner. She sent a cheerful wave to Jack as she hustled Eric through the doorway.

Night fell and Jack ate a simple meal alone on his porch, even though it was a little chilly. He looked up and down the quiet street, saw Linda and Tom's big TV light up in their family room, saw Eric's bedroom light go on, saw Claire and Andy drive up the street, listened to the peepers, heard an owl and a distant howling that might have been coyotes. And he thought about how everything would change the next day when they all learned what Maud had done.

Stealing mail: what could be worse? People couldn't stop talking about it once the news broke, and Chatty Joan broke it before the guy at the garage heard it on his police scanner and days before the newspapers got hold of it. As Rebecca had feared, it made the national press. No news bureau could resist the story of a small town post mistress tucking mail away for years without apparent motive. Jack thought Maud had been trying to protect him when she took that letter from Cate, apparently one of the first, as all the other mail was postmarked after that. Because he had his own shame to deal with, he felt inclined to forgive her.

But that was until he got the letter that the shelter had sent two years ago, asking him if he would consider taking Conway back as things were not working out with the family who had adopted her. Not working out! What did that mean? He immediately called, but the staff had changed, the records were all a mess from that flooding back in March, and they could tell him nothing. A terse woman advised him to drop it. Surely another home had been found. He should not worry. Not worry! It amazed him that people who worked in shelters could be so insensitive.

He had another letter, this one only five months old, from Trip Skye and a lawyer. Some Burnside parent was suing the school and Trip, claiming he'd touched their boy, and others, in inappropriate ways. Jack remembered Trip's hand on his shoulder to steady him before a meet. He remembered the fond pats after victory, but none of it had ever alarmed him. Dig hard enough, he thought, and you'd find some awful parent who didn't think Trip had coached their boy into early acceptance at Yale. Trip had been asking for a letter on his behalf. Jack's position as a former student and colleague would hold weight; a letter from him could influence things, but it was probably too late now. Jack thought back to the night he drove around Burnside and saw Trip walking along the path, alone. Most of his peers had already retired. But Trip had never married, and he'd made his whole life at the school—a life that had to be lonely at times, especially during the holidays. After leaving Burnside, Jack had meant to keep in touch, but with the twins and the land, it just hadn't happened. What a shitty way to come to the end of your career, Jack thought, and he promised himself he'd call Trip soon.

Because of email and follow-up calls, the card advising Claire that she needed her teeth cleaned mattered little, but the letter from the editor at the online magazine astonished her. They wanted to pull her essays together into a book. She had not even realized that she had a dozen. A published book would mean everything. It could get her a job teaching at the community college. The administration at Burnside would be shocked, and then they'd publish news of it in the newsletter and on the website. She'd enjoy all the attention and then quit. Brad would be jealous. Andy would be so proud, or maybe mortified. She'd written about his hilarious bathroom habits. If they were going on a trip, they had to get up at five in the morning in order to leave the house at eight, because the earth would stop turning if he ever had to use a public bathroom. Not until they were safely ensconced in a five-star hotel could he relax, and then in the morning, before they could go sightseeing or anything, they had to wait again, for total evacuation, which in Andy's case, took time. It was a family trait. All this had been written under her maiden name and she'd never told him.

It was one thing to have these online under another name, and quite another to see them in a book with her name on the cover. She sent an email to the editor explaining that she had just now received the offer. That editor might have moved on by now. Perhaps she was no longer interested. If that was the case, the decision would be made for her and Claire would be relieved, but also disappointed. She folded the letter and put it away in her desk. She opened the drawer, unfolded it and read it again.

She'd put aside the small pile of letters from Lizzie. Each word would bring back the months of anguish. Not yet ready to face them, Claire put them in a small basket for someday.

Jess and Mary found a thick envelope two years old containing plane tickets so they could visit Mary's parents. They also found out that all the pictures they'd so carefully wrapped had never been sent. Once they called and explained everything to Mary's mother, there had been tears all around. True, Mary's mother had said she hated their whole way of life, but not anymore. This was all because her best friend turned out to have a gay daughter, and although these two women had been life-long friends they were also fierce competitors. So, when her friend celebrated her daughter's coming out by giving her a party, and later organized a lovely commitment ceremony, because gay marriage was not yet legal in Michigan, Mary's mother had bragged that her daughter was legally married in Vermont, not understanding the difference between marriage and civil unions, and that had inspired the plane tickets. When she'd heard nothing back, she'd assumed Jess and Mary no longer wanted anything to do with her.

After the whole mess involving lost letters and plane tickets had been sorted out, and she heard that they were thinking about another child, she offered to help them out if they needed a bigger house. For about a day, Jess argued that Mary's mother was on board for all the wrong reasons, but Mary told her she was being ridiculous, and Jess backed down.

Linda learned that her last Pap test had been suspicious, and she needed to come in for another; and Tom found out his cholesterol levels were still high despite the new diet and exercise regime. Tom started taking statins right away, which meant he could eat anything. With a backlog of desire, he gobbled bacon cheeseburgers and thick marbled steaks with glee.

Linda didn't like it. Fat was fat, she said. It was still linked to cancer, and she could not eat this way without gaining a ton of weight. Tom said life was short, and he was fine now. He wished they had bought stock in the drug company that made what he was taking instead of buying the houses over in Woodside.

If a UFO had been spotted over the meadow, it could not have generated more conversation than Maud's crime. Speculation about what had made Maud do it and what else could be going on right under their noses had an irresistible force, along with all the gossip about people whose lives had been changed by the discovery.

Cooper Hill had been on CNN. Linda and Tom's house had been shown in one of the film segments edited to show how small and tranquil the place was. Amanda Sloane had been interviewed, and she'd said nothing like this had ever happened in all her years of living in the city. She had been looking for a safe small town and in just one year her house had been robbed (though she couldn't say of what), she'd broken her shoulder, a rabid skunk had nearly attacked her, and now this. She was going to Boston, where she would feel secure!

Linda thought they all needed a party. She felt like spreading all the people she could around her, like a thick warm blanket, and she invited everyone who lived along the common. They had a perfect day. No clouds and little wind. Only tiny patches of snow remained around the garage. The long stretch of lawn on the south side of the house had been clear for a couple of weeks, though still a little soggy. Mindful of the time of year, Linda chose symbols of rebirth. She dyed eggs in tea and set them out as a centerpiece. She and Tom bought two legs of lamb and pierced them, filling the holes with garlic and rosemary. Then they placed the roasts cut-side down in a marinade for hours. Tom lit the grill so the coals would be perfect before they put the meat on. They would serve it with mounds of asparagus and new potatoes. For the vegetarians, they grilled peppers and eggplants, mushrooms and sweet white onions, and served the mixture over couscous with a yogurt sauce made with dill and lemon juice. While shopping they laughed. You could never go wrong with lamb. All their semi-vegetarian friends loved it and Tom had a tee-shirt made that said Baby Animals Taste Better. Linda said he couldn't wear it with children there.

Tom bought kites for the kids, and the adults watched Eric and April and Hannah run across the grass with the streamers flying in the gentle breeze. In a quiet moment, Linda looked around at the assorted people, and it stunned her that they looked so alike—not in the way siblings would, but as members of the same tribe. Except for Amanda, who had put a maroon stripe in her black hair and wore dark red lipstick, there was not a spot of makeup among the women. Their hair had been cut to chin length or grown long so it could be pulled back. They wore expensive limp clothing that hid the lumps and bumps of middle age. The men had beards and mustaches tinted with grey, and their once long hair was cropped short. No comb-over in this group. They wore jeans or khaki with cotton shirts and sweaters ordered from LL Bean. Men and women alike had good teeth, caps and bridges where necessary. None could be called fat. They were religious about sun screen. Suddenly Linda felt the weight of boredom. She missed the dirty noisy streets of Brooklyn. She missed the slick wax-paper napkins that people got when they ordered pizza, wafting along the sidewalk smeared with tomato sauce. She missed rude young people on roller blades and the sound of rapid-fire Spanish spoken between teenage girls. Did community mean this like-mindedness, look-alikeness, a self-sorting group with more in common than not?

And yet Linda could differentiate her closest friends to a stranger. Claire was the aggressive atheist, well read, witty and scathing when the mood hit her. Patty had been everyone's sweetheart for her whole life. Wasn't it perfect that she made the desserts for the book group, lofty yellow cakes swirling with innocent butter-cream frosting and peach pies to die for. Melanie was their warrior woman. Linda would describe herself as the peacemaker, the one who took the most care to make everyone comfortable, crafting her home into a nest. But Linda had to admit these were pretty subtle differences among all these white women. Had Cate lived, she would have stood out some at this party, mostly because of her amazing face with those sea-green eyes and the natural arch of the eyebrows that framed them. But she'd also be wearing tan linen. Was looking forward to years and years of parties such as this enough?

Eventually this awful war in Iraq would end, Linda thought. Global warming and population growth would continue as issues worth discussing. The *New Yorker* would come each Tuesday. New restaurants would open, and they would all go and offer opinions. Talk would continue as the pastime of choice. Aching backs and cholesterol tests had already entered the conversation. Could assisted living communities be far behind? Just a few days ago at Stop and Shop, Linda had noticed that the paper products were displayed with a certain sequence in mind. Little starter tampons gave way to pads and maxi pads and then to adult diapers, and at the very end of that same aisle someone had made a small display of bran flakes and boxed prunes.

Her father had died young and her mother mercifully in her sleep. Linda had no instructions about growing old, only instincts, and those told her to surround herself with good people. These neighbors and these book club friends were good people, but as she walked from one group to another to fill glasses and take plates, she listened to scraps of conversation and realized she could finish their sentences for them.

Not a good way to start a party. Linda shook herself, bent from the waist and tossed her hair over her head so it would look fuller when she stood up. Amanda was drinking wine straight from the bottle. She had spice. And she was leaving. Just leaving. It seemed like another lifetime when Linda had been able to put most of her stuff into a small trailer and take off. She shook herself. What was this all about? Her favorite season had arrived. The flowers would be gorgeous this year, and she and Tom were planting more of them and fewer vegetables. She would enjoy the deck and the gardens for months. She'd see more of Claire, and Melanie, when she was around. Life was good. Life was fine. If she could get a night's sleep free of night sweats and get through a day without hot flashes, life would be perfect.

Jack was not the first to arrive, but not the last either. Linda gave him a slight hug, but tried not to make a big deal of it and Claire did the same. After all this time, the worst thing would be if everyone said, "Jack, how amazing, how wonderful to see you here." When Hannah's kite got caught in a tree, he went to free it. When Eric fell and got his pants all wet and muddy, and Eric's mother wanted to bring him home right away to change, Jack said let him be, and advised Eric to stay in the sun until he dried off.

Amanda brought him a glass of white wine, but he already had a gin and tonic made by Claire. He gravitated to Andy who was deep into a conversation about the war with Hannah's mom, who was saying she wanted to move to Canada. The three of them agreed with one another about the state of the world until Linda came over and jerked her head in the direction of Patty and said it might be better to stay away from politics for the day. That left the Red Sox, and there was always plenty to say about them. Passionate debate about the Yankees and the Red Sox began. The children joined in, with Eric insisting this would be the year for the Sox, and Hannah surprising Jack and her mom by quoting all kinds of statistics that proved the Yankees had the edge. The child who could barely read loved numbers, Jack noted, and in his mind he began to revise his poem about Nina and Conway. Perhaps it should have less to do with language and more to do with math, but how could he do that in a poem? It would be fun to try.

Tom kept returning to the grill to be sure the lamb didn't overcook. Nina made five turns before settling herself in a shady spot where she could see everything. Eric gave her a piece of cheese and was running back to get more when Jess stopped him.

"Make her work for it," she said, and she showed Eric how to make the sit command. He did it perfectly, so April had to try and then Hannah, and for each of the children, Nina obeyed as if she'd been trained for Westminster.

The young couples who had never been to Linda and Tom's asked for a house tour and Linda was happy to oblige. Trailing behind her, Eric's mom and Sarah and the others learned what could happen with patience, money, and hard work when the bones of these old houses were revealed. The gorgeous wood floor in the kitchen was the result of weeks of work. Vinyl flooring had covered two layers of old linoleum, which Tom and Linda had stripped away without realizing they were filled with asbestos. "If I get lung disease someday, this will be the reason," Linda told them, but anyone could tell she didn't believe this would happen. The tin ceiling had also been covered with an ugly dropped ceiling. All that remained from the original kitchen was a huge enamel two-sided sink—the kind that would now cost a small fortune at a specialty plumbing supply. The two old bathrooms had been redone with tile and marble, and a new one added. In the dining room and living room, rotting plaster had come down and the chestnut beams exposed.

It was a marvel. Linda watched Jess turn to Mary with a look that said *See what we can do if we stay*, and Mary answered with an exquisite raised eyebrow that said *If we had a lot of money and no child to put through school and the skill AND all the time in the world.*

When Linda had gone into the house, all her guests had been talking in small groups. When she finished the tour and went out onto the deck, the silence hit her. People were standing in a circle around Jack and Patty. In the short time that she'd been gone the conversation had turned back to the war. The news had been awful for months. Every morning's report began with casualties caused by suicide bombers. It appeared that the evidence for attacking Iraq had been faulty at best and a pack of lies at worst. It was inevitable that this group would want to talk about it, but Linda wished they wouldn't. The food smelled wonderful, the sky still shone a perfect blue, and it could all be ruined by bad feeling if this went on. But it had been years since Linda had witnessed Jack in what he called "a teachable moment."

Patty's face wasn't puckered in anger as it had been that night at book group. Jack was saying, "This isn't about being a Democratic or a Republican. It might have been during the election, but not now. This is about an inept president who has surrounded himself by a bunch of criminals, and Patty, you love this country; I know you do, so you have to let yourself see that, because these guys are stealing the country you and I both love."

Patty didn't answer, so he went on, "I know there are people who think that only bad news gets broadcasts and there are good things happening in Iraq, but pictures don't lie. The country is starting to look like Dresden, and to tell you the truth, I don't know what ought to happen next. Can we pull out and leave all that rubble behind and live with the genocide that will follow? Probably not."

Patty said, "We need to win before we can pull out, Jack. America can't afford this defeat."

Where Linda might have scoffed and Claire might have said something sarcastic, Jack just asked a question, "What would wining look like? How would we know we'd won?"

"Well, all these insurgency attacks would stop."

"Because?"

"Because they will eventually understand that we mean business, and we won't let it continue."

"Should we use nuclear weapons then, to stop it once and for all?"

"Well, no. I would never suggest that. I don't even think we should have bombed Japan, even though people say it ended the war."

"So, how does this one end?"

"The Iraqis take over."

"Which ones, the Shiites or the Sunnis?"

"That's for them to decide."

"Are we helping them decide?"

Patty didn't cower, and she didn't say "Oh, Jack Walker you are so smart," like someone who had just been saved by the love of Jesus, but anyone could see that Jack had made her think.

Linda let her breath go back to normal. This wasn't going to become a big fight. Patty wanted to end it, and Jack wasn't the kind of person who needed to be right all the time. So when Patty said, "I think it's time for me to go ask Linda if she needs some help," he said, "Good idea."

Patty followed Linda into the kitchen, and Linda handed her a basket of cutlery to put out on the table. Before heading out, Patty turned to Linda and said, "I think it's my turn to host the next book group. I'll call everyone next week to find a time."

"We never chose a book last time," Linda said.

"So, let's use one meeting to choose the next twelve books. Then we won't use up so much time deciding." Linda was happy. Book club had been going on for eight years, but after the March meeting she was afraid it might be over.

*

*Nobody wants to leave. The air is so soft and scented. They eat everything and find the stash of Scotch and brandy in the pantry and pour that to drink with dessert, which has of course been supplied by Patty. Strawberry shortcake with homemade biscuits and real whipped cream. Sinful and totally satisfying. At a certain point when darkness falls and everyone still lingers, getting drunker all the time, Linda and Tom make eye contact, and it is like the holidays when the house is filled with friends and family. Tom makes the slightest motion of his head, and Linda understands perfectly.*

*Upstairs, with the help of a little personal lubricant, Tom and Linda come together like teenagers. For less than a second, as she reaches for the tube of KY, Linda gets sad that her body has betrayed her so. The juices have dried up. Tom makes it all better. He takes the tube from her hand and squeezes a big hunk of the stuff onto his fingertips. Then he pushes them gently into Linda and moves them around and she almost comes right then. But she waits and he slides inside her. From their open window they can hear the conversations below. From the edge of the yard, they can smell a cigarette burning. Claire most likely. Linda shudders. Tom places his hand gently over her mouth, and his whole body goes into spasm. Enough, thinks Linda, letting out a long deep sigh. This life of ours is more than enough. Laughing they pull their clothes back on and walk downstairs holding hands.*

*

Jess used the same donor Mary had used so the children would be truly related, and they all went to get the canister of sperm at the airport. It looked like a small fire hydrant. Mary strapped it in the back seat next to April's car seat and made the mistake of telling her that her little brother or sister was in there.

April said, "That's ridiculous."

Mary started an explanation about sperm and eggs meeting and growing and April glanced over at the canister and said, "If you can believe that, why don't you believe in Santa Claus?"

"You'll see," said Mary.

"I don't want a brother who comes from a big thermos," said April.

"What if you get a sister?" asked Jess. April ignored the question. She had already decided on a brother.

"Did you find me this way?" she asked.

Mary and Jess both nodded. "We looked in books and read all about donors and picked the very best one."

"Hannah says the daddy has to put his thing inside the mommy."

"That's when a man and a woman make a baby," said Mary.

"But the donor is a man, right? Why doesn't he just visit and do it the way Hannah says?"

"Because men and women only do that when they love each other, but Mary and I love each other instead," Jess said.

"So how does the sperm get in?" April asked.

Mary began to carefully explain the procedure, but April interrupted, saying "I don't want to hear about this before we eat lunch." After that she fell asleep in the back seat.

As the days warmed and grew longer, Linda found herself often at the base of the weeping cherry, talking to Greylock and remembering him as a kitten. She liked telling the story of how he'd been found. She began thinking of kittens. Soon the farmers market would open, and there were always boxes of kitten there. She'd mentioned this to

Tom. A kitten in their huge house would hardly make an impact, and they had such a great yard and the neighbors had a barn filled with mice. What worried them both was the fisher cats, lumbering, snarly creatures with jagged pointy teeth; they were known for preying on small animals.

Tom said, "I don't want a cat if it can't go out."

Linda reminded him that Greylock had lived many years without encountering a fisher cat, but Tom reminded her that there were more of them around now, and Greylock had been an imposing and amazingly intelligent cat. These words meant he wasn't ready. Greylock still owned the place in his heart reserved for cats. That was okay. Linda decided to wait a while and try again.

## *May*

The Morris Dancers came down from the hills to lead the May Day celebration in Cooper Hill. Their bells jingled as they leapt into the air. Dressed in white with bright blue vests, some dancers also wore stags heads. They feigned battle and clicked sticks upon sticks in an ancient ritual of rebirth. All along the common, old Saabs and Volvos sported every kind of political sticker. Like Halloween, Cooper Hill was also a destination point for May Day. Men with beards and women in soft long skirts all wore sandals or flat cotton shoes made in China, except for the dancers who wore boots. Fat pink breast-fed babies rode in slings. Dogs with flower garlands sniffed each other. The fiddlers played while children danced around the maypole, and it all looked festive and sweet, but Claire knew it for what it was and understood its power.

Many years ago she'd attended her first May Day celebration; she'd been dating one of the dancers, and they had decided to break up but not until after May Day. He had been one of those sweet valley men incapable of making any kind of commitment, and Claire could not see herself growing old at the end of a long line of contra dancers, all comparing notes about the musicians they'd been with. So she'd told her dancer that this was the end.

At that fateful May Day, she had tasted the fertility cake, laughing as the crumbs dropped down the front of her soft peasant shirt. The dancer had hoisted Lizzie to his shoulders. She was laughing. Claire had braided flowers into Lizzie's hair and her own. That night she had enjoyed one last night with this man, and she'd taken all the usual precautions, but the cake's power had been stronger than her diaphragm and three weeks later she missed her period. Two weeks after that, her fears were confirmed at the clinic; and it had been Cate Walker who pulled her through the awful decision and the procedure that followed.

It had only been a few months later when Cate introduced Claire to Andy and after they became serious, she told him. "I guess it was the right thing. Otherwise I'd be pregnant now." She'd expected him to agree, but Andy had said it wouldn't have mattered to him, and that was the moment she fell in love.

May Day. Lizzie had been around for the last one, helping April and other young children with their ribbons. She'd been less than a month away from graduation and just a week away from getting caught drinking at school. She'd worn a blue linen dress and little flat cotton shoes for the dancing. Amanda came, too, and made everyone stare because nobody went to May Day in black stretch pants and a tank top. Jack had been up on his porch, watching quietly, but he had not come down to talk to anyone. He was different this year. He'd picked up a penny whistle and joined in with the music makers.

Claire watched April dance her way around the pole, ducking under the person in front so that the ribbons twisted and wove a rainbow. This year, April didn't need any help with her ribbons, and she didn't need her mommies either. She danced with the other children while Jess and Mary watched. In front of all the houses that lined the common, people had put out tables filled with tag sale stuff. Five years ago Lizzie had come home with six ceramic ducks and a set of cookie cutters shaped like dog bones and mailmen. She had wanted to make treats for Nina. Claire still had the ducks, but couldn't have located the cookies cutters for anything. The church was selling baked goods, and Patty was there with a tray of lovely little fruit tarts.

Claire breathed deeply and raised her face to the sun, trying to get control of herself, but she missed Lizzie in a gut-wrenching way. She missed Lizzie as a five-year-old who had not had the chance to dance around a maypole, because those had been the bad times before she met Andy and they moved to Cooper Hill. She missed Lizzie rowing. At this time of year on a Saturday she would have had a race. She missed Lizzie slamming the door to her room and playing loud music. She tried to tell herself to stop. If Lizzie was away at college, she'd be missing all these same things. Time passed. Parents had to learn to let go. Yes, they did. No matter what. Even if both mother and daughter had been robbed of some of the best years. You couldn't get them back. Her job now was to set Lizzie in the right direction and push her off. That she could do. That she could manage, but this drifting and not knowing hurt; and also, she felt ashamed, even though Andy and Amanda said she shouldn't. Having a daughter who hates you enough to run away shamed her. The day that had started off nicely, with Claire dressing in a new cotton skirt and tying ribbons around the brim of her old straw gardening hat, started to sour.

She'd lost Andy in the crowd and she was feeling too warm, so Claire decided to head home and rest for awhile. Halfway down the street she saw Andy who had stopped to talk to Jess. She walked more quickly and caught up with them. "Didn't I just see you up on the common?" she asked.

Jess said yes, but she had to eat something right away or she'd throw up again. Jess had conceived on the first try, and according to the doctor, things could not be progressing better. Her constant nausea was normal, but she told Claire she didn't understand how the baby could grow healthy when she couldn't keep anything down.

"It's like that for some women," Claire said. "I was like that with Lizzie, and then she weighed more than eight pounds at birth. The baby takes what it needs."

With Claire and Andy still standing there, Jess turned and ran into the house with her hand over her mouth.

The last time Jess had a session with Nina, she'd thrown up, right on the sidewalk, and Nina had lapped up the mess. It was more than Jess could take while pregnant and she'd decided to take a break from working with Nina, who could now walk nicely and perform a reasonable sit-stay just as long as the paperboy was nowhere in sight. She was almost eight years old and neurotic, but the chances of breaking old habits seemed slim. Claire and Andy were actually relieved since they no longer thought Jess was helping, but they hadn't wanted to end the training sessions and deprive her of income. Mary didn't earn much, and now they had another child on the way.

Jess came back out looking better. She had a handful of saltines that she nibbled around the edges. "Where's Nina?" she asked.

"We couldn't chance bringing her to May Day. The paperboy might show up," Andy answered.

"Would she freak out even if he wasn't delivering papers?'

"I'm sure she would," Claire said. "She goes nuts when she sees his mother's car."

"How does she know?"

"His mother drives him around the route on rainy days."

"Someday this will make sense."

"Or it won't," said Andy. "It's okay. Even if she didn't bark and pull, she'd still eat all the little bits of food on the ground and get sick. She gets this awful diarrhea; it's just fluid but the smell."

Jess's face changed color. "Please, I don't need to know." Claire could not believe Andy had said that.

They made their way back to the house, noting how much Jess had changed. Andy asked Claire if she would mind if he played tennis later.

"It's really hot out," she said.

"The heat never bothers me."

"Don't forget to bring water. You always forget to drink."

"I will. What will you do?"

"I'll read or maybe work in the garden. I'll be fine."

"What does Mary do for a living?" Andy asked.

Claire wasn't sure. "She worked for a dentist for awhile,

answering phones and making appointments, then she took a job over in Woodside at the yarn shop. I think she's still there." Her voice dwindled, "Actually, I hardly know anything about her, and now they're leaving.

"Really?" Andy said, "Why?"

"The schools clinched it. They can't afford private school for two," Claire said, and that made her think about how Jack had helped Lizzie get into Burnside and it had made all the difference. She'd been miserable at the regional school over in Woodside, where one of her teachers calmly told them not to worry about her math grades, because girls didn't do well in math after grammar school. Jack had written a recommendation, Claire's position at the school took care of tuition, and Andy took care of everything else. Lizzie had thrived there, until everything fell apart.

Now that they were on the subject of schools, Claire said, "I wrote to Lizzie about Princeton again. I know you said not to, but I couldn't help it. She hasn't written back. I think I've had it. I cried for months but now I'm mad. Those letters of her's hardly said a thing, just don't worry. I'm safe. No explanation. Sometimes I feel like I raised an ungrateful little bitch."

"You don't mean that," he said, as they passed Linda and Tom's place.

"Maybe I do. Unconditional love can only go so far. All she's done is try to hurt me. She knew going to Brad's would cut."

"Come on, Claire. Was going to her father really such a bad idea? Do you want her to go through her whole life feeling abandoned by him, having no relationship with him at all?"

"He has no right to swoop in and make everything better after all this time."

"But she went to him. She found him on her own. And he did not turn her away. People change. Maybe he's become a better person."

"Now that it's easy." Claire stopped walking and wrapped her arms across her chest.

"Easy? An alcoholic eighteen-year-old isn't easy. Whatever he's done or not done, Lizzie is safe and sober." Andy was using his calm doctor's voice. Claire hated when he did that.

"And wasting her life."

"How?" he asked, even more softly.

"You know how."

"By not going to Princeton? Claire don't you think that's your dream more than hers? Leave it alone."

"That's easy for you to say with your degrees from Michigan and Columbia." Claire knew she was building this fight, stoking it as carefully as a low-burning fire and threatening to ruin the day, but she couldn't help it. It was as though once she'd allowed herself to get angry at Lizzie, she couldn't stop; and her anger extended to Andy, and Lizzie's advisor at Burnside, who never saw any signs of trouble, and everyone on the common pretending they lived in England five hundred years ago, and even to Tom and Linda who had more money than they knew what to do with. She felt fury swelling inside in waves, like labor, and she only wanted to push.

Andy, who still thought there was some reasonable, conversational way out of this said, "I knew what I wanted. Lizzie doesn't."

"Places like Princeton help you figure out what you want to do."

"But people can also do that on their own. Just let her be. She has all the time in the world."

He shouldn't have used the word time. To Claire, time was an enemy. "But she doesn't. That's just it; we all think we have endless time and then you find yourself in some stupid job you just fell into, like mine, and there's nothing satisfying about it, but there's nothing else you know how to do and it's too late. Too late to go back to school, too late to change because no one reading resumes can make the leap and see that one set of skills would work in a completely different area. And then you are trapped."

"You could go back to school if you want. We can afford it."

"Sure, and I could study anthropology, like I wanted to when I was younger and the departments discouraged women, and then I can go and study cultures around the world and leave you alone and stop worrying about whether Lizzie ever comes home or not. Doesn't that sound like a wonderful plan?"

"Well, it wouldn't have to be that extreme," said Andy

"Really?" Claire raised one eyebrow. "You mean I could get a nice degree in English and go teach somewhere and get a job with mother's hours. Give me a break, Andy. It's kind of you to suggest; and yes, I know we can afford it because you make plenty for both of us, which means I don't really have to do anything at all, but don't you see what I mean? We all get tracked and trapped. Even you. All that school and training, and you just do the same things over and over again every day, and if it wasn't for tennis you'd go out of your mind."

"But that's how it is, Claire. What are you thinking? That Linda and Tom wake up each morning excited about their work? That these anthropologists you envy make discoveries every day? Mostly they watch minute details and graph them statistically and prove what has been intuitively known all along."

Andy thought he was making good arguments. She could tell by that satisfied look on his face. He wanted her to think that she lived on a fantasy of fulfillment that simply didn't exist. He wanted her to see that insisting on this could push people away, but she would not yield. They had arrived at their house and he looked relieved. Claire had been talking louder and louder as they made their way down the street, and if there was anything Andy hated, it was a scene.

Finally Claire hurled Cate into the argument. "Cate felt like she was doing important work, but she had a great education and the skills she needed, and somewhere along the line her parents or a teacher told her she could do something that mattered. Nobody ever made me feel like that, and now it's too late, and I don't want the same thing to happen to Lizzie. "

"So that's it," said Andy. "We're back to Cate Walker again. But you've got it wrong. Most of the time Cate felt her work was futile, a Band-Aid on a larger problem. When a woman comes in for her third abortion, because she's on welfare and can't afford birth control pills, it gets a little discouraging."

"And you would know best how Cate felt," Claire said, her eyes shining.

Nina howled when she saw them turn into the driveway and ran to get her toy, then appeared at the window. Claire had to laugh at the sight of her big brown eyes appearing above the body of the stuffed toy. She'd had about six of these "babies" since they got her, all the same; no other dog toy would do.

After the big greeting, Nina went back to being her languid hound-self and sprawled on the sofa. Claire asked Andy if he wanted some lunch. They moved around each other awkwardly, getting out bread and a can of tuna, a knife, the Hellmann's, a tomato. Andy picked up the phone to see if they had any messages and they had four. Two were from Claire's mother, and two were from her nurse who had just been fired.

"Is this the fourth or fifth?" Andy asked.

"I've lost count," Claire said, "But we need to see what's going on. I can go myself this time."

"No, I'll call David and ask if he if he can switch our on-call days. I don't want you to go alone."

"I'll call Jack and see if he can take care of Nina."

A stranger walking into the kitchen at that moment would have felt the love and purpose. Claire would have hated making the trip alone. Andy always needed a job. His job was to care for Claire, to hold her when she cried, drive her to her mother's, do the grocery shopping when the roads were slippery, walk Nina, choose the wine, talk her into buying expensive clothes, figure out when they could buy a new car, listen, and understand or pretend to.

Claire's job was much more simple. She only had to appreciate the good man who stood before her.

Jack and Nina were walking nicely. At midday on a Monday, no paperboy could be near. Nina stopped and sniffed the ground every few feet, but Jack didn't mind. Walking Nina was not exercise, just a way to enjoy the May sun, a clear blue rain-washed sky, and the lacy pale green trees. Nina took him off guard when she began to strain and lurch and howl at an unmistakable figure standing at the end of Claire and

Andy's driveway. Tall broad-shouldered Lizzie crouched down and called Nina by name and Jack knew. He let go of the leash, and Nina bounded to her

She looked a little tired and her clear eyes owned a new, wise sorrow. Always polite, Lizzie said, "Hello, Mr. Walker, how are you?" Then, before he could answer she barraged him with questions. "Where's my mom and Andy? How come the door's locked? I didn't know we even had a lock. Why are you walking Nina? What's with all the For Sale signs around town? I thought nobody ever moved from Cooper Hill."

"Feel like going for a walk?" he said.

"Not really. I got here about an hour ago and I've been walking around. Can you let me into my house?"

"Sure can," Jack said. "Your folks are away at your grandmother's and I'm taking care of Nina."

Lizzie's face clouded. "Did she die?"

"No. Not yet. She's had a few bad spells this year, and your mom and Andy keep going off to say goodbye or make sure she's getting the care she needs. She's weak and taking a lot of morphine, but she's holding on."

Lizzie took that in. "My mom didn't tell me."

Now Jack could have said, "What good would that have done? You would have raced home and then felt like you'd been tricked," but he didn't say that. "It's been up and down like this so many times. I don't think your mom wanted to worry you," he said. "If your grandma was dying, she'd call and send a plane ticket." Then he wondered how Lizzie had gotten here.

"I flew into Burlington and hitched a ride from there."

Jesus, thought Jack, for all her good grades and fine writing, Lizzie was still capable of stupid mistakes. He didn't even want to think about her journey to Pennsylvania.

"Where's your stuff?" Jack asked as he opened the door. Nina was still staring at Lizzie with her tongue hanging out.

"I just traveled with this backpack. My dad's sending the rest of my things. There isn't that much, really. Mostly when I was there I wore his girlfriend's clothes."

"That was nice of her."

"It was, but she still didn't last."

"No?" Jack took care not to sound too interested.

"Oh, she would have stayed. She would have married my dad if he asked her, but he met someone else."

"Did she share her clothes?"

"No way. She didn't even want to share my dad. If we went out together, even for a little while, she pouted and whined. He's stupid to be with her."

So now Jack knew why she'd come back. There would be plenty of time to learn what she'd been up to and what she planned to do next. He wouldn't prod. But Lizzie had something she needed to say. After standing in the kitchen for a few minutes, just looking around, she asked if he wanted anything, some coffee maybe. She had learned to make coffee this year. Everyone drank it all the time at AA meetings. They drank coffee and smoked up a storm, but she had definitely not started smoking. Jack said some coffee sounded fine. He fed Nina and filled her water bowl and found her brush.

After Lizzie placed the cup in front of him and set out milk and sugar, she started, while he brushed Nina. In his years working with teens, he'd learned that they liked to know you were listening but got startled, like some dogs, if you looked them in the eye.

"First of all, Mr. Walker, I want to thank you for helping me get into Princeton. It's an incredible honor and I know people like you get asked to write recommendations all the time, and you can't do it for everyone, and you decided to do it for me because you thought I had a good shot. It's like, you know, I really am grateful, but I'm not going. I wrote to them a few weeks ago, and I wanted to tell you first. My mom will be so upset. She thinks it's the best thing for me, and I know it's an incredible school, but with what I've been through this year, I just can't picture myself there. I don't even know if I can still row. I'm so out of shape, so maybe they wouldn't want me anyway."

Jack continued to brush Nina's shiny coat and waited. Lizzie took a breath and barreled on. "For one thing, the whole idea of going off to college to row seems really stupid now. It's not like I could make it into a career, and you have to get up at dawn and work out on the ergs, and it seems pointless when I don't even know what else I'd want to be doing there. Some of my friends say it doesn't matter what you study, because after a place like Princeton, especially for athletes, the Wall Street firms come running. They figure you're competitive and a team player and you have the pedigree. But I never ever want to work on Wall Street."

Jack thought she'd had this conversation before, maybe with her dad or in front of the mirror. She topped off his coffee cup and her own, and gazed across the table at the wall of pictures. "We were all so happy," she said. "How can you stand it?"

Jack said, "I have no choice."

"Me neither," Lizzie said. "I'll never ever be able to go to a party and have a drink or two or even enjoy a glass of wine with dinner in a nice restaurant. I'm like someone with a life-threatening food allergy, and it will always make me different. That's the other thing about going to college right now. I feel a lot older than the other kids my age. AA meetings are interesting, you know. I thought there would be a lot of down-and-out people, but that's not so. There are all kinds of people, but the ones I liked best had lived hard lives. I met a woman whose kids had been taken away from her. There was a guy who'd been sober three times and then went back to drinking, and I thought he was so brave to keep trying. He was the one who finally made me want to stop for good. I don't know why you didn't start drinking after the accident," she said, bringing the conversation back to Jack as if she suddenly realized that losing your whole family was not the same as losing your ability to drink socially.

"I just never much liked it," Jack said. "If I'd had a habit in place, it would have been a problem."

"You didn't used to talk to anyone in town. Everybody worried about you. I really missed talking to you, but we all knew you didn't want to see anybody, so we left you alone. How come you are taking care of Nina?"

Jack told her about the old lost letter from Cate and the rest of the mail Maud had stolen. "It meant so much to have that letter with all her life in it, to remember all the good things. I can't quite explain it except to say that it woke me up and made me lonely."

"So what else are you doing?"

Of course, for Jack, this was always the most difficult question. "This and that," he said. I've been having a good time tutoring some of the children in town. Given the state of the public schools around here, it's the least I can do. I take care of dogs and houses when people go away, and of course there's the foundation Cate's parents started. I have to read all the applications every year."

Lizzie's brow wrinkled, "And that's all?"

Jack laughed. Here was a teenage runaway who had put her family through hell and just turned down four years at Princeton, who didn't seem to have a plan, who had met full-grown men and women struggling with addiction, and still she had that innocent faith that adult lives were well-organized and purposeful.

"That's all for now," he said, "What about you?"

Lizzie stretched her arms behind her head and knotted her long hair into a twist. "I'm going to need some kind of job. I think I want to take some classes at UVM. I'll need more science if I want to get into Tufts vet school, which is what I think I want. I really do."

"Large animals?"

"I'm not sure about that; maybe just dogs and cats, except I love horses, so maybe."

"How would you like to go see your grandmother?" Jack asked. "I could drive you down today."

"What about Nina?"

"We'll take her. I'll leave you there and drive back in the same day; what about it Lizzie, want to surprise everybody?"

"Oh, Mr. Walker, that's a lot of driving, and I'm a little scared. My mom must be so angry."

"Well, she's had a hard year. I'm not going to lie about that. You know she never got any of your letters. Maud took them, so it was awful for her, especially when they found those bodies out in Iowa. You know, it might be easier to just surprise her at your grandmother's and let her be thrilled. The two of you will need to sit down for a long talk at some point."

"In the letters I gave her my cell phone number. I was waiting for her to call. When she didn't or Andy either, I figured they were too mad to talk to me."

"And you never thought maybe she didn't get the letters?"

"I thought that about the first and even the second, but I wrote eight times. Then I just gave up. Things got pretty bad. I lost the phone after a while." Lizzie sighed.

Jack knew she'd tell the whole story someday. "Look, this may be your last chance to see your grandmother alive."

"Can I take a shower first? I've been traveling for the whole day."

"Sure, but hurry up." Claire and Andy called every afternoon to check in, and Jack did not want to speak to them. He hated lying, but this was not the kind of news to deliver over the phone. He turned off his cell phone, and while Lizzie showered he packed some food for the trip.

Linda could not stand her catless house any longer. She had vacuumed everywhere, and still tufts of Greylock's fur appeared and made her sad. They wafted up from the heating vents or appeared in an old shoe. When she pulled a sweatshirt she hadn't worn in months from the back of her closet, it was covered in cat hair. In the very back of the pantry she found an old catnip mouse, and then she found a real mouse in the cellar and told Tom, and they both remembered all the rodents Greylock had killed in his time. On Monday, after making one of her periodic inspections of the houses over in Woodside and visiting a family who wanted their living room redone in earth tones, she found herself heading for the shelter. Just to look, she told herself. There were always kittens in the spring. Tom would object to a kitten, she knew. Kittens shredded the furniture and climbed the curtains, but they also hopped sideways at imaginary prey and their lives, so filled with empty melodrama, made them irresistible.

The day could not have been more beautiful. She drove through the family neighborhoods in Woodside and saw lilacs and tulips everywhere. It really was a pretty town with good old housing stock, and even the homes that begged for some fresh paint looked nice at this time of year. Thinking about her unsold houses, she wondered what was going to happen to the land where the old factory had stood. When she and Tom bought the houses, she thought they had value because the plant had been torn down, allowing all that sunlight in for the first time in a century, but now she wondered if their failure to sell was due to the barren landscape they faced. There had been talk of a park or a movie complex, but all progress in Woodside got mired in politics. Everybody wanted better schools, sidewalks, and services. Nobody wanted higher taxes, and all efforts to zone certain areas for light industrial use that would have brought both jobs and tax revenues, had failed. She had to drive through some of the poor neighborhoods to get to the shelter. She passed blocks and blocks of three-decker houses with sagging porches and dirt-packed yards. She passed a trailer park, an abandoned Honda dealership with weeds growing up in the parking lot, a place that rented RVs, and finally turned down a narrow side-road to find a sorry-looking cinderblock building with long chain-link kennels out back. The sound of dogs' plaintive barking surrounded her as soon as she got out of her car.

Inside, two women behind a long desk were talking about all that had to be done that day. Two workers had called in sick, leaving these two to cover the desk, feed the animals, and clean the kennels. The place smelled ripe and fetid, and Linda almost left, but then she thought about the animals needing homes. They would not let her look before she filled out a number of forms, but finally one of the woman led her to the cat section and it nearly broke her heart. She saw kittens and old cats, and some that needed medical care. One cat had been burned, and though the skin had healed, she had no fur on her left side. One had a battered ear. A fighter, the woman said.

"Where do they all come from?" Linda asked.

"From all over. These are the lucky ones. All over the country cats are roaming around, or whole litters get drowned. People have gotten a lot better about spaying dogs, but they don't bother with cats. They just let them breed." The woman looked exhausted.

"How long have you been working here?' Linda asked.

"Nine years and you don't want to know the awful things I've learned about people."

Linda knew that with just a little coaxing this woman would tell all, and she couldn't bear to hear, so she looked at her watch and the woman understood and she let her scan the cages alone. Linda asked to hold a tiger-striped ball of fur, probably about eight weeks old, and as she nuzzled it, the other woman who worked there came from the dog section followed by an old Newfie. Her eyes were clouded over; she walked slowly with an unsteady gate, and her once lovely coat was matted and dry. Linda held the kitten closer.

"Oh, you don't need to worry," the woman said. "We keep most of the dogs in cages, but this one likes to follow us around and she's so gentle; she's no problem at all. Sweet old girl." Linda stared at the dog for a long time. Of course all purebred Newfie's look the same she told herself. She was being ridiculous. But Conway had followed Jack and Cate around in just this slow and steady way, never taking her eyes off them.

"How long has she been here?' Linda asked.

"Oh, close to a year I'd say."

"And nobody's wanted her? A beautiful dog like this."

"We're a no-kill shelter, so we'll hold onto her, but nobody's going to take this old dog. She's nearly blind, she can't hear, and she has a terrible case of heartworm. We can't even treat her for it; she wouldn't survive it."

Linda put the kitten back into the cage and knelt beside the dog. "What's her name?"

The people who brought her in called her Nellie, but I think she's had about three names."

"Why did they bring her in?"

"She has accidents. She's old. There's lots of people who use up animals and then toss them away. They got her from some people with kids who thought a dog would be so great and realized pretty soon how much work went into them."

"I think I know this dog," Linda said. "It sounds crazy, but I think I do. I mean, how many people even have Newfies; they're big and expensive. I can't imagine they're very popular."

"No they're not. It's Goldens and Labs that most people want." Linda had learned that the woman's name was Sheila.

"Sheila, do you mind if I make a phone call? It's local."

Sheila said, "Not at all," but Jack's phone rang six times and then the machine came on. Linda decided not to leave a message. She'd go see him instead. Linda left the shelter with the kitten and confused feelings. If it was Conway, how would Jack feel? He'd been doing so much better; would the dog bring everything back and force him into retreat again?

While Jack's home phone rang, he and Lizzie were making good time. He figured they'd do better by taking the ferry to Long Island from New Haven to avoid New York traffic, and he'd been right. But later, on the trip home, he found out the ferry schedule would not work. Nina, who sometimes got sick in the car, whined as they crept through traffic the whole length of Connecticut. When he could, Jack pulled over to give her a chance to walk and get some air, but that bad leg made getting in and out of the car into a chore. After the third stop he said, "That's it girl. We're not stopping again until we get home."

It got dark and Nina fell asleep. The roads cleared up after Hartford and he opened the car windows. They breezed through Springfield and through Easthampton, where you could finally see the mountains. Jack drove through the scented spring night smiling to himself at the look on Claire's face when Lizzie stepped from the car. First she'd seen the car and looked terrified, anticipating news so bad that he'd made the drive to tell her in person.

Then she saw Lizzie. No questions. No reprimands, just joy. It was rare to bring that kind of joy to another person, a rare and beautiful gift.

When Jack got home the light on his answering machine was blinking, but there was no message. In the morning, Linda called and asked if she could come over. She took such a long time describing her trip to the shelter and the kitten she'd found that he began to lose interest, and then she finally came to the part about Conway. "It probably isn't her. I know you took her to the shelter in Russell and that's thirty miles away, but still, there's something familiar about her. I could go with you if you want, Jack, in case I've set you up for a terrible disappointment."

It was a kind offer, but this was a trip Jack needed to make by himself. Linda gave him directions and said she'd go over and feed Nina and let her out into her yard.

Jack knew the instant he saw her, sweet wonderful dog, and Conway knew too. She was sleeping in one of the kennels when he got there, but by the time he made his way past the other cages, she'd pulled her aching body to the gate and pushed her nose up against the chain link so that her black nose poked through the opening. From deep inside her chest came a low moan and then squeals. Sheila unlocked the gate, and Conway stood on her hind legs with her paws on Jack's shoulders and licked his face over and over again.

Sheila said, "My, we didn't even think she could stand up like that; she's so sick." Jack tenderly pushed her off and lowered himself to the cold cement floor. Conway stood over him, her big head nuzzled into his neck and then. Jack pressed his face into her chest and cried like a baby. Sheila gracefully retreated to the front desk area.

He wanted to know everything, but they couldn't tell him much. It was against the shelter's policy to give out the names of the people who left the dogs there or those who adopted. They told him what they knew. She'd been passed around to at least two families. Along the line someone had neglected to give her heartworm pills, and she had a very bad case. They'd been afraid to treat her. She was weak and her lungs had already been compromised. He had to fill out forms before taking her, and when Sheila logged on to the computer she found Jack's name.

"We wrote to you when her first family brought her in," she said. Jack told them that he'd only recently received the letter and when Sheila checked his address and saw that he lived in Cooper Hill, she said "That awful woman who stole people's mail?"

Jack nodded. Because of Maud Crowe he'd lost two years with Conway.

"Did you have her as a puppy?" Sheila asked. Jack still found it hard to talk but he nodded. "So how old is she now?" Shelia asked.

"Almost nine."

"Well, that's old for this breed. She's had a hard time of it, but she's held on."

During this conversation Jack never lost physical contact with Conway. He had his hand on her head, her back, her haunches. He scratched the base of her tail. He could feel her spine. She was too skinny. He asked her to sit, but she didn't. "She's deaf," said Sheila. He tried hand commands, but she didn't respond to those, either.

"We think she's nearly blind," said Sheila. None of this mattered to Jack one bit. Conway had held on. She had cared for his babies when they were small, watching them every minute, pulling them away when they tried to crawl too near the wood stove, making a cage of her body if they got too close to the pond, and he would care for her now.

She could not get into the car and he had to lift her onto the back seat. Pulling away from the shelter, his heart ached to think of the months Conway had spent there. The people had been good to her, but it was such a dank, forlorn place. He couldn't imagine going to work there every day, surrounded by the cries of homeless animals and trying to keep those cement floors clean while ignoring the mold that grew on the cinder block walls. The place had been cold, even on this lovely May afternoon. There weren't enough windows, and the ones they had leaked. The computer had been old and slow, and the boxes of files had been stuffed. He was surprised that they had records of dogs adopted over in Russell. It was amazing that they'd even managed to try to contact him. That Sheila was a good person, overworked and underpaid. She had a mouth filled with teeth that needed attention, and she had clearly loved Conway. A small comfort, but it helped a little.

On the way home he stopped to buy food, bowls for water and food, a thick dog bed covered in sheepskin, and a ramp. When it was time to get out of the car, Conway let herself be led down the ramp. Jack placed her feet and she let him lead her, but getting into his second-floor apartment was another story. He thought he'd just carry her up the stairs, but she still weighed close to a hundred pounds, and he could not really get a firm grip on her and also navigate the stairs. Conway felt his unease and struggled to get free. She'd break a leg or her back if he dropped her. So Jack and Conway stood there, twenty steep steps from the comfort of home, looking lost.

All Jack wanted to do was settle Conway down and stroke her soft muzzle. He wanted her to feel safe and comfortable. He wanted to see her eat and drink and fall asleep with her head between her paws.

Linda, who had been working on the flower beds in front of her house, saw them and walked over. "Stay with us tonight," she said. Jack was touched and grateful but he really wanted to be alone. "I've got to go check in on Nina. I think I'll call Claire and Andy, and see if we can stay there. Conway and Nina were great friends."

"They'll be happy to let you stay," Linda said, and she didn't seem at all put out. Though not a dog lover, Jack figured her long life with Greylock helped her understand.

He pulled the dog bed and the feeding bowls from his car, and they set off down the street, walking slowly. Conway peed three times and stopped to sniff. Jack waited. She became more animated as they turned into Claire and Andy's driveway, and when Nina came to the door both dogs stood nose to nose, tails wagging.

"So Nina, you have to be gentle with this old girl," Jack said, but he didn't need to worry. Nina had slowed down, too, since the days when they tore through the woods, but beyond that she seemed to understand. He poured food for both dogs, but Nina did not eat until Conway finished. He put out Conway's new dog bed, but Conway found her way to Nina's and the two curled around each other, with large parts of Nina spilling over the edge. After fixing himself a sandwich, Jack felt spent and turned on the TV. Both dogs followed him to the living room. Conway managed to get up on the sofa, and Jack moved to the far end, squeezing himself into the few inches left after Conway sprawled, full length. Nina slept at his feet. Jack clicked through the channels for a while and drifted off into sleep, but was awakened about an hour later by Nina's whining. She looked at him and then at Conway and then at the door. It couldn't have been any more clear if she had words.

They made their way around the block with Jack scooping poop for two dogs and went back to the house. Still exhausted from the long drive the day before and the day itself, Jack decided to go to bed. Andy had said he could sleep wherever he chose, but all the bedrooms were on the second floor, so Jack found a light quilt and some sheets and made up his bed on the sofa. He fell asleep on his side with one arm dangling down, stroking Conway's fur, and his last thought before deep sleep claimed him was that he'd have to give her a good brushing in the morning, and he'd probably need to cut out some of those mats.

After nearly a year of solitude, Claire and Andy suddenly had a packed house with Lizzie, Jack, Nina, and Conway all living there. Jack went back to his apartment each day for a little while, but he didn't want to leave Conway for long. Lizzie spent a lot of time on her computer. Jack took Conway to the fields in the afternoon and spread a blanket by the stream and read while Conway slept in the sun until she got too hot and then moved herself to a shady spot. By dinner time everyone was back in the house, mostly in the kitchen. Conway had some sight left and navigated the house quite well, but liked to spread herself out in the middle of the floor between the stove and the refrigerator. Nina sprawled nearby so that Claire had to step over the dogs while she cooked. After dinner, Lizzie walked up to the church for her AA meetings and came home reeking of cigarette smoke and also hungry. Claire began to shop differently; she stocked the house with cheese and sandwich meat and watched what Lizzie did not eat disappear into Nina or Conway's waiting mouths. Both dogs drooled.

Jack was looking for a new place to live, one without stairs, but Claire was in no hurry to see him leave. Lizzie was another story. She stayed out late, left dirty dishes in the sink, dropped wet towels on the bathroom floor, acting in every way like a normal teenager, and Claire had been secretly happy to learn that she planned to find a job and an apartment. Knowing she was fine was one thing, living with her, another.

For all her love for Lizzie, she could not quite get over the fact that Lizzie had cut deep and might do it again, anytime she was crossed. Claire found herself timid around her daughter, afraid of saying the wrong thing and setting her off. She couldn't ask a single question about Brad without inviting trouble; she felt guilty when she opened a bottle of wine for dinner, and if she said anything about the dirty dishes or the towels, a voice inside told her to shut up and be grateful her daughter had come home unharmed. Where a child's personality began and ended and where a parent's influence irrevocably marked that personality confounded Claire. She didn't know if she'd succeeded or failed as a parent.

At one time, Claire had thought the substance of her relationship with Andy consisted of family. He was so good at packing a picnic lunch for the game, taking Lizzie to the dentist, talking to her about her classes at Burnside, grocery shopping for everyone, and remembering Lizzie's favorite shampoo. Claire had feared that she and Andy wouldn't have enough to bind them all by themselves, but she'd been wrong. They had endured. She wouldn't have made it through without him. Her future lived in Andy and his in her. They would grow old together, care for each other, travel, buy wine by the case, and make love as long as their bodies wanted them to, no matter how wrinkled and saggy they got. Work or love could take Lizzie far away. Their relationship could be reduced to holiday visits. She remembered *The Prophet* and the poem about children going forth into the future, and after years of thinking that this work was a tired fragment of the sixties, Claire dug it out and found more truth than she ever realized

Lizzie's news about Princeton had not surprised Claire. At the sight of her daughter alive and well, she'd let go of that wish. She'd been granted one; better not to ask for two. On the last Sunday in May, Lizzie went to Burnside's commencement. It was a tradition for the previous year's seniors to show up for their friends who had been juniors when they graduated. Claire worried a little that Lizzie would meet all her friends who'd gone to college and feel lost, but Lizzie came home after lunch unimpressed. Apparently most of them, more than well prepared for the academics of college, had spent their freshman year partying. It seemed that the hardest part of places like Harvard was getting in.

Unused to large classes and anonymity, many of Lizzie's friends were disappointed and talked instead about internships, school-year abroad, and graduate school.

"Can you imagine that?" Lizzie said, "It's as if they've already written off the next four years."

It was the best spring in years, everybody said. Twenty days of rain in April resulted in lush lawns, leafy trees, and huge hostas. Eagle chicks had hatched at Lesley Cove and you could see them on the public access TV station. A pair of cardinals made a home in Linda and Tom's yard, in the tree nearest their deck. Over in Woodside, a family of coyotes took over the park. Signs had been posted warning dog owners not to let their pets off-leash. There seemed to be more bears than ever, walking around town rather boldly. People put their bird feeders away, but the bears, with their great sense of smell, pawed the ground where seeds had fallen in the winter. Walking Nina one morning, Claire and Andy turned a corner and thought they saw two huge dogs at the end of the street, but soon recognized them as cubs. They lumbered across the road and through the fields that led to the river, with mama following. Soft air, tee-shirts and shorts, bare feet in sandals—time to consider vacations, or not. Perhaps two kayaks instead, as a way to get on the river. Tennis outside. Frustrating wind carrying the ball in unpredictable ways. Fiddlehead ferns for dinner. Baby lettuce and arugula at the farm stand. Life felt hopeful in Cooper Hill and a mystery would soon be solved.

At six-thirty one morning Lizzie said she'd walk both dogs. They were filling the yard with poop and eating it. It was disgusting. She'd rather walk them and bag it.

Andy said, "I'll go with you. At this time of day the paperboy comes by. You won't be able to control both dogs."

Lizzie looked insulted. "You just have to let her know who is boss."

Andy explained how hard they'd tried. "Well, this was never a problem before. The paperboy must have done something to Nina."

"We've been over it time and again and there's no way. He's only around when he delivers the papers. And it's only this one paperboy. Nina never did this with the others."

"She just decided to take advantage while I was away." Lizzie said. She had been the official morning dog-walker all through high school, even when she had to be at Burnside at eight.

"Well, I'd enjoy a morning walk, whether you need me or not," Andy said.

Jack and Claire also liked the idea. The day would get hot later, and afternoon thunderstorms had been predicted. It would be nice to get out at this soft part of the day and walk around Cooper Hill together.

Maud's house had a SOLD sign out front and so did Amanda's. Andy told Lizzie about Tom's plan to buy it. "Good thing he didn't," he said, "The place needs new wiring, a roof, and a furnace. The people who bought it plan to do the work themselves, over time. Jess and Mary took their place off the market after people at the last town meeting voted to keep the elementary school open. April really wants to go there. She said she loves her room, and if they made her move she would paint her room in the new house black."

Lizzie laughed. "When April wants something, she usually gets it. She's always been that way."

Linda and Tom's house looked amazing with its flowering fruit trees, and Jack told Lizzie about Greylock and the new kitten, Hastings, named after the street over in Woodside where they'd bought their first house. "The fisher cats have come back, so they don't let her out by herself yet," he said.

Lizzie was curious about the big old ruin that someone was restoring. The town's recluse had lived there alone for years after a commune disbanded, and he'd died there two years ago. Claire told her about the filmmaker who'd moved to town and planned to spend half a million to fix it up.

"I've been away for less than a year and so much has changed," said Lizzie, and Claire was tempted to say, "What did you think? That the world would stop while you were gone?" Feeling terrible for thinking such a thing, she reached over to stroke her daughter's hair and pull a piece away from her eyes.

Lizzie pulled the piece of hair back to where it had been and said, "I like it that way."

They all looked up at Jack's apartment windows. "I am so glad you are here with us now," Lizzie said. "All that time you just sat up there watching everybody made me so sad."

"Well, I was missing you, too, only it took me a while to realize it."

Andy considered their little group, almost like old times. Cate could have been off somewhere with the twins and joining them later. Nina walked a little bit in front of Conway, as she always had. Conway stayed steady at Jack's side. If she had full sight, he could have walked her off-leash, but he didn't want her bumping into things. Lizzie was right, thought Andy, an extraordinary amount of change had occurred in a short time.

Suddenly Andy said, "Uh oh," and reached for Nina's leash that Lizzie was holding. The paperboy had just cruised out of a driveway up ahead.

Lizzie held fast.

"We should turn around," he said, but Claire reminded him that it would do no good. At this time of day the paperboy delivered to the whole village, and if they tried to avoid him, he'd come swooping out of a side street. "Just hold her tight and talk to her, and we'll get by him," Andy cautioned. They got closer. The paperboy waited, as he sometimes did, afraid that Nina might break free and topple his bike. They got closer still, and Nina did not pull or bark. The paperboy had a strange look on his face as he took a step towards them. Still Nina failed to react in any way. She just sat there quietly.

"Hey," said the paperboy, pointing at Conway, "Where'd you get that other dog? He leaned his bike against a hedge and came closer. "I used to have one just like it. Her name was Nellie."

Conway started wagging her tail. The boy knelt in front of Conway and pushed at her upper lip to reveal a broken tooth. Nina just watched. "This *is* Nellie. Hey old girl, how did you get here? How are you doing?" He looked up at Jack and Claire and Andy and Lizzie, and he had tears in his eyes, this skinny boy on the border of adolescence, with a few angry red pimples and slightly long hair. "This is the best dog in the world." He wrapped his arms around Conway's huge neck. Conway was licking his face.

"Where do you live?" Jack asked.

"Up on the hill."

"And this was your dog?"

"She's supposed to be dead. My mom took her to put her down, but that's her. I'm sure. Look in her mouth. See that broken tooth. That proves it."

Jack didn't need to look. Conway had broken the tooth years ago, retrieving a rock he'd thrown into the pond. He had a million questions for this kid. He asked the others if they minded if he stayed behind, and he asked the paperboy if they could talk a while.

## *Conway's Story*

On that late summer afternoon when Jack learned Conway had been adopted by a family with children and felt so glad, neither the people at the shelter nor the family was lying, but truth bends. Barbara and Sam Howell did have a fenced yard and children, but the dog had been Sam's idea, not Barbara's, and she was terrified to let Conway too near her children, ages two, four, and seven. One swipe of those big paws could rip a baby's face. One toss of that huge head would topple a toddler. So, inside the fenced yard, they placed a chain-link kennel, just eight feet long and six feet wide, and from that space, so small compared to the forty acres Conway once roamed, the dog who loved children, watched the children play. When she saw the toddler wander too far, she barked. When the oldest boy punched his brother, she barked.

It made Barbara Howell crazy. "Look at her barking at the children. I told you it wasn't safe to let her near them," she told Sam and anyone else who would listen.

Barbara Howell had no time to walk Conway, and Sam had promised he would. In the morning he took her round the block. When he came home from work, if the weather was nice, he did it again. Sometimes on the weekend he'd take her for a longer walk, but never off the leash. He was afraid she'd run away. In their yard he'd tried to see if she would come when called. He'd let her out of the kennel and she'd run to the children at breakneck speed, terrifying Barbara. Their oldest boy threw a ball and she fetched it. They she ran and got a stick, and Barbara screamed that she'd poke the baby's eye out with that thing. Frantic from so much inactivity, Conway had started running laps around the yard, with the two older children following, laughing. She'd ignored Sam when he called her. She'd dodged him when he came after her with the leash, and it had taken him more than an hour to finally get her back into the kennel. So much for that, he'd thought. No off-leash walks.

Dogs do not like to soil their surroundings, so Conway waited and waited, but often Sam worked late, and if it got too late, she could not hold herself any longer. When that happened and nobody cleaned the waste, the ground inside her kennel became fowl. She would make herself as small as possible to keep from touching the piles of excrement, but after the rain the ground became muddy, and it all mixed in and she had nowhere to go.

At first Barbara had allowed Conway in at night to sleep in the cellar, but once Conway began to smell she no longer permitted this. While the weather remained warm, Sam could hose her off on the weekend, but it got cold, so Conway remained soiled and smelly and learned to sleep outside. When it got really cold, Barbara worried, but Sam said Newfies were bred for the cold, known for diving into icy water; she'd be fine. Sleeping on the cold hard ground like that? Barbara asked. Sam told her not to worry.

On walks Conway would try to clean herself by rolling in dirt, but Sam, who had no experience with dogs, thought she was just getting dirtier and held her back. The three children who had been so excited to have a dog, lost interest. What good was it to have a dog you couldn't play with? Barbara Howell kept track of the cost of food and soon stopped buying the good stuff the vet had recommended, and speaking of the vet, his bills were ridiculous. Shots for this and pills for that. She barely had time to get the kids to their scheduled doctor's visits and dentist visits, soccer, and ballet, and that was after she did the grocery shopping, laundry, and cleaning. When Sam noticed that Conway had gone a few months without her heartworm medication, the vet said they should not renew the pills until she tested negative for the disease. Barbara made an appointment to take her for the blood test, but had to cancel because her youngest had strep throat, the next time the middle child was in a ballet recital that day. Barbara gave up.

Still, she spent the most time at home, and she was the one who began to feel bad about the bear-sized dog who lived in the yard like a creature in a petting zoo, only worse, because nobody paid any attention to her at all. Sometimes, when the kids were otherwise occupied, Barbara went out into the yard to visit. At first Conway would rouse herself and come to the fence and lean into it so that Barbara could scratch her ears, but after a while she just sat there, looking at Barbara, making her feel bad.

Winter passed. Conway slept burrowed into the snow. Spring came, and she got soaked in the pelting rain. Again Barbara spoke to Sam. "Shouldn't we get a dog house or put a roof over the kennel? Sam said a dog house big enough for Conway would take up all the room in the kennel, but he fastened a tarp over the top of the kennel. Sam had no skill in these matters. He should have fashioned some kind of peak. During a heavy rain the flat tarp held water until it sagged, and after a while its weight pulled the ropes that held it free, and Conway got deluged.

One April afternoon, after nearly two days of rain, Barbara could stand it no longer, and she brought Conway into the house and led her down the cellar. An entire winter outdoors had thickened Conway's coat and doubled her undercoat, and in the unaccustomed warmth of the cellar Conway began to shed. Barbara couldn't believe her eyes when she went down to give her some food and water. Dog hair practically swirled in the air. The laundry she'd hung down there was covered, the rug looked matted. Appalling as it was, she knew what to do and went to find a brush, but it was hopeless. Each stroke drew enough hair and fur to render the brush useless until it had been cleaned again.

At this point Barbara and Sam had had Conway for nearly nine months. Enough time to make another whole human being, Barbara thought, and enough time to ruin a lovely animal.

When she told Sam Conway had to go, he said, "Well, you never wanted her in the first place," and got all sentimental.

But really, Barbara acted from a better part of herself than Sam when she brought Conway back to the shelter on a Sunday, while Sam took care of the kids and told them someday they'd get another dog, a better dog, you'll see.

The people at the shelter in Russell dutifully wrote to Jack as promised. They let him know that they had Conway, and just in case he might be traveling or something, they put a hold on any adoptions for thirty days. During this time they examined Conway carefully. She passed her temperament test with flying colors. You could push a rubber hand right into her food dish while she was eating, even if she hadn't eaten all day, and all Conway would do was look up and wait until you were done with whatever foolish thing you were doing. She was behind on all her vaccinations and the vet who volunteered at the shelter took care of those and also took a blood test. It was he who discovered Conway had heartworm. And a pretty bad case at that.

The treatment was a painful and difficult process that involved a deep muscle injection of an arsenic-based poison, followed by at least six week of inactivity, and that just killed the adult worms. Another shot later killed any remaining larvae. As the worms died and passed through the heart there was always the danger of arterial blockage. Also, the disease affected many body systems. Conway was now six-and-a-half years old, well past middle age for her breed. The vet sampled her blood at the end of the treatment period and pondered the options. She still had some worms. The poison that had sickened her had not killed them all. Another course of treatment might kill her. He suggested that she be transferred to the no-kill shelter in Woodside, since it could be a while before anyone came along who wanted to take an old sick dog.

The Woodside shelter had slightly more funding and could arrange adoptions without any fees for dogs and cats that fell into special categories.

Conway spent eight months in Woodside, needing treatment and getting sicker, sleeping on concrete, but winning the love of Sheila and the other two people who worked there. During the day Conway spent most of her time off the leash placidly following them on their rounds. She adopted a kitten. The lower cages were just her height, and she poked her head in one day and pulled out a grey kitten that had been crying, brought it over to her blanket and licked it into sleep. Sheila took that kitten off the adoption list, and until the day the board president came by and complained about the lackadaisical way the shelter was being run, it followed Conway all through the day and slept beside her at night.

In January, 2003, a family that had just bought one of the new houses in the subdivision above the village of Cooper Hill came to the shelter looking for a puppy, but the shelter had none. They had four rescued greyhounds and Conway. The boy, who looked to be about twelve, at first wanted to leave if there weren't any puppies. Sulking, he wandered off by himself. He said the greyhounds gave him the creeps. They didn't even know how to climb stairs. His mother read a poster about the Golden Years adoption program at the same time she learned that rescuing a shelter dog did not mean there weren't any fees. If they did have puppies, it would cost about two hundred dollars to bring one home. They'd just bought the house and spent a little more than they'd planned.

"Jimmy, why don't you take a look at the big black dog over there," she said. "She looks like a purebred to me." Jimmy sauntered up to Conway and looked her over. His mother looked on hopefully, but his dad turned to her and said, "That's too much dog for us."

Sheila told them about Conway's health. "She's big, but gentle as a lamb, and she won't need much in the way of walks. But she has heartworm. There's been a lot of damage to her lungs." The she told them that the vet thought she might survive another treatment if she lived with people who would be vigilant about her care.

"Another treatment! And how much does it cost to feed her?" said the dad, clearly ready to leave, but Jimmy had crouched down next to Conway and seen something in her. "If we get her, I could get a paper route to help pay for stuff," he said.

His mother smiled, but not his dad. "A boy ought to have a dog he can run around with, toss a ball with—not an old invalid."

Jimmy, who wanted to act like a grown-up and not a crybaby, nevertheless felt hot tears begin to slide down his face. This dog already loved him. He could tell, and he loved her, too. It was just something that happened. If it happened in a movie or a song he would say it was stupid. But this was a great dog, and maybe she was sick, but she was bigger than any other dog he'd ever seen and his friends would be amazed. " I think we should call her Nellie," he said. "She looks like grandma."

"Jimmy, that's an awful thing to say," said his dad.

"No it's not. It's a compliment."

. Jimmy's mom and dad went over to the side of the office and had a talk. When they came back his mother was smiling a lot and his dad a little.

"And you'll be sure to get her to the vet soon," said Sheila.

"Monday morning," said Jimmy's mom.

So Conway entered her third home, if you didn't count the shelter. This family let her live in the house. Jimmy wouldn't hear of anything else. And they called the vet on Monday as promised and made an appointment for the following Saturday. The news was not good. The injection option would not work, and Conway, now known as Nellie, needed an operation in which they would open her jugular vein and attempt to pull a large number of the adult worms out of her heart and the surrounding arteries. Not only would this cost more than a thousand dollars; the vet could not guarantee that she'd survive.

"And if we don't do it?" Jimmy's mom asked.

"Then just keep her comfortable; don't let her run around, though I doubt she'd want to, and wait. She's got a cough now. I expect it will get worse. She's probably got some liver damage. But she's also a very strong dog. Her size helps. This many worms in a small dog would have killed it long ago."

"What would you do if she were your dog?" Jimmy asked.

"I'd take her home and give her the best of everything and love her a lot."

Jimmy's mother and father wouldn't let him apply for a paper route until summer, knowing that they'd end up driving him around on bad days. When he finally got the application in that spring, he found out they had another boy, and they only needed one. Jimmy mowed lawns that summer and shoveled driveways the next winter, and he used all his money on Nellie. He bought her rawhide chews and liver treats made from real liver. When his mother went grocery shopping, he went with her and went to the pet store where he bought dog food made from venison and duck. For a very short time, he tried a raw food diet and it didn't agree with Nellie at all. Three times a day or more he took her for a gentle walk, but they never made it into the village where they might have passed right by Jack Walker's porch.

By the time Jimmy got his paper route his skin, clothing, hair, probably even his bike were ripe with the scent of Nellie. Later Claire would insist that Nina had smelled Conway on the paperboy, and was trying to tell them something. Jess and Andy would accuse her of anthromorphism, and she would shoot back, "Then you come up with a better explanation," and that would silence them.

When Nellie began to have accidents in the house Jimmy's mother didn't know what to do. Jimmy adored the dog, but her rugs in two rooms had been stained forever, and on certain days, despite all her scrubbing, the smell of urine and feces wafted up from the fibers. They got a baby gate and contained her to the kitchen where the floor could be easily cleaned and Jimmy took care of it whenever he was home, but school and the paper route meant he couldn't deal with it every time.

The breaking point came very early one morning when Jimmy's dad stepped over the gate to make coffee and his foot landed in a soupy mess of diarrhea. "This dog has no life at all," he told Jimmy. "She's suffering. You're not here to take care of her most of the time. We have to do something."

"Like what?" Jimmy sat on the floor with Nellie's head in his lap. When she breathed, he could hear it. He loved Nellie, but she also made him feel guilty.

Later that night after Jimmy had gone to bed, his mother and father decided that putting her down would be the best thing and Jimmy's mother said she'd take her to the vet on Wednesday when she only worked for half the day. Jimmy would be in school. On Tuesday night, Jimmy fed Nellie a small steak and let her eat a bowl of ice cream. That Wednesday morning, after his paper route, he said goodbye to Nellie. He'd gone online to learn what happens, and knew she wouldn't feel any pain. They could get another dog, after a while, his dad had said, a young healthy dog. Jimmy had to get to school and at school he couldn't be crying. He was thirteen now; his dad said he had to buck-up.

It turned out that his mother was not as strong as she'd thought. She and Nellie rode to the vet with Nellie in her usual car position. She sat on the back seat with her head between the front seats, resting it on the driver's shoulder, drooling. Halfway to the vet's, Jimmy's mom changed her mind and headed for the shelter. The people there had loved this dog and she had seemed content. They had cement floors and hoses and could clean any mess she made. She didn't seem to be in pain. As she turned into the driveway, Nellie began wagging her tail, and she got out of the car and walked right up to the front door where Sheila hugged her and roughed her coat and found treats in her apron pocket. "Hey Conway, good to see you old girl, how're ya doing?"

"We named her Nellie," Jimmy's mom said.

"She still responds to Conway. Dogs are like that," Sheila said. She made Jimmy's mom sign a form and led Conway inside.

Later that day, Jimmy's mom told her family that it had been very quick and the vet said it was time, and that is why Jimmy, the famous paperboy of Cooper Hill, had been so surprised to see Conway walking down the street, very much alive. She also looked better. Her coat had been brushed to a shine and her teeth had been cleaned. Jack was gentle with the boy. He told Jimmy he could visit any time.

"My mom and dad said she was suffering. They said putting

her down was the right thing to do."

"Well, I'm sure glad they didn't," Jack said, "but they weren't completely wrong. She won't be with me too much longer, sweet old girl."

Jimmy asked if he could walk Jack back to his house, and Jack said fine. Conway couldn't go fast and that gave them time. Jack told the boy that he'd be with Conway most of every day; she'd never be lonely or need to mess the house, because he'd be there to walk her or let her out.

"I was going to do all that," said Jimmy

"Of course you were, and you did a lot; you did the best you could," Jack said and then he said it again and waited until he saw the boy smile. "Aren't you late for school now?" Jimmy looked at the clock atop the church steeple and jumped on his bike, while Jack and Conway made their way home.

## *June*

Claire and Lizzie were watching the news together when a story came on about a teenage runaway who'd been abducted, sexually abused, and finally found in a crawl space in some psychopath's house, alive but near starvation and covered in filth. Claire felt her throat tighten.

"That could have been you," she said.

"Here it comes," said Lizzie. "I know you've been waiting to tell me how stupid I was."

"It's not that at all. I never thought you were stupid, but look; these things do happen and every day you were gone I thought about them happening to you."

"Well, you should have had more confidence in me. I took that self defense course, remember? Plus, I'd never get close to a weirdo like that."

"That's not the point. You know I worry. How could you have

gone so long without calling?"

"I wrote those letters. You were supposed to call me."

"But when I didn't?"

"I was afraid you didn't want to talk to me."

"How could you ever think that?"

"I don't know. At first I was just so mad at you for what you said about Mrs. Walker and for sneaking around in my room, and if I called, you would have asked all kinds of questions."

"How did you live?"

"I had some money. I met people."

"What kind of people?"

"You really want to know? You'd better be sure before you pry everything out of me, Mom." Claire pulled a cushion up against her chest and hugged it.

"I think I only need to know things you want to tell me, and I need to know if anything awful happened, if you need to see a doctor or talk to a professional."

"I don't need to talk to anybody. Time went by. The more time that went by, the harder it got. I can't explain it. I just started feeling like Cooper Hill didn't really exist. That the high school kid who lived in this house and got good grades and did everything right didn't exist any more. And you loved that other Lizzie, the one who made you proud all the time, but once I made a mistake you'd never trust me again and you'd be snooping and watching me every minute like some sort of criminal."

"But I had to watch you. You were drinking. It's not as though I accused you falsely."

"But you gave me no chance to work it out on my own."

"Alcoholics don't work it out on their own."

"But I did. At Dad's I went to meetings, and he didn't ask me every minute how I was doing and I got sober. He gave me space."

"Well," said Claire, "He's certainly always been good at that." The minute the words came out she wanted to bite her tongue off.

"There you go. You can't stand for me to have a relationship with him. You're jealous, just like you were jealous of Mrs. Walker. It's always about you, isn't it, Mom? Jesus, maybe I should have stayed there."

"Maybe you should go back then," Claire said, this time from plain old exhaustion.

"No Mom, really, that's not what I want."

"Am I ever going to know how you lived for all those months before you went to your dad?"

"Maybe someday, but not now. I can't talk about it. Can't you just relax? I'm here. I feel like I have to start my whole life over again. I need you and Andy, but not like when I was little and not like you're my best friend, either."

"So I'm not a mom and not a friend; then what am I, a cook and housecleaner?"

"That's not fair; you're exaggerating. Of course you're a mom, just not a mommy who needs to know every minute where I was and what I was doing and where I'm going. I'm not ten."

"But you aren't twenty-five and living on your own."

"I'm going to find a way to take care of myself." Claire looked at Lizzie then, so stubborn and closed, but still and always her daughter, and she wanted to offer comfort.

"I don't want you to rush anything. There will always be room for you here. I'll back off, I promise. I will. Lizzie, I missed you so much. We were terrified. I love you so much. I haven't made a single decision in my life that didn't take you into account. Can't you just let that in a little? Can't I hold you, stroke your hair, let you cry if you need to?" For the first time in this conversation Claire saw Lizzie falter.

"I wish, but no. Don't you see that I have to learn how to comfort myself—not with a drink, not with hugs and kisses from you or anyone else? I need to find something in me to be proud of again, and you can't do it for me." Now Lizzie had tears spilling from her bright blue eyes and streaming over her lovely face, and Claire was crying, too, but neither mother nor daughter reached out to touch the other. Claire thought it was probably the most honest conversation they'd ever had, which was ironic considering the fact that Lizzie had not told her a thing about those months away.

Claire sniffed suspiciously. Sophie Weis's office smelled like insecticide. The beams had been sprayed and injected and the whole foundation had been treated.

"I am a complete hypocrite," she told Sophie. "I'd never poison my house. I won't even spray my roses and there are ugly beetles all over them. We eat all organic food, and then I smoke and drink."

"Oh, give yourself a break," Sophie said. "You'd spray like everyone else if you found vermin crawling all over like I did."

"No, we had ants and I made little cotton balls soaked in Borax and water and brown sugar. The Borax is safe for people but toxic for the ants. They died."

"Well, I don't have the patience for that," Sophie said

"But you don't smoke."

"If it makes you feel so guilty, why don't you stop?"

"That's another conversation entirely. I have stopped, then started, then cut way down, but this year I've been awful."

"Is that what you want to talk about today?" Claire said no and told Sophie about her recent conversation with Lizzie.

"She's just establishing boundaries," Sophie said. "A lot of mothers and children have this problem after a divorce. They live for a time like roommates, the moms share too much with the kids. It's not the natural order." This was one thing Claire liked about Sophie. She didn't just sit there repeating your last three words back to you like some kind of machine.

"But I may never know what happened all those months."

"She'll tell you some day. Are you sure there's no guy involved? The whole thing doesn't come together unless she had someone to take care of her between the time she left and when she showed up at Brad's."

Linda and Mel had both thought this, too, and it made sense to a degree, except that Lizzie didn't even have a boyfriend in her last year of high school. She'd been far too busy.

"She traveled in groups like the kids do these days. I even asked her friends if they thought she was going with anybody and they said no."

"Kids lie."

"Andy always says that, but these kids were worried about her, too. If they had a clue they would have told me."

"So how long are you going to obsess about this before you can move on?"

"When I'm not thinking about it, I'm trying to figure out why in the world she chose Brad."

"Maybe because your opinion of her is the most important thing in the world and you have so much power."

"I don't feel like I have any power at all."

"But, you do, and you always have. Lizzie hated it when you left her father, right?" Claire nodded.

"And was there anything she could do about it?"

"No. Was she getting even?" Claire asked.

"Maybe, but not on a conscious level. She also must feel guilty and ashamed."

"Guilty I can understand; what she did was awful. But ashamed?"

"Alcoholics always feel ashamed. They think they're weak, since so many people drink and don't get addicted. For a person like Lizzie, varsity athlete, honor student, it's a larger blow than it would have been for someone less determined."

"But she went to her father, of all people."

"She had unfinished business there. And his opinion of her matters less than yours. Do you know why she left?"

"Apparently she didn't get along with his new girlfriend, no surprise there. I wonder if she told Brad where she was before she got to his place"

"Claire?"

"What?"

"How are you going to deal with her privacy?"

"Is it really a matter of privacy? How come I feel like she's punishing me?"

"You need to let go of that. Lizzie loves you, and she doesn't want to talk and that's that. Claire, are you going back to work in the fall?"

"I guess."

"That's a good thing. You need to start having your life."

"I hate my job."

"Then find another, but do something, start swimming again, paint your whole house; it really doesn't matter as long as you get up each morning with something to do other than go over every sad detail of this year."

"It has been a sad year, for all of us," Claire said, "Except for Jack Walker; did I tell you he found his dog?"

"You did, but we weren't talking about Jack."

"I keep waiting to feel better," Claire said, "I don't think this therapy is helping. I wasn't going to come back after last time. Then I did." Claire let the sentence dwindle.

"It takes a while to see how therapy is working," Sophie said. "Will you be back next week?" That was Sophie's way of saying her time was up. Claire said she wanted to skip a week. Maybe move on like Sophie had suggested.

When she got home the house was quiet. Andy was working; Lizzie had gone off somewhere, and Jack and Conway were also out. What a perfect June day. She looked at her garden and felt tempted to spend some time there, but instead she ignored the tyranny of perfect weather, pulled the shade down, crawled between sheets that had been dried on the line earlier that day, and had the most restorative sleep she'd known in months in the peace of her empty house.

Jack and Conway had headed over to Burnside. Normally he ignored reunions, but it was his thirtieth, and more importantly, a memorial service had been planned for Trip Skye, who had died in the spring, shortly after announcing his retirement. Many people thought his heart had literally broken at the thought of leaving Burnside, and Jack knew that this "retirement" had not been Trip's idea at all. By the time Jack got the letter from Trip's lawyer, it had been too late. A mediation had taken place and a sum agreed upon. No charges had been made; in fact, verifying the charges did not even matter once the issue had been raised. Jack would never believe Trip was guilty of abuse of any kind, but a letter from him would not have mattered. Burnside had been ready to get rid of Trip anyway. He could no longer do dorm duty or drive the varsity team van, and enrollment in Latin and Greek was failing.

Jack skipped the morning symposiums and the afternoon lobster bake and got there in what he thought was plenty of time, but he circled the campus again and again looking for a place to park before deciding to head down to the big lot by the football field. He found a spot at the very back of the lot and worried about the long walk for Conway, but she placidly walked beside him, stopping to sniff and pee every little while. He figured her kidneys were failing; she urinated so often, and he paused at one of the fountains to let Conway drink. He never considered leaving her at home. One of the quirky wonderful aspects of boarding school life was the constant presence of dogs, mostly golden retrievers and chocolate Labs. They followed teachers to class, they slept in department offices, they trod with muddy feet on expensive old oriental carpets, and nobody ever complained. It seemed almost a miracle that he had never known a student to object due to allergies or fear of dogs.

They arrived at the school chapel where Jack and Conway confronted the stairs, a steep set of granite rising in front of them, almost an impossible impasse. Then Jack remembered the handicapped access ramp around the back. He and Conway went in through the rear, and the entire chapel was packed, with plenty of people standing in the back. He found a place off to the side and Conway settled down on the cool floor. The bells rang. The headmaster climbed to the podium and asked in the gentlest voice if all who knew it would please join him in the school song, so loved by Trip and generations of alumni. Voices faltered at first and then gained strength. By the third verse, all were singing as they had at their own graduations, when they'd been coached for weeks by the choirmaster.

The power of the place overwhelmed Jack. Family, club, and cult all combined, Burnside claimed the hearts and minds of its students and created ever-loyal alumni, and they'd come back to say goodbye to the one most essential element of the school—a teacher. Yes, the buildings and impeccable playing fields made them proud. The accomplishments of their former classmates, duly reported in the alumni magazine, also fostered pride, but the heart of the place resided in the one-on-one relationships between teachers and students, so that each person in the room felt that he had a unique bond with Mr. Skye, and he would remain Mr. Skye no matter how many years they were out, unless they came back as Jack had and enjoyed equal status as colleagues. Then and only then would he be called Trip. Trip had embraced new teachers and mentored them throughout his career.

Jack had been part of this and could be again. He could devote the rest of his life to wonderful girls and boys who would someday come to his memorial service offering memories and tributes. It would take just a phone call and he and Conway could move onto campus, and if she made it to the fall, would be loved in all her waning days. He already knew they had an opening in the history department, unusual at this time of year, but young love had compelled one of the junior members of the faculty to follow her sweetheart west.

It would be so easy, but not right. Jack checked in with himself and had one of his imaginary conversations with Cate. She said, "Go ahead if you want. Don't pay any attention to those things I said. Maybe we were wrong to leave, if you consider what happened."

Yes; that was probably what she'd say, but he hesitated. Something told him this embrace would eventually crush him. Driving around Burnside looking for a parking space with Conway had given him a still blurry vision of something else he might do with his life. He stood there watching men of all ages dressed in khaki pants and blue blazers and Burnside ties, just as they'd dressed as boys, and he understood that he'd moved on.

Moving on meant leaving the lovely village of Cooper Hill. He had looked at every available apartment and house and none met his needs. The next day he called Linda about those houses over in Woodside. "One looks like a bungalow," he said and Linda told him it was, with a nice bedroom on the first floor. "In that case, I'll buy both houses," Jack said. He next called the broker handling the property of the old tap and die, offered a little less than the asking price, just on principal and waited. In twenty-four hours he had an accepted offer. His next step involved a trip to the bank and a transfer of funds. By selling stock and annuities, he had the cash he needed right away. Jack and Conway moved into the bungalow three days later. He didn't have much stuff. Lizzie helped and said, "You're going to live like this?"

"No, not for too long, but this will do for now," he said.

"And what are you going to do with the other house?" She asked.

"I was hoping you would agree to live there."

"And?"

Jack told her the plan. On the land he would build a combination shelter, training facility, and boarding kennel. All dogs would have lessons every day. No dog would ever go up for adoption if it couldn't sit, stay, and heel. No dog would be free for adoption if it didn't know how to live properly in a house, which is where Lizzie came in.

"I see that house as a foster care situation. A family comes and wants a dog that is already pretty well trained, but it's important to see how it does in a family situation. So the dog or dogs live with you, and you invite people over, take the dog for walks, bring lots of noisy children over, and continue the training. If the dog chews a slipper, you correct her. If there's too much barking after the animal gets territorial, one of the trainers will work with you and the dog. The adoptive family can visit and walk the dog, hang out for coffee if they like. The point is that no dog that leaves this facility will ever get brought back because it can't behave, and no family will ever trot home with nothing but a leash and collar and no idea of how to care for a dog. Are you interested in helping me with that?"

Lizzie nodded, but she didn't look very convinced, "Who's going to pay for all of that?"

"I am," Jack said. "I can do all this with money to spare, though after a while I'll set it up as a non-profit and do some fundraising."

"Why go to all that trouble?" asked Lizzie who had participated in phonathons at Burnside in which students called wealthy alumni and told them how much their support meant to the school.

"It's good to keep the community involved. No matter how careful we are, someday some dog will break free and run around the neighborhood, and if nobody has had anything to do with this place, they'll turn against it."

"Like, how much money do you have, Mr. Walker?" Lizzie asked. Ever the teacher, Jack repeated the word "like" with a frown. It didn't matter where they went to school. All teenagers talked this way now. Take the blazers and pink shirts off the Burnside kids, and set them loose at the mall, and they all looked and sounded the same.

"You know what I mean," said Lizzie with that smile he hadn't seen in a long time. She mashed her lips to the side so she looked happy and quizzical at the same time.

"So much that it makes money all by itself every day."

"But, like—sorry. How much was there to start?"

"I couldn't even tell you. My great-grandfather invested some money and bought some timberland, then his son did it, too, then my father. When I was sixteen, just three years younger than you, my dad tried to explain it to me."

"And?"

"He said, 'Let's put it this way. You really won't ever have to work if you don't want to, nor will your children, and unless something catastrophic happens, their children won't worry about making a living either.'"

"Amazing, I wish someone would say that to me," Lizzie said. Jack looked at her with his most serious face and said, "No, you don't, Lizzie girl, you really don't."

Jack moved into the bungalow with Conway two weeks later after buying some furniture and laying wall-to-wall carpet over Linda and Tom's carefully restored floors. Conway didn't like slippery surfaces. He had not been this busy since he lived on the land and the summer months filled with urgent chores as he grew vegetables, put them away for the winter, chopped firewood and tried to keep the twins happily occupied in activities that did not involve tubs of boiling water for canning jars or the chain saw. Leaving his perch above the life of Cooper Hill didn't turn out to be as hard as he'd imagined. For one thing, he went back every day so that he could walk Conway in the fields or rest with her on the common. Most of all, he no longer needed to be someone who watched life happen all around him. He had so much to do. Getting permits turned out to be a full-time job, and the city council wasn't happy about his plans to turn the place into a tax-exempt nonprofit, so he abandoned that plan and figured he'd live with the consequences and deal with them when he had to. He set up an endowment to pay for operating expenses, and went to talk to Sheila, who agreed to start working there as soon as the place was ready. He talked to the board of the old Conway shelter, and they agreed to a merger. The dilapidated old shelter sat on a valuable piece of land, which they would sell. They'd use the proceeds to help build the new facility and also for outreach for the Dixie Dogs program. Down south where people had not yet absorbed the importance of spaying dogs, strays ran wild and joined packs that soon threatened neighborhoods. Bringing them to Vermont was expensive, and sometimes these dogs, mostly hounds, did not make good pets. They'd been on their own too long. But Nina had been a Dixie Dog, and Jack had a special affection for her, so he gladly embraced the program.

When he went to talk with Claire and Andy about his plan for Lizzie, he could see they were torn, ready to see her leave the house, but even as they held that thought, missing her. Frightened, too. Would Lizzie stay sober if she lived all alone? In the end, it would be her choice, but Jack was damned if he'd employ Lizzie without Claire and Andy's okay.

"She won't be alone much at all," Jack told them. "She'll have responsibilities. She won't neglect a dog entrusted to her care; you know that as well as I do. She's been sober for months now. I'll make sure we have relief staff so she can go to classes, and she'll be fine."

Because Claire had been avoiding any conversation that might lead to confrontation, she did not know that Lizzie had enrolled in three courses at the university, two in science and one in math, in preparation for acceptance at the vet school at Tufts in a year or so. Just hearing that she still included school in her plans was enough to put Claire's mind to rest.

"It will be a few months before she can move into the other house, but she could come live with me now and help take care of Conway. I have all these meetings and it's too hot to leave her in the car. Municipal buildings don't welcome dogs unless they come at the side of a blind person. I don't like leaving her home alone."

Now there was just Claire and Andy again, and Nina, who no longer barked at the paperboy or pulled with all her might to get to him. Claire could walk her by herself, and on a hot Friday afternoon she took her to the river. Nina was beautiful to watch off leash, and her leg had healed well enough to let her run. Setting her free like this would probably mean that it would take Claire an hour or more to get her back. Nina had no recall. She went into hound zone when she was free and didn't recognize her name or Claire's voice, or even respond to liver treats. In her own time she'd come home, and Claire would have let her be, except for the road that ran in front of the house and Nina's complete lack of street-smarts. Whether it was her hound blood or lack of training had been an ongoing source of conversation. In any case, getting her back on the leash so she could be safely led home involved ignoring her and walking slowly in the other direction until Nina got curious or insulted and came close enough to grab. She fell for it ever time.

Claire kept her on the leash until they had crossed a field and descended into the meadow bordered by the river. Nina didn't like to swim, but she enjoyed wading in the shallows. A bridge had once crossed to the other side, but it had crumbled during that heavy snowfall back in March. Now the field on the other side had grown up in brush with only a narrow path through it, made by those who waded across the river. Claire took off her shoes and hobbled over the slippery rocks, and Nina followed once she saw that it wasn't deep. Bees hummed among the wildflowers, and Claire and Nina made their way along the path that led to a small hill. From there she could see the meadow, the river, and the rooftops of the homes in Cooper Hill, even her own. Under the bright blue sky, surrounded by fragrance and silence except for the gentle buzzing and the sound of her own footsteps on the soft earth, a profound sense of well-being came over Claire. She savored it and exhaled.

Nina, who usually bounded through the high grass and into the woods, circled back close to Claire, stood in front of her and snarled, making a sound Claire had never heard. Her upper lip rolled up, showing her sharp incisors. Claire took a step back. Nina had never once growled at her. Nina held her ground, and Claire took another step back and looked around. All was silent except for the guttural sound coming from Nina. Then she saw the bears over by the wood line that followed the river. A mother and cub lumbered through the little stand of chestnut trees at a bend in the river. The cub, a hunchy brown ball smaller than Conway, looked like some toddler's dream toy. The mother shambled along, looking back over her shoulder every once in a while, and casting her gaze towards Claire and Nina too, just checking.

Had Claire continued on, her path would have put her right between the mother and her cub. Nina's hound blood had mixed with enough German shepherd to make her very smart and protective. Good dog, thought Claire as she turned around and headed back and Nina followed. They crossed the river downstream from their original spot to keep a safe distance. They climbed the hill that would take them to the side street, and Claire hooked Nina's leash. "You great girl," she said, trembling a little. Shaky but also gleeful that she had such a fine story for Andy; Claire made their way back to the path that led to home. Nina, the languid dog who barely roused herself when they came home, who claimed the sofa with her full length and slept as though it was some kind of work, had rescued her, had literally shepherded her away from harm.

Amanda would have been so affronted by a bear in their tranquil meadow, she thought, but Claire felt nothing but glad that in this place, just thirty minutes from a university, a mall and a highway, bears still roamed. Of course they were there because their habitat had been slowly diminished by all the home building, but still, it was good to be reminded of another wild world. Linda had been fighting the deer who wanted to munch on all her ornamental trees. Andy had sworn he saw those coyotes in the winter. That rabid skunk had nested on Amanda's porch, and the squirrels in Maud's yard had never quit, not even in the face of her efforts to annihilate them. In April the local paper had reported a bobcat sighting, and fisher cats were a real threat.

Around the block, one of her neighbors kept chickens. In March, Jess and Mary had tapped the sugar maples in town and boiled down the sap. Each family got about eight ounces of syrup, and they savored every drop. In their small yard, Claire and Andy had planted six tomato plants and clumps of basil. All the woodpiles were shrunken now, but sometime in the fall, trucks would come and chain saws would whir on Sunday mornings. In the hill towns just thirty minutes north and west, farmers had started raising grass-fed beef and lamb and free range chickens along with their eggs. Handmade cheese, organic and locally-produced, could be purchased at stands or at the nearby co-op. Soon the farm stand just half a mile outside of town would have the midsummer abundance of tomatoes and zucchini, cucumbers, carrots, and corn—the best of all... Claire had already bought spinach and early peas. All this and great bookstores, too, and a restaurant carved from an old mill and built out over the same river she'd waded across that afternoon.

Claire believed she lived in the best place in the world, which is why just that morning she'd been shocked when Andy had said he'd like to get away for a while. With Lizzie back in body and Jack back in spirit, he thought they could leave Nina with them and go somewhere. At first Claire had thought he meant a vacation.

"No, more than that," he'd said. "I was thinking about the Peace Corps."

Claire's immediate reaction had been to bring up Cate, since joining the Peace Corps was just her kind of thing, but she held back and let Andy talk. She hadn't realized how bored he was, or how filled with good will. All his skills and education would mean so much more in some village in Latin America. He'd read Tracy Kidder's book about Paul Farmer, and been inspired. He had, he'd said, just so many years left when such a thing would be possible. He reminded Claire how much she hated her job, and how she might work in a local school, helping children learn to read. Claire had once volunteered over in Woodside to help Cambodian immigrants learn English.

"Leave Cooper Hill? For how long?" she'd asked.

Andy, whose eyes were bright with hope, said a year.

Just thinking about a year away from home made her sad, and Claire knew half a dozen ways to put this to rest right now. She could say she would be too worried about Lizzie; she could say it was wrong to leave Burnside so soon after Lizzie had received free tuition for four years; she could say Lizzie had felt abandoned once, what would this do to her? And if none of that worked, she could ask Andy how he could possibly manage his irritable bowel in a place with pit toilets. But she hadn't used any of those excuses yet. Ever since they met, each time some choice had to be made, Andy made it in favor of Claire and Lizzie. His on-call schedule had not often interfered with one of Lizzie's games or the nights Claire needed to be at the library. He only scheduled tennis after checking with her. Even getting Nina had not been his choice, and then he'd become her greatest fan. Claire could not just dismiss this without thinking about it some more and talking to Linda and, of course, Lizzie and Jack, who would have to care for Nina and the house if they went.

No place could be quieter than Cooper Hill on a weekday afternoon. It was too pretty to go inside, so Claire and Nina walked over to the town playground where the volunteer fire department had begun stacking wood for the Fourth of July bonfire. At this particular time most people in Cooper Hill couldn't summon much enthusiasm for the traditional fireworks. When you got right down to it, it was just a celebration of war, and the war in Iraq that started off with the "Shock and Awe" bombing that riveted the nation like some sort of video game, continued to take lives, sixty-five one day, fourteen another, one hundred and three on the day after that, and on and on. She and her friends talked about it less and less. It had become ugly background noise, but over in Woodside, outside the VFW building, a man had been placing flags in the ground each time a soldier died, and now there were more than two thousand.

Cooper Hill had always had the Fourth of July bonfire. Some years it rained, but the fire department soaked the wood with gasoline so it would burn. And some years, it was so hot out that the idea of standing by the enormous fire didn't appeal at all. But no matter the weather, she and Andy would go, so would everyone else in town, and Jack would bring Conway, and since she no longer chased the paperboy, Nina could come, too. They'd stretch out on blankets and watch the sparks fly into the air while children ran around and mothers warned them not to get too close.

Claire thought about the comfort of predictability and the joy of contrast; bears and domesticated chickens, dogs and coyotes in the same town, cruel war in one part of the world and a placid bonfire in another. As she often did, she put some sentences together in her head, but as she was doing that she found herself letting go of the experience she was having right at that moment. The effort to package it and pin it down somehow diminished the real thing. She wondered if anyone's story, once written, lost something, just as a movie made from a book never came close. What if every articulation of an experience reduced it? Name the flower, and it becomes only a word. String words together and the noise of the sentence drowns out meaning. If this were true, would there be any point in writing, let alone talking? Which brought her to the subject of her book. She'd sent one message to the editor asking if she could delete certain essays and still have enough for a book. If she could take out the one about Cate, the one about Andy's bathroom habits and the one about Lizzie, it might be alright. She had not been surprised when the editor said no.

Because they had their own business, Linda and Tom had to file quarterly taxes. When Linda came in from the garden, covered in mud and sweat and at her most happy, Tom made the day even better when he reported on their finances. They had not bought Maud's house, but they had listed it, and done some of their magic to bring buyers to the door, and even they were surprised that Rebecca got her asking price. Amanda's place had sold within two weeks of its listing, and because everything had so recently been redone, a bidding war had taken place between two buyers that raised the selling price above the asking price, even though this was also above the appraisal.

Once again, they congratulated themselves on not buying Maud's place. The insurance companies had just raised rates on homes with knob-and-tube wiring and they would have been killed trying to deal with that. The nice energetic couple who bought the house would take down walls, and redo it all. It was great that Jack had still not closed on the two Woodside houses, since two more sales in this quarter would push their taxes to the sky. All that, and they had obtained three new listings this week.

"It feels like old times," Tom said and Linda had to agree, though Tom said it didn't make sense. The economy was weak and every body said the real estate market had gone belly-up.

"Not in Cooper Hill," Linda said. "People still want community. You can take away any notion of privacy, have a crazy old lady stealing mail and killing squirrels, stay up half the night because of dogs barking, and it doesn't matter a bit if there's something that makes it feel like community, even if we only stop to talk when the dog walkers are out."

The phone rang and Claire asked if she could come over. Linda took a quick shower and met Claire on the deck that looked out over their deep yard. The perennial garden in full flower glowed in the slanting late-day sun. Both women sighed and sipped their drinks. Linda told Claire about Tom's news, and Claire asked if they would retire soon. Linda said not soon, but they might take on a partner and cut back on their hours. They might think about going away for January, February, and March, when the market died.

"No snow to shovel," Claire said. "Who will look after your house?" Linda thought Jack might be willing. "Would you buy another place?" Linda thought not. It would be more fun to pick a different place each year. Sicily, Arizona, the south of France. This led easily into the reason Claire had come, and she told Linda about Andy's idea. Linda knew without asking that Claire didn't like it.

"I don't think you should say no without thinking about it," she told Claire. "First of all, it would be interesting. It would be new. You've picked up and changed your whole life before. When's the last time you had an adventure?"

"It feels so far, far and foreign. Being away from Lizzie makes me nervous. And Nina; what would she think? She could forget all about us. And leaving the house—anything can happen. What if a pipe bursts and floods the basement? What if the roof starts leaking? Then there's my mother; she could go any time."

"You sound like a text book agoraphobic."

"No I don't. Those things could happen."

"What if they did? If your mother dies, you'll fly back. It's not likely that you'd be at the bedside anyway. You've been on watch for years, and it's just going to happen someday when you least expect it."

"But I go see her."

"How often?"

"Most of the time she doesn't even know me. She sees horses on the street and a little girl standing in the window."

"Sweet," Linda said.

"What a year it's been," Claire answered.

"I can't believe Amanda is moving next week," Linda said.

"She'll be here for the fourth, though. I wonder what she'll wear?"

"Well, her city look hasn't won Jack over; maybe she'll try something new. Imagine Amanda in a pastel cotton sun dress?"

"I can't," said Linda. "She'd look like Halloween with that hair and her almost black lipstick. But, you know, I think it's great actually. How many people move out here and remain completely unchanged? I heard she went to one contra dance and swung her partners so hard that a guy nearly fell over."

"That had to be before she hurt her shoulder."

"Yeah, I think it was her first year. We should think about the new people moving in," said Claire and then her voice trailed off.

"So what will you tell Andy?" asked Linda. Claire didn't answer right away. She thought about the long winter months without her best friend. She thought about how fast Lizzie's time away had actually passed, though within that year certain days had seemed endless. She thought about Burnside and the repetitive school cycle and the library director who never gave her credit for any of her ideas, even the website that she'd designed. And she wondered what it was that really held her here in Cooper Hill, where she'd always felt so safe. They all locked their doors now. The mystery of the intruder had never been solved, if it had even been real. She thought about all the times she'd urged Jack to move on and start living his life.

"I guess I'll say it's okay, if he really wants to go."

Linda smiled. "You'll have great stories when you come back, and maybe you'll write."

"Maybe," said Claire. She still didn't feel ready to tell Linda that she had been writing, but she knew that if she went away for a year the book deal would be over. She would have to tell Andy about it. It was too big a secret to keep from him.

"I could light the grill and cook some chicken if you want to stay for dinner," Linda said. Claire offered to go home and get Andy and make the salad. Andy wouldn't feel like coming, but he'd get into it.

On her way down the street she met Peter and Melanie. Claire wondered what Peter would say about their leaving for a year. The guys started playing outside as soon as the snow melted off the courts, three sets two or three nights a week after work and five set marathons on Saturday morning, right into December if the courts were still clear. Then they went indoors to play without the glare of sun or distraction of wind, and they liked it, but it wasn't like playing outdoors.

Claire liked Melanie. They called each other tennis widows and enjoyed chiding "the boys" and egging them on. Melanie had not been able to join the book club due to a long-standing feud with one of the members, but she read on her own, and she and Claire talked about books, daughters—Melanie's had changed majors three times—and mothers. Both dying slowly. Shy by nature, Melanie had seemed standoffish at first, but the boys' tennis had created conversation and the rivalry between two men old enough to know better made them laugh. Claire invited Peter and Melanie to Linda's, knowing it would be fine, and Melanie went to her garden to pick corn.

On her way back from the garden, Melanie met up with Ethan Sykes, who was new in town and had moved into Jack's old place. She thought the group would like a chance to know him better and invited him to Linda's. Ethan offered to bring some hamburger meat he'd been planning to cook that night and asked if he could also bring his girlfriend who'd come up for a few days. She'd be moving in soon. Once Linda found out that the party had grown, she called Amanda and Jack. Jack said Conway was not doing well and he needed to stay home, but Amanda said yes right away and left her house with four different kinds of cheese and a baguette.

By the time everyone had a drink in hand, Linda had worked magic in the kitchen and produced a tray of marinated shrimp, a bowl of tiny savory meatballs in some kind of wonderful sauce she made from opening random jars of condiments she always kept handy, and a plate of thinly sliced apples and red onions to go with Amanda's cheeses. Tom lit the grill and let the coals develop into a fiery heap and then put the chicken on. When Linda figured out how many people would be eating, she thawed two small strip steaks and six pork chops in the microwave. Ethan had brought lean hamburger from grass-fed cattle, real dill pickles that his girlfriend had brought from New York, and a pot of black beans. The smell of meat spiraled into the smoky air.

"Look. Here come the bats," said Andy. Amanda ducked, disgusted, but the rest roamed out into the yard and then crossed the street to watch the bats swarm from the church steeple. This happened every summer night, and people stared each time as if they'd never seen it before. Ethan's girlfriend, whose first name was Morgan and who aspired to become a naturalist, loved the bats. They came close enough so that you could almost feel their furry bodies whirring past your ears.

"If they get married, her name will be Morgan Sykes. I think that's beautiful," said Melanie.

"Unless she keeps her own name," said Claire.

"Which is?" asked Linda.

"Saltonstall," said Claire. "She'll probably keep it." Claire knew this world of names. They were all over Burnside—last names as first names, middle names made from maternal last names. Money people did not name their children Barbara Ann or Lizzie Sue.

"She seems nice," said Melanie.

"But young," said Linda. Then she reminded everybody that it was time to eat.

They sat around tables covered in old linen. Candles glowed. Conversation slowed as people began to eat with serious intent. And then a little voice interrupted from the darkness. It was April, from across the street.

"How come you're having a party when it isn't the Fourth of July yet?" she yelled.

"How come you're not in bed?" Amanda said under her breath. April looked both ways and crossed the street.

"What's up? said Andy, who was rubbing his shoulder, still sore from the match two days ago.

"Jess is throwing up again. It's disgusting," said April who had in the last year abandoned the Mom and Mamma distinction.

"Have you had your dinner?" asked Claire.

"A very long time ago," said April, sniffing the air and eying the dessert table.

"Well, we have plenty, what would you like?" asked Tom who'd gotten up to serve himself another pork chop.

"What do you have?" asked April. "I had tofu for dinner. We don't eat meat."

"Hmm," said Tom, "We have beans and cheese and bread and corn. What will it be?"

April paused, looked back at her house, and then asked for a hamburger, "A big juicy one, please. Maybe with lots of catsup and a pickle, like Eric always gets to eat at his house."

All the adults looked at each other. Feeding a child food against a parent's wishes presented a moral dilemma. But all the meat at this party had been raised humanly, without hormones or antibiotics, and April had asked. Jess and Mary always said that they'd let her sample meat if she asked.

"What the heck," said Tom, making a plate for April. In minutes April had meat juices running down her face; she looked like a happy wolf. Soon afterwards Claire noted the time and sent her home, and about two hours later the party dispersed.

After Claire and Andy left, Linda started to get ready for sleep. In her opinion, the witches in *Macbeth* were really menopausal crones who resented all that passion between Macbeth and his Lady, and cursed them in spite. Feeling like some kind of witch herself, she began a ritual that consisted of an oatmeal bath, black cohash tea mixed with warm milk, guided visualization and chanting. On a good night she would sleep from ten to four A.M. before the night sweats turned her into a soggy, thrashing mess and chased Tom from their bed. By the time she got into bed, Tom was already asleep, snoring lightly. Linda lay flat in the dark thinking about Claire and Andy in Latin America and she and Tom somewhere warm in the dead months of winter. The image felt more unsettling than seductive. Change came hard. In the middle of her night sweats, she sometimes tried to submit to them as she imagined some women submit to childbirth, but in the end she had more fight in her than yielding. She'd encouraged Claire to go with Andy, to give him this chance, but she hadn't said how much she would miss her. As sleep finally let her busy mind rest, she remembered snow, falling gently on the rooftops and blanketing the trees in Cooper Hill; she thought about how much she hated flying. Maybe Tom would be happy with just a month away in Savannah or Charleston, even Florida. They could make it into a road trip. There were health clinics down South where Andy could make a contribution. Maybe Claire could convince him. Sleep.

## *July*

Jack and Conway didn't make it to the annual July fourth bonfire. On a pallet on the kitchen floor, next to Conway who could not get up, he stretched his full length and listened to her breathe.

"Nine's a pretty long life for you, you big old giant dog," he said. "You've done alright even with the heartworm." Conway wagged her tail. Jack stroked her shiny coat. After a while she struggled to get up. She could push herself up with her front legs, but her back legs collapsed under her, and she went back down again with a pitiful whine and a trail of urine spread out on the floor. Jack got up and mopped it with a rag. Conway would not look at him.

"Don't be ashamed, Conway, you couldn't help it. You've always been such a clean dog. I think we got you house-trained in about a week. You were much much easier than the twins. I used to tell their mother they'd never get out of diapers. Remember that? Molly would walk around in her big girl panties and then ask for a diaper so she could poop. Sometimes, when she or Zeke needed changing, you'd let us know. You'd poke that big nose of yours into the diaper area and stare at us, as if you were saying, what's wrong with you people?"

Conway relaxed and rested her head on Jack's leg. Her eyes fluttered open and then closed in sleep. She continued to take in long labored breaths.

After a while Jack said, "Think it's time? You can go now, if you want. I'll miss you but I'll be okay. You can go anytime you like, and I'll be right here with you, and when you're all done with that tired old body, I'll take you back to the land and put you in the earth right on that little knoll overlooking the pond. I'll do that and pat everything down, just so, and you can rest there."

Conway opened her eyes one last time. Jack put his face up against her snout and rubbed her ears gently, and he felt the long exhale and a slight shudder and then she was still.

Knowing it would happen soon, that she really couldn't hold on any longer and shouldn't, didn't make it any easier. He had to clean things up. With that last sigh, Conway had let go of her bowels. He didn't mind. He cleaned the floor and her coat and then wrapped her in a flannel blanket. It was stupid, he knew, but before leaving her there alone in the kitchen, he put a small pillow under her head.

He had planned for this. In the morning he called the people who had bought the land and told them when he'd be there, then he went to wake Lizzie, who still abandoned herself to sleep like a teenager. He climbed to the third-floor bedroom she'd claimed for now. It was too soon to move into the other house. What a good kid, he thought.

She'd not only been caring for Conway when he had to be away, but she'd also proved adept at sorting through the permits and paperwork required to get the new shelter up and running. They would break ground in a month. He tapped on her door and there was no response and he finally had to bang, which felt wrong with Conway's body heaped on the kitchen floor.

Lizzie took it alright. They'd talked about it a lot. Together, they lifted Conway's body into the van. "Do you think I should call Mom and Andy?" she asked. "They'd want to know."

"If it's okay with you, I'd rather just do this myself."

"You don't want me to come with you?"

"No, Lizzie; I want to do this by myself."

For just a minute Lizzie looked like she might cry, but she straightened and shrugged. "I can see that," she said.

So Jack took off alone to drive to the place that held such wonderful awful memories. He had a dirt shovel in the car. He had thought about building a small wooden coffin and discarded the idea, but he would wrap her in an old cotton sheet. There was no way he could shovel dirt over Conway's face.

Of course his story followed him everywhere. The people who bought the land had almost pulled out of the deal when they learned what had happened there. On this day they greeted him uneasily, but were glad to be able to do this one small thing. The place he had in mind, however, might be a problem. They'd put a picnic table and arbor up there in that spot. The best spot on that land, anyone would agree. True. Jack walked around; the picnic table sat right on the place he'd had in mind. Conway's spot. But then, hadn't Conway loved the whole place border to border? He didn't want to put her too close to the pond, and he didn't want her in the deep woods, but about thirty yards away from the picnic table there was a small stand of tamaracks. Conway had loved their shade and the soft earth beneath them. If he could find a place to dig between the roots, it would make a fine spot. The owners agreed, and he poked his shovel a number of times before he found soft earth.

Because it was not snowy or mud season he could drive very close to the spot. He carried Conway the rest of the way and did what he had to do. He began to sweat and took off his shirt and the sweat bees came after him. He didn't care. If he'd had his way, Cate and the children would be buried here, too, and not in that sterile place all in neat rows with their tender bodies filled with chemicals. Cate's parents had pretty much taken over back then, and he just didn't have it in him to fight. But he would have washed the bodies and laid them out in the living room and watched over them until it was time to put them in the ground. He would have rubbed the frozen skin until it softened and washed the pond water from their hair. Life in America in this century did not permit that—not with people. So Conway got the burial Jack thought all loved ones deserved, and he settled the most loyal of all dogs into the fragrant pine-scented earth with the utmost care and covered her, feeling gratitude for her huge tender heart.

Lizzie organized a memorial service for Conway, which had at first seemed silly to everyone until they got to the spot in the meadow she had chosen. The river made a wide sweep at this spot and could be seen from the knoll beneath one of the tall pines. The brown needles made a dry soft seat for the circle of friends: Claire and Andy, Linda and Tom, Amanda, Mary, Jess, and April, Eric, Hannah and her mother, Sarah, Jimmy the paperboy and his mother, and Sheila from the shelter. Lizzie had gathered wildflowers and springs of sage, lavender, and rosemary from her mother's garden and tossed them in a heap next to a vase filled with clear river water. Lizzie told everyone what to do. It was simple. As words and memories formed, each person would speak and then place a flower in the vase. Jack would speak last and also bring the flowers home and hang them upside down to dry, and they would hold all good Conway memories and Cate and Molly and Zeke memories, and the flowers would release these along with their fragrance, as they dried. In this way every part of Conway's dog life, which would be woven forever with all of Jack's life, got remembered and named, and Jack loved Lizzie for arranging it.

With Conway gone and the permitting process over, there wasn't enough for Lizzie to do at the house in Woodside. Promising that she'd be back when the shelter opened, she moved in with friends who had an apartment near the university where she'd signed up for classes. This would be so much better than driving back and forth, she said. Claire told Jack she didn't like this idea at all. The people she'd be living with were all older. Bars lined the main street of the town and the drinking culture of college life could be seen everywhere. Jack had come by with his van to pick up a dresser Lizzie needed for her clothes. They talked while he tied it down so it wouldn't bump around while he drove.

"But you have no choice but to let her go. She'll do it one way or another," he said, not needing to remind her of what had happened last time her mothering pressed in too closely.

"I know, and she keeps saying, 'It's my life,' but she's still on our health insurance; we're paying for school, and she needs to borrow some money for this move, but it's her life anyway. Sometimes that makes no sense at all to me. Lizzie has a disease. Does she even know where the AA meetings are?"

"She'll figure it out."

"And if she doesn't?"

"If she slips she'll steady herself again, like she did this past year. What does Andy say?"

"He's so focused on this trip and getting someone to replace him for a year in the practice; he's not really paying attention. He wants this to work out for Lizzie, so I can go away with peace of mind, but I felt a lot better when she was living with you."

"She's coming back in the fall when we open the shelter. Two months, maybe a little more, and you're not leaving until September. Claire, relax." He regretted the words as he said them, remembering all the words that had come his way. After a while they had no meaning at all. You might talk a person off a bridge or get them to dive into the deep end of the pool, but you could never talk a person out of feelings. It was like shouting in a foreign language.

"Want to come to town with me?" Jack asked.

"No, she'll think I'm spying." So Jack waved to Nina, who still looked at him oddly when he showed up without Conway, and he drove off.

And it turned out that Claire had reason to worry. Jack saw it right away. She'd been gone just three weeks, but Lizzie was pale and the slight shaking in her hand told him she'd been drinking again. He pretended not to notice and asked all the polite questions about work and school. It was eleven-thirty in the morning and one of her roommates straggled bleary-eyed into the kitchen and peered into the refrigerator, weaving slightly. Lizzie introduced them. The girl, named Jennifer, nodded and asked him if he'd like a beer. He declined and asked Lizzie if she felt like going for a walk. She said she had to get ready for work; she had a job at a restaurant and she had to prep for dinner. She asked how the work in Woodside was going and he said fine. They'd be open in October if all went well.

"Did you hear about Mom and Andy? They're going away, either to Nicaragua or Africa. Andy wants to join Doctors Without Borders for a year."

Jack told her he thought it was a great idea.

"Mom doesn't really want to go, but I told her she should. She never goes anywhere."

"Well, she's really never had a chance before now. I told them I'd take Nina. If you come back she won't be too lonely."

"What do mean if I come back? I said I would."

"Things come along, life gets complicated. I don't want you to think you have to." Jack said, hoping with all his heart that this sweet, basically good kid would come back to Woodside, where he could keep her busy from morning to night and the needs of the dogs and cats would keep her from drinking. This environment was not good. The shabby house looked neglected. The bathroom had mold growing in the shower stall, and if Claire ever dropped in as he just had and saw Lizzie's morning shakes, she'd never go away with Andy.

It had seemed almost story-book simple when she first came home, sober and chastened. Jack had forgotten the long struggle of alcoholics. One of his friends had fought it for years and then succumbed again for no apparent reason and finally died of liver disease. What he knew from books and life is that nothing he or Claire or Andy or anyone could say would make a difference until Lizzie wanted it to, and she was just eighteen, a bad age to find out that you can not join in with the crowd and have the same sort of fun as everyone else.

Molly had had a peanut allergy. It had not been a problem as long as he and Cate controlled everything she ate, but they had worried about future birthday parties or Easter baskets or even a careless friend packing peanut butter and jelly sandwiches for a play date. It was one reason, among many, why they'd considered home schooling. Had she lived, Molly would have always been set apart by this. She would watch kids dive into food with abandon, and she would always have to ask if the food had nuts or had been made in a facility with nuts. She could not go to an ice cream stand where the scoops were rinsed all together in one bucket. She could not have the grilled chicken if the grill might be contaminated with sesame oil. She could not eat store-bought bread. Until you read the labeling carefully, you would never suspect all the foods that came into contact with nuts.

It would have made her angry, just as being a person who could not drink made Lizzie angry. He could see it that morning in her grey-blue eyes. She wanted it not to be true, and she would test herself, tell herself that she could have a single drink and stop, until she finally accepted that she could not under any circumstances, and that a drink for her was as toxic as a single peanut had been for Molly. Jack wondered if there was any way he could remind her of Molly's allergy. Lizzie had taken such good care of the twins, and when people came to the house for a pot luck she'd checked all the dishes like a general. At the moment, he couldn't think of any graceful way to insert this into the conversation, and he had to be careful. Lizzie would run and hide if she didn't want to confront this now. She might not run away again, but she'd go into another kind of retreat where nobody could help her.

He headed back to Woodside feeling tired. Jack passed the turn off to Cooper Hill and thought about the endless quiet days on his porch there. Coming out of his solitude had turned out to be exhausting. Lizzie was now a person he worried about. Amanda had moved back to Boston but she called all the time. She had decided to keep some of her clients and had hinted and hinted until he finally said he had plenty of room if she needed a place to stay. She'd be coming up this week, and he wished Lizzie was still there as a buffer. It was not that he didn't find Amanda attractive; he just knew they had no future. He'd told Claire and Andy that he'd gladly take Nina while they were away. Linda and Tom had asked if he'd take care of their house if they went away for the winter, and Mary and Jess kept asking him to dinner, having decided that April needed men in her life. Cate's parents called all the time, too. They gushed about how happy they were that he was getting his life back in order, but never failed to mention Cate's foundation or what would have been the twin's birthday, or their anniversary, or Cate's birthday, or some holiday they hoped he would spend with them.

He did not want to forget Cate and the twins, but he had not married her parents. In fact, he and Cate had put strict limits on the time they spent with them, since some always led to more, and one summer Cate's parents actually looked over the land and started talking about how they could build a nice cabin over by the pond and come for a couple of months in the summer. He'd felt his blood run cold, and Cate had laughed that night in bed and consoled him. "They have all these ideas; then they get over them. Last year it was a place in Italy. Stop worrying."

His parents had started calling often as well. His dad worried about the amount of cash he'd sunk into a project that would not make any money. He wanted to know why Jack hadn't borrowed the money. "Never spend your own, when you can spend the bank's money," he said, pointing out that the interest he would have paid on the loan would be less than his investments had been yielding. Jack didn't know why this should matter when he'd barely made a dent in his funds. He liked owning it all outright, and his ability to pay cash had made everything go faster. His father sighed on the phone, and Jack could hear failure in his breath. His fucked-up son was off again, swept away by some high-flown plan that made no sense to him. To his dad, the one shrewd thing Jack had ever done was to buy the land and then sell it at such a profit, and until the day he died, he would never believe that Jack hadn't grasped the resale value on the day he signed the purchase and sale agreement.

When he got home Jack made a fresh pot of coffee and spread the building plans out on the kitchen table. The architect had sited the shelter and training wing in a way that left room for a two-acre fenced dog park with a small pond in the middle and an agility training area. An addition to his bungalow would provide a place for grooming. The floors in the kennel would have heated coils beneath the floor, and though not air conditioned—Jack didn't believe dogs liked it—windows would be placed for maximum cross-ventilation. Staff members would have private offices where they could interview people who came to adopt, and nobody would walk out of there with a dog without knowing about site visit inspections, follow up calls, and when inoculations were due. Though he'd charge for some classes and for grooming, he'd never make a cent on the place. The whole project could only lose money, but not at the rate that his money made money, so what did it matter? This was not a strategy for happiness that his father would ever understand, but then again, he didn't need to. He made a note for the architect, approving cedar siding, triple-glazed windows, cherry trim inside, and an expensive, but environmentally responsible, green roof.

## *August*

Wet heat clamped down on Cooper Hill and the rest of the river valley. Windless grey mornings swarming with mosquitoes made people want to stay in. Weeds overtook gardens untended for even a day. The zucchinis grew huge and hollow. Lettuce bolted and went to seed. Tomatoes developed black patches and rotted near the stems. Dogs pawed the earth, dug out a cool spot and panted. By four each day the rain came but it brought no relief. Afterwards the sun came out, sending the moisture back into the air where it hovered until four the next day.

People tried not to complain. They tried to remember winter and be grateful. "Hot enough for you?" they said to each other as they passed on the street, when they went out. They acted as they did in winter and stayed inside a lot. The small town library ran out of new books and free videos. In Jess's vegetable garden, Swiss chard, collard greens, peppers, carrots, and broccoli flourished, but one night she picked broccoli to serve raw with a yogurt dip, and after they had eaten most of it, she saw the small white worms on the plate. Maud's house was a mess because the new owners who were tearing off the old asphalt shingles had stopped working because of the heat. The people who had bought Amanda's house also had a place down on Cape Cod, so they were hardly there. Ethan Sykes and his girlfriend spent all their spare time down at the river, so the porch once quietly inhabited by Jack Walker seemed deserted. When Claire and Andy walked Nina, they talked about how uninhabited Cooper Hill could seem sometimes.

The people who went away chose this time. Normally Claire and Andy would go to Maine, but not this year. They had too much to do. On a Tuesday night in the second week of August, Andy lingered at work. He didn't need to go to the clinic and Peter couldn't play tennis, so he could have gone home at four after his last patient left—another overweight white male who would rather take cholesterol drugs than do a single thing about his diet. Earlier that day he'd seen a woman with a sore throat, a man with wax in his ears, a woman with a small goiter, and another woman who was developing carpal tunnel syndrome. A man who said he had a hard time walking had to have his corns trimmed. Most of his day had been spent writing referrals. His nurse had removed the ear wax. Andy sat at his desk at four-thirty reviewing the day's paper work and occasionally folding and unfolding the flyer that had caught his eye and made him want to get away to a place where life seemed more urgent.

He could never ever let Claire know that the idea had come to him via a flyer addressed to Cate Walker. Some non-profits never revised their mailing lists. Lizzie still got enrollment reminders from a teen camp she'd attended when she was nine. Cate had been on every list you could imagine. Usually people at the clinic just threw away the junk mail, but this one for Doctors Without Borders had made it through, and the photographs of children in Africa with amputated arms were as compelling as anything he'd ever seen. Africa had been his first choice, but he knew Claire would think it was too far away, whereas Haiti was separated from Vermont by just one time zone.

After lengthy conversations with Linda and a lot of quiet brooding, Claire had finally agreed to go, and Andy felt grateful, but her acquiescence reminded him of a date he once had with a women who took him to her bed afterwards as though it was the least she could do after the expensive meal. Even as Claire read the first draft of his application and went to the Post Office to renew their passports, he knew she was hoping he'd change his mind. The other day she'd asked if he had thought about working on an Indian reservation out west, and he hadn't, but it wasn't a bad idea. The poorest people in the richest country in the world lived on these reservations, where diabetes had become an epidemic. There would be plenty to do there, too, but he was not drawn to the barren western landscape filled with trailers and bars. It made him feel a little guilty that he did not want to spend a year in a place that didn't appeal to his aesthetics, and he began to question his motives. Was he just a middle-aged do-gooder looking for some adventure? If the desire to do good really compelled him, why wouldn't he want to serve wherever he was needed? Plenty of people in Woodside could use a free clinic. They could go live in New York City, and he could work with babies with AIDS; why did they need to go so far? He knew this was what Claire was thinking as she struggled with the thought of leaving her friends, their house, Nina, her mother, and most of all, Lizzie.

Andy was not accustomed to forcing his will on anybody. He couldn't even close on a set if Peter got truly upset when Andy had him 6-1. He'd get rattled and hold back a little and sometimes lose. If he could make himself believe that in the end Claire would be glad they'd gone, it would be okay. But since that could not be known, it didn't help. He had to pee. Washing his hands afterwards, Andy looked in the mirror and saw a man much older than he thought himself to be. He saw saggy jowls and pouchy eyes and almost no hair. He saw unfocussed disappointment. How many years of schooling had he had so that he could do work better left to a nurse? He even saw a little unfamiliar anger. Didn't he deserve a chance, just one, to follow a dream? How corny did that sound? If he wasn't careful he'd break into song. Jesus, he'd just finished washing his hands and he had to pee again. Every man his age went through this, but that didn't make it any better.

He heard the phone ringing at his desk, but didn't finish in time to get there. It had been Claire: when was he coming home and did he want to get together with anyone for a cookout? He didn't want to get together at all and especially not for a cookout on such a hot night. Why had they gotten central air if they intended to stand around a bunch of burning coals on one of the hottest nights of the year? He had already said everything he could ever think of saying to his friends and neighbors in Cooper Hill. He had read this week's *New Yorker* cover to cover—undoubtedly most of them had—and so they knew all the same things. The casualties in Iraq continued, those stated and the civilian ones never mentioned. The state budget was a wreck. The residents of Cooper Hill had voted themselves an override and so their taxes would increase, but what about Woodside and Russell and the hill towns, where people made it through the winter in trailers? Ritalin was over prescribed for young boys, and global warming and extinction seemed inevitable. Why did Claire continue to enjoy these evenings? If he asked her she'd say, well then, what do you have in mind? And that's when he'd lose because he'd just get mildly drunk, watch an hour of TV, and go to sleep. Sleep—he could sleep right now for hours, right there on the waiting room sofa. Andy had been tired lately. He blamed it on the weather and the stress. Summoning his last shred of positive energy he called Claire back to tell her he'd be home soon and she should invite everyone to their house where they'd all be cool. Linda could use a break. In turn, she reported on the status of their passport application, clothes she had ordered online that had insect repellant imbedded right in the cloth to keep you safe from malaria, and that day's conversation with her mother. She'd been trying to get her to understand that they were going away. It wasn't easy with a person who had lost her memory and her sense of time. He knew it wasn't easy to leave. He knew it, so why did she have to keep sayings things to remind him? And all that stuff she kept ordering—they were going to look ridiculous in all that gear.

Andy knew he had to calm down. Tomorrow night he'd play tennis. It always relaxed him.

On his way home the sky turned green, the wind picked up and it rained so hard that he had to pull over. In twenty minutes the sky cleared again, and he made his way along a road covered in fallen branches. When he turned into his street he saw a gathering of people standing down the road where the Mill River usually ran under a small bridge. The road and the bridge were covered with water. On the other side of the flooded road, water had reached the porch of a small house built too near the river. The DPW truck with a bucket loader had parked, and they were trying to help the young family who lived there get out, but they weren't really needed. The couple, carrying a baby, waded through the water and up to the road, but the bucket loader, perched precariously on the side of the road that that been washed out, began to tilt. Cooper Hill had an event. Everyone offered advice and slowly the huge truck ground its wheels and backed away from danger. Everyone stood there watching the swirling water. Their little river, the place where golden retrievers chased rocks and children waded, had become menacing. In such a short time. And it was a good thing the bridge on the other side of town was so high, or the town would have been cut off with no way to get in or out. Since they were all safe, this was a thrilling idea. After a while Andy and Claire gathered up their friends and headed home.

It rained again on Wednesday night and Thursday. Friday night, Peter and Melanie had something to do, so Andy and Pete couldn't play until Saturday. The temperature hit eighty-two by seven in the morning. Claire reminded Andy to fill his water bottle. Andy left without telling her that with three long tennis-free nights to think things over, he'd decided they should put off the idea of working in a foreign country for at least a year. Give Lizzie time to settle in and take care of Claire's mother in the months she had left. It had been an unsettling year, to say the least. He didn't have to push this now. No need. But he wanted to tell her on Saturday night when they always made a special meal and broke open a very good bottle of wine. He wanted to deliver this news and then make love in their nice, quiet empty house with nothing more intruding than the sound of Nina's toenails on the wooden floors.

Energized by this decision and the relief it would bring, Andy came out strong and took the first two sets. Then Peter rallied and took the next two, winning in tie breakers. They played long games, each determined not to let go easily. In the fifth set, Andy had Peter 6-4 when Peter began lobbing the ball from the baseline so that Andy could either hit an overhead but get blinded by the sun or go back behind the baseline and wait for the ball to come down. He took one of the balls high and drove a passing shot down the side. Peter aced his serve. Andy's shoulder was still bothering him, and Peter returned a weak serve with a shot straight to his feet. After three and a half hours of play they were tied at 6-6 in the fifth set. Andy's green shirt had white salt rings all over it.

Melanie called Claire. "Are they still at it?" she said. Claire told her she was beginning to get worried. "When the phone rang I thought it might be the hospital."

"We could go over to the courts and watch," said Melanie. This had never occurred to Claire. Tennis seemed so much like Andy's private thing. What if they distracted them at a critical moment?

"C'mon, they've been at it long enough. Let's go." Melanie said, and they did.

First Andy and Peter looked terrified, as if the women had come to tell them someone had died. Then they merely looked annoyed, but Claire and Melanie settled on a bench and knew not to talk.

It was amazing for Claire to see Andy like this, so concentrated and totally wrecked. Both men were limping. They looked like warriors after a long battle and the tie breaker score stood at 11-12 in Andy's favor. One point would end it, but Peter scored next, so either man now needed two points to win. Claire played a little, but never like this. It occurred to her that she did nothing with this intensity, and her heart filled with joy for Andy, for his need to win this match, and for his need to have something like this in his life. To feel this alive more often. Just before he won the next point she promised herself that she'd stop whining and start to show some enthusiasm for the adventure ahead.

The people he could help with all his years of education and practice deserved it. Andy deserved this chance. And she feared that he'd kill himself on the tennis court if he couldn't express this kind of passion elsewhere.

As if she'd channeled her thoughts, Andy summoned the last bit of strength left in his injured shoulder and sent a serve right to the T. Peter barely saw it. If people still jumped over the net to shake hands, Peter would have done it. Laughing, the guys poured water over their faces and began to relive certain points.

That night Andy prepared to tell Claire his news, but before he could, she produced a plate of smoked salmon and capers and an icy martini along with their passports and a smile. Andy let that soak in. He remembered how she often came slowly to new ideas and then embraced them like some kind of convert. But still, he wanted to be sure. He wanted her to know she had the choice. Because he had truly let go, he felt calm. Things would be fine either way. They had a good life. He told her so. It took her back. For a moment he could feel her waiver.

At this moment Claire and Andy, perched on stools at their kitchen island, kept interrupting each other with, "But you really don't have to. Really, I've thought it through," until each forgot what they were arguing or apologizing for. The setting sun streamed into the kitchen from the window over the sink behind Claire, and it made a red gold halo around her head and caused Andy to squint, so that for a moment he looked angry—that or very confused. He had now made such a strong case for postponing a year of service that Claire wondered why she had agreed to go in the first place and questioned herself as both mother and daughter—how could she even think of leaving at this time?

If the situation were music, it would be annoying jazz. If it were a poem, it would be concrete poetry, forming a shape with words, and the shape would be that of a wall of peeling paint. With the salmon eaten and dinner forgotten and a second round of drinks, a solution emerged. Andy turned on the computer and went to the Doctors Without Borders website. Claire stood over his shoulder and they read together. They didn't have to commit to a year. Some programs lasted just six months. And they could leave in January or February instead of

October. Claire liked the idea of Haiti, where she could use her high-school French. Andy said there were French-speaking countries in Africa, too. Like people planning a vacation, they clicked from country to country reading of compelling need everywhere, even in places with beautiful beaches.

Andy suggested they go out to dinner, to the restaurant on the river they thought of as their own neighborhood place. They liked to eat at the bar. There they continued the conversation. "If we go in January, I'll be back in time for tennis," Andy said.

This made Claire laugh. "Do you think most volunteers make a commitment based on their tennis schedule?" she asked.

"Who knows why anyone does anything," Andy said.

"Does this mean you think my Mom will be gone by January?"

"If she isn't, her mind will be so far gone that she won't even know we've left." Sagging a little from the drinks at home and the glass of wine in front of her, Claire said, "We are not nice people."

"Yes, we are," Andy said, enjoying his wife, the idea of their future, and this particular moment. He was in no way ready for her announcement that she and Melanie were going on a river trip together.

"When did you decide this?"

"On our way over to the courts. She suggested it and I said no way, but then I saw you playing tennis like that, and I remembered how much we loved that kayaking trip."

"But that was an afternoon on estuaries; where do you and Melanie want to go?"

"The Allagash."

"You're kidding. That's white water."

"Some, not all. Melanie's done it before; we'd be part of a group."

"And camp out."

"Of course. That's why I didn't even think about asking if you and Peter wanted to come."

"When?"

"Maybe the third week in August, depending on the weather." It has to be after Old Home Days and during a stretch of clear weather.

We don't want to be out in the woods in the rain. You and Peter can play marathon tennis while we're gone."

"How long is the trip?"

"Ten days. Ten days on the river and there are loons and moose in the woods and by late summer all the black flies are gone."

Claire had this big goofy grin on her face, and he knew she was serious, and it really didn't surprise him. She was a water creature. Put her by a lake, river or pool and she stayed in till she turned blue, like a kid. "You haven't been camping in twenty years; it's pretty gutsy to do this. You don't want to start with a one- or two-day trip?"

"No. I want to do this. It will be great and I have all that gear I ordered for our trip. I just need a new sleeping bag and tarp. Melanie has an extra tent and cook stove and all the rest."

Andy looked at Claire's soft hands. She wore gloves when she gardened. She'd recently had her hair cut, and it had been shaped perfectly. He had a hard time imagining her not showering for ten days, not washing and conditioning her hair, but of course she'd swim every day. He thought this was great.

"You're not afraid at all? What about bears or if the boat tips over?"

Claire only laughed. "Andy, hundreds of people do this all time. Aren't you afraid to go some place where we might get malaria or dysentery or bitten by some poisonous spider, or worse, caught in the middle of some civil war? I think we should each do something that scares us each year for the rest of our lives. Next summer I want to learn rock climbing."

"What about sailing?"

"We can learn to sail."

"I'll never go camping."

"That I know."

Their food arrived and Claire and Andy ate in silence. They were both starved. Enough had been said to last a while, Andy thought. His wife, who had been so filled with fear, now seemed equally filled with joy. Had it been those sessions with Sophie or merely time? Had she really relinquished her need to hover over Lizzie, or had Lizzie simply worn her down? Actually, he thought; it doesn't matter. He made a forkful of steak and mashed potatoes with truffle butter, savored the taste and watched the baseball game on the TV over the bar.

The heat broke, as it often did, right before Old Home Days. Tag-sale tables lined the street. Linda and Tom got out early. Linda always found things there that others would miss. April had three dollars and she used two to buy a basket of toys for "her baby," even though Jess said her brother wouldn't be able to use them for a long time.

"But I will show him how to play," April said. With the other dollar, she bought a ballerina costume for Halloween.

"You don't want Mary to make a costume?" Jess asked.

"No, this one is better," April said, patting the sequins and the net skirt.

"Little girls can be anything they want to be; you could be an astronaut if you wanted," said Jess.

April looked at Jess like an adult summoning patience and shrugged. "I know that. But if I can be anything, then I can be a ballerina."

The day began with a road race, and then, of course, the auction. Quite a few things on offer came from Maud's house, and whispers passed through the crowd.

Maud's story had became one of the village stories, and people would know about it forever along with the story about Hugh Blanchard who survived a torpedo attack during the Second World War and lived for a week in a small raft in shark-infested waters, and Otis Clark who loved opera and once saw Ted Williams play baseball. Maud would be the lady who killed squirrels and stole the mail, and she would take on the characteristics of some witch. She'd get uglier in the telling. She'd have warts on her chin. Clearly those thick drapes had concealed horrors—oh, what her children must have gone through, people would say, when they talked about her, but they would not talk all that much, and at the auction, they held back from bidding on any of her things.

Claire and Andy had a seat in the back. They had told Jack they'd look for stuff he might need at the shelter. Although he was sparing no expense, supporting the auction appealed to him along with recycling things that might otherwise end up in the landfill. He had told Andy and Claire and the others that he had something to do, but he'd be back in the early afternoon for the band concert. Claire raised her face to the sun and pulled a cotton shawl around her shoulders. This always happen in mid-August. The mornings became cool and people began to think of fall and bright leaves and crisp days. Without saying much about it, Lizzie had moved out of her friend's apartment and moved in with a single mom who needed some help with her two children. She'd signed up for fall classes and told Jack she wouldn't come to work at the shelter until the woman she was living with could get childcare. It wouldn't be long; she'd put in an application for a subsidy.

In just a week, Claire had to go over to Burnside and start to get textbooks sorted for the new students. She would request a leave from the director and it would be granted, because Burnside would be proud of what she and Andy planned to do. Really, she shouldn't complain so much about her job, she thought. Some people spent their working lives knee-deep in fetid water at chicken-processing plants. Every day, she drove fifteen minutes to a gorgeous campus where she worked with smart, polite children and enjoyed a free lunch. What more could she ask for? There was more, but she'd decided that publishing a book could wait.

Enough had happened in just one year. Too much, really. To squander her current contentment for a book that would upset everyone she loved, be remaindered in two weeks most likely, and make no money seemed like a stupid risk. Andy had his bidding card in the air. They were auctioning off a set of camping cookware. "You could use it on your trip," he said. Claire took his other hand and kissed his palm.

While Cooper Hill observed a day that once celebrated the harvest season and set everyone's mind towards fall and the cold, silent winter that followed, Jack went to the cemetery to visit Cate and his children. He had not been there since the day they were buried or "laid to rest," as his in-laws said. He didn't like the neat manicured rows. He did not believe that the lovely view from the hilltop meant anything to the dead. He did not believe they were resting at all; those had been the minister's words, not his. Nevertheless, he was drawn there on this day that ended a year in which he'd done shameful things and wonderful things and decided to live in the world. He'd been having regular conversations with Cate and felt no need to address any feelings to a particular rectangle of earth, but he was happy to see that the lilac bush he had had planted had survived, and someone was keeping the weeds down.

Over on the other side of the cemetery he saw a hearse, followed by a long string of slow moving cars. He watched for a while. A man about his age got out of the car and helped a woman of the same age. He held her tightly as they approached the grave site. Children were lined up as well, dressed in dark clothing. So this funeral seemed to be in the natural order of things: a grandmother or grandfather had died. Jack knelt down so he could touch the stones above Molly and Zeke's grave. He closed his eyes and read their names with his fingertips. He told them about Conway—not the sad parts, just that she had lived a long life and died in his arms. It felt good to say this out loud, even if it was not the whole truth. Then he left.

He'd told Claire and Andy he'd stop by and then Amanda was coming to his place later in the afternoon. He'd begun to admire the woman's persistence. She'd given him her piano, such a lovely instrument, and when she stayed at his place, they sometimes played simple tunes together. But more often she asked him to play for her, and he enjoyed it. He had still not touched her and would not unless a time came when he could tell her why her door had blown open on a day that was not all that windy. He hoped she would laugh and suspected she might. She was happier in Boston. He had not caused her to leave Cooper Hill but perhaps supplied the excuse she needed. He'd told Cate about her. She would have warmed to Amanda after a while, as everyone in Cooper Hill had. She would have liked her honesty.

Jack drove slowly through the cemetery, past the group he'd

observed from a distance and through the gate, where he exhaled, feeling like he'd been holding his breath for a long time. He chose back roads that took him through Russell and around Woodside, and finally meandered back to Cooper Hill. He pulled into Claire and Andy's narrow driveway, where his car fit the paved strip with little room left over, the way earth hugs the sides of a coffin, the way death presses on life evenly, so you always know it's there.

Lee Wicks is a writer living in Western Massachusetts. Her non-fiction work has appeared in the *Boston Globe*, Salon.com, the *Daily Hampshire Gazette*, and the *Amherst Bulletin*.

§

PRINTED IN THE UNITED STATES OF AMERICA
TIGER PRESS
NORTHAMPTON MASSACHUSETTS
OCTOBER 2008